Ceremonial Magic
&
The Power of Evocation

OTHER TITLES FROM THE ORIGINAL FALCON PRESS

By Joseph C. Lisiewski, Ph.D.
Israel Regardie & the Philosopher's Stone
Kabbalistic Handbook for the Practicing Magician
Kabbalistic Cycles & the Mastery of Life

By Christopher S. Hyatt, Ph.D.
Undoing Yourself With Energized Meditation
Energized Hypnosis (book, audios and videos)
Radical Undoing: The Complete Course for Undoing Yourself (audios &
videos)
The Psychopath's Bible: For the Extreme Individual
Tantra Without Tears
Dogma Daze
To Lie Is Human: Not Getting Caught Is Divine

By Christopher S. Hyatt, Ph.D. with Lon DuQuette & Aleister Crowley
Aleister Crowley's Illustrated Goetia

Edited by Christopher S. Hyatt, Ph.D. with contributions by
Wm. S. Burroughs, Timothy Leary, Robert Anton Wilson et al.
Rebels & Devils: The Psychology of Liberation

By S. Jason Black and Christopher S. Hyatt, Ph.D.
Pacts With the Devil: A Chronicle of Sex, Blasphemy & Liberation
Urban Voodoo: A Beginner's Guide to Afro-Caribbean Magic

By Antero Alli
Angel Tech: A Modern Shaman's Guide to Reality Selection
Angel Tech Talk (audios)

By Phil Hine
Condensed Chaos: An Introduction to Chaos Magick
Prime Chaos: Adventures in Chaos Magick
The Pseudonomicon

By Peter J. Carroll
PsyberMagick
The Chaos Magick Audios

By Israel Regardie
The Complete Golden Dawn System of Magic
What You Should Know About the Golden Dawn
The Golden Dawn Audios

By Steven Heller
Monsters & Magical Sticks: There's No Such Thing As Hypnosis?

**For the latest on availability and pricing
visit our website at http://originalfalcon.com**

Ceremonial Magic
&
The Power of Evocation

by

Joseph C. Lisiewski, Ph.D.

THE *Original* FALCON PRESS
TEMPE, ARIZONA, U.S.A.

International Standard Book Number: 978-1-935150-86-2
Library of Congress Catalog Card Number: 2004108844

First Edition 2004
Second Printing 2006
Third Printing 2006
Fourth Printing 2009

This story is based on true events. Names and locations have been changed when necessary to protect the identity of the participants.

Cover design and illustration Linda Joyce Franks
(illustration of the "Devil" from the artist's Tarot in progress)

The paper used in this publication meets the minimum requirements of the American National Standard for Permanence of Paper for Printed Library Materials Z39.48-1984

Address all inquiries to:
THE ORIGINAL FALCON PRESS
1753 East Broadway Road #101-277
Tempe, AZ 85282 U.S.A.

(or)
PO Box 3540
Silver Springs, NV 89429 U.S.A.

website: http://www.originalfalcon.com
email: info@originalfalcon.com

Dedication

This book is dedicated to Christopher S. Hyatt, Ph.D. as a token of my respect and gratitude for the friendship and personal instruction he has unselfishly given me throughout so many years; and to my first mentor in Magic, Dr. Francis Israel Regardie, who guided me in the Secret Work throughout the last fourteen years of his life. In the end, his greatest gift to me was his friendship.

Table of Contents

Illustrations

WARNING!

PLEASE READ THIS CAREFULLY! This warning is given in earnest. It is not like other gimmicks meant to sell a book. You now stand at the opening of a portal that will lead to personal power! If you decide to undertake what is written herein, you begin an incredible journey that can lead you to material fulfillment and magical power. It is a book that describes the evocation of long forgotten spirits; beings who have as much objective reality as you do. But it contains much more than that. It will enable you to design your own occult system of personal development which is the only kind that can truly work for the individual. You are warned that by following these instructions you *will* produce the magical phenomena described, and can most certainly succeed in obtaining your heart's desire. In short, you, dear reader, may very well have your wishes fulfilled. But there is an old admonition concerning wishes which you will do well to heed as you read and work from this strange text: "Be careful what you wish for, because you just *may* get it!" Mark this charge well!

Introduction

D r. Joseph C. Lisiewski first met with Dr. Francis Israel Regardie during the week of October 8–13, 1973. Joe flew from his home in Selinsgrove, PA to Studio City, CA to meet the world famous Occultist; this, the result of a two-year correspondence that had passed between them. They spent those days at Regardie's home at 7332 Coldwater Canyon Avenue. Among the many subjects discussed, Francis had confided in Joe (and in myself) that in all of his years in the occult, he never knew of anyone who had attempted the Abramelin Operation as it is given in the *Book of the Sacred Magic of Abramelin the Mage*. Regardie went on to say that those who did attempt the operation always modified it in one way or another, causing him to be extremely suspicious of their "results." This idea of altering the magical operation left a marked impression on Joe, who told me years later that it was this one statement of Regardie's which later formed the basis of his belief—and later experimental verification—that systems of magic must never be altered or mixed. Put quite simply, this is the basis of this wonderful book: full and completely unaltered Magic.

Although Joe and I began corresponding in April 1985, a month after Regardie's death, our first face-to-face meeting did not occur until April of 1986, approximately 13 months after Francis' demise. He flew to Phoenix from the East coast. I picked him up, took him to my home in Sedona, AZ, and our intense magical times began.

During our early correspondence, Joe stated to me that he was one of Regardie's students as well as his alchemical consultant. While I normally would have been cautious of such claims from most people—even likely to reject them outright)—I knew of Joe through Francis before he knew of me, as Regardie had talked to me about him a number of times. Indeed, I was present at Dr. Regardie's home during several of their marathon telephone discussions.

Privately, Francis told me that Joe was one of the few students of the occult who he respected. He "knows his stuff!" he said, "...particularly in the areas of alchemy and evocation." He also confided in me that Joseph Lisiewski had attended Frater Albertus' school of alchemy, and was one of the few students Frater Albertus respected greatly. In fact, Joe had completed the entire seven year cycle of alchemical instruction in six years (1975–1980).

Thus, Joe became part of the inner alchemical circle which included some of the Dallas people (such as Hans Nitzel), along with Dr. Regardie, and of course, Frater Albertus himself. All of them communicated regularly with each other, sharing the results of their secret alchemical experiments.

As you may know, Dr. Regardie became a strong supporter for physical alchemy. That is, he simply didn't see it as Jung and others saw it—as a form of archetypal psychology—even though Regardie's earlier book on alchemy did originally support that view. Time and direct experience changed Regardie's stand on the matter. Like Joe, Francis also had his own alchemical laboratory, in which he carried out a number of both basic and advanced alchemical works. In fact, as Regardie personally told me and a few others, it was actually an alchemical experiment that put him into the hospital, and was the causative factor behind his emphysema. Joe later criticized Regardie to his face for doing this dangerous experiment in closed quarters without proper ventilation.

Beyond this, Regardie later confided to Joe what actually happened as a result of that experiment. This is what Joe told me, as Regardie explained it to him:

> Francis' lung condition was not due to his years of smoking, as he first told me and everyone else. The fact of the

matter is, he quit cigarette smoking in his 40's, and took up a pipe throughout his 50's, which he then gave up.

As time passed, and we became closer in our alchemical and magical work, he finally explained that his lung condition—and the need for an oxygen tank—was not due to his years of smoking. He told this to people as a dodge: he didn't want to have to explain the real reason. He further told me that he did not have emphysema at all. Instead, his lung condition was caused by an alchemical experiment gone bad. Specifically, he was calcining Antimony Trisulfide ore. This ore, coming directly from a mine, contains naturally-occurring arsenic compounds that must be removed through a special calcination process. He did this same experiment many times before in his small shed; but this time, instead of leaving during the lengthy purification process and only checking on it intermittently, he remained inside. The arsenic vapors caused him to nearly pass out. He was unable to breathe as well. He made his way the few feet back to his house, and called for medical attention.

In the hospital, his lungs were determined as having been "burned" badly by "some caustic agent," as he explained to me. The condition deteriorated as he got older. Not only was he adamant about not explaining this to others but, for some reason I could never fathom, he would not publicly admit to his involvement in physical laboratory alchemy either. Hence he made up the story of having emphysema as a result of smoking.

Returning to Jung's work and physical reality: While Regardie respected Jung's work, insights, and metaphorical model, in the end he abandoned Jung's methodology as being extremely flawed, and chose Reich's psychotherapy methods instead. Here, again, we see Regardie accepting the physical over the metaphysical—and this is one reason he admired Joe. For not only was Joe performing magical evocation and doing real alchemical experiments, he was also being educated as a physicist at university while yet carrying on his own scientific work: applying what he learned to his own ideas in physics.

Both Dr. Regardie and Dr. Lisiewski did agree on the fundamental issues underlying the practice of magic. One point that was extremely important to both was that there is no such thing as "Magick Without Tears." To them, Magic is serious business; and considering how difficult it is to perform a genuine ritual, and how exact results of even serious ritual and ceremonial work are in large measure unpredictable, both Regardie and Joe felt that what most people called a "magical ritual" is, in fact, nothing more than an exercise in futility and ego gratification. Joe, Regardie, and I would often smile at what most people called "Magic," and that included Crowley's Gnostic Mass and adorations. In our view, these performances are not true magic but, rather, mysticism interlaced with religion, and placed within a framework meant to elicit a scandalous reaction from the general public. Regardie, Joe, and I felt—and Joe and I still do—that this is particularly true of those individuals who identify themselves with the New Aeon—where magic is nothing more than a watered-down form of Christianity. In fact, neither Crowley nor the so-called "New Aeon" provide much credence for hardcore Magic. Dr. Regardie would often say to me that the New Aeon and the New Age were co-extensive, and referred to it as "Cosmic Foo Foo."

This view did not make Dr. Regardie popular with many of the Wicca people nor with the OTO, which Regardie supported, nonetheless, out of his commitment to his memory of his Guru, Crowley. In fact, to this day, while it was Regardie who helped bring Crowley and his work into the public eye, most high-ranking members of the OTO despise Regardie for having psychologized Crowley, as he did in his biography, *The Eye in the Triangle.*

While it is true that Joe practiced Golden Dawn Magic for many years under Regardie's direct tutelage, and was both a member and officer of Crowley's A∴A∴, he found both systems of magic to be utterly lacking in accomplishing what he wanted: reliable results. This is where Dr. Regardie and Joe disagreed, as Regardie was highly supportive of the Golden Dawn. Yet their disagreement only strengthened their friendship. It did not end it, as the history of Magic has shown is almost always the case.

My view is that whatever disagreement there was between them was due to a confusion between initiation ritual and the techniques of practical magic. Joe is not given over to the pomp and pageantry that underlies Golden Dawn initiations. Francis was. It is important to remember, however, that both Regardie and Joe agreed completely that the old grimoires were the key to functional, practical, and verifiable magic.

Regardie would always tell me how beautiful he found the rituals of the Golden Dawn, both the initiations and the religious-type rituals such as Corpus Christi. (Joe couldn't have cared less. His position was, and is, intensely practical, always looking for the underlying principles—just as a physicist should!) However, when it came to practical magic and the accomplishment of a given end, Regardie always fell back on the older, more complete systems as represented by the older Grimoires.

There existed yet another basic disagreement between Regardie and Joe, and that was the nature of the beings evoked to physical manifestation through the act of evocation. Regardie felt the nature of the demon being evoked to manifestation was psychological, thus favoring Crowley's view as given in the *Goetia*. He also preferred the use of the full Qabalistic theory in an evocation, once again, as Crowley gave in the *Goetia*. For example: that the number of candles, the color of the candles, etc., must correspond to the planet the demon is under. Joe, however, never favored this, arguing that the Old System—the grimoires themselves—very rarely call for any such significance. In fact, Joe argued that the Grimoires have their own requirements, and very few of them are Qabalistically-based. An example of this can be found once again in the same *Goetia* concerning the times for evoking a demon of a given rank. In this scheme, Qabalistic Planetary Hours are *not* used. Instead, a different set of times for evoking a being of a given rank are presented. In both my opinion and Joe's, Francis' stance here again was a reflection of his dedication to Crowley.

At other times, however, Regardie told Joe and me that he was actually uncertain as to the nature of the evoked beings; and yet still there were other times when he felt they were objective beings. Put simply, Joe did—and still—views the beings manifested through evocation as being purely objective in nature, and refutes their psychological basis completely.

Regarding alchemy, Joe explained to me that Francis was responsible for getting him into the in-residence, seven-year cycle of alchemical instruction at the Paracelsus Research Society. As Joe explained,

> It was in October 1974 that Regardie and I discussed the issue of alchemy, and my interest in it. I told him of the basic experiments in alchemy that I had already conducted at that time—which came from Rosicrucian Order AMORC instructions. Francis insisted that as I was a physicist in the making, it was vital that alchemy be brought under the aegis of the Hard Sciences, and strongly lamented the fact that he had not gone this route himself (he was very interested in chemistry, and I sense he would have liked to have become a chemist instead of pursuing the career he chose.) As a result, he informed me of Frater Albertus and PRS, and asked me if I would be willing to enter the seven-year cycle of instruction. I immediately agreed. Regardie then contacted his very good friend Frater Albertus, and made the arrangements for me to begin with the Prima Class (first year class) in February 1975. I completed the seven-year cycle in October 1980 after 6 years, having taken two, two-week classes back-to-back in 1978 (the Quarta and Qunita classes.)

There is much, much more that I can say and reveal, as Joe was—and is—part and parcel of the modern history of magic. At the time of this writing, he is 55 years old; and like myself, has been involved with serious magic for well over forty years now. However, as I have stated, he is absolutely unlike most practitioners. He is for real. He knows his material, and practices what he writes in this, the first of his many books to come from The Original Falcon Press. I will now pass the ball to my associate S. Jason Black.

— Christopher S. Hyatt, Ph.D.,
June 2004

If There Are Spirits In Your Head, I Have A Bridge In Brooklyn For Sale, Cheap

"Any sufficiently advanced technology
is indistinguishable from magic."
— Arthur C. Clarke

One of the most recurrently frustrating features of my involvement in esoteric groups for the past thirty years is the irritating, and seemingly inevitable, tendency of people to simplify esoteric practice to the point of eviscerating it.

In largely Protestant America, even Christianity—a religion already simple well past the boundary of stupidity—has been reduced from the elegant ceremony of Catholicism and the Episcopal church, to congregations which merely sit in pews to be yammered at or, at most, driven into (often fake) hysterical fits in a Pentacostalist hall.

In a culture already used to lazy superstitious religious traditions, and almost completely alienated from ancient esoteric practice, it is no surprise that even the most serious occult streams have suffered from this tendency.

Since I began by studying alone in the Midwest, finding classic sources only with great difficulty, I was shielded from the moralizing and "*blandizing*" that was already taking place in movements like Wicca by the late 1970's.

One of my first encounters with this phenomena came early in my involvement with an occult order after my move to Southern California in 1978. A man was in conversation with another about the *Goetia* (the *Lesser Key of Solomon*) and I overheard him explaining that "the magic circle can be anything you want it to be. Pretend you've laid out the circle while putting on your belt if you want to."

And this was in a Crowley group, at that time, about as hard-edged as you could get short of one of the Satanist orders. This same group, however, for some considerable time, met twice a week to experiment with John Dee's Enochian system, so there was still serious practice occurring for years to come. This, unfortunately eroded over time. Much of this deterioration can be laid at the door of Aleister Crowley himself. In 1903, when "editing" the *Goetia*, which he would eventually publish (it has been suggested he stole it from MacGregor Mathers), he wrote in the introduction: "The spirits of the Goetia are portions of the human brain."

This single remark has mislead thousands of sincere seekers, and created an excuse for even more thousands of dilettantes. Never in his life did Crowley have any real familiarity with psychology (this is demonstrated by his fear of hypnosis), and he himself cites numerous occasions in his biographical writings when he has experienced physical phenomena in connection with the conjuration of spirits.

He also says, in the same introduction: "Our Ceremonial Magic fines down, then, to a series of minute, though of course empirical, physiological experiments, and who so will carry them through intelligently need not fear the result."

The only true thing in this remarkable bladder of hot air is the word "empirical." As far as the practitioner not needing to fear the result, *nothing* could be further from the truth. Fundamentalist churches are full of converts who were told spirits are psychological, and found out otherwise. I've been acquainted with many.

In nearly thirty years of active practice, I have witnessed poltergeist phenomena, apparitions (usually in broad daylight), and successful death spells as the result of ceremonial evocation. The result of mishandling or ineptitude can be disastrous so far beyond belief, that only other people who have had the experience are likely to believe your story should it happen to you.

As a particularly mild example, many years ago, I participated in Aleister Crowley's Rite of Jupiter, one of his series of "Rites of Eleusis." I was one of the three major male characters in the drama (though I no longer remember which one) and along with some others, I placed a Jupiter talisman under whatever passed for the central altar. Well, all in all, it must have been one of the most half-assed evocations ever done. Within 90 days, all three of us had lost our jobs.

One very important thing about Dr. Lisiewski's book, *Ceremonial Magic,* that one rarely finds in occult books (other than books about ghosts) is the author's emphasis on material manifestation of the spirit.

In the surviving grimoires that have been published, which are by and large, merely outlines of ceremony, not philosophy or, indeed, teaching, the manifestation of the spirit is a given, and not elaborated on. Since Crowley's "brilliant" remark, recent-generation "magicians" have spent their time pondering what the writers "really" meant by this. In a talk I gave awhile back, a girl asked me if I thought the instructions of the old books were "really blinds"; my response was: "For what purpose? And have you tried following the instructions?" The first question she couldn't answer, the second, of course, was "No." Dr. Lisiewski, being a physicist, and trained in scientific method, as well as being the personal student of two of the greatest occultists of the twentieth century, and not being a lazy man, made no such assumptions. He followed the instructions, and got the results indicated by tradition, as did I, as I will show later. Incidentally, Dr. Lisiewski is not the only physicist that I know of involved in the practice of ceremonial magic. There is little in the traditions of magic that contradicts modern physics.

This "it's all psychology" thing has not been such a problem until now, as earlier writers, such as Dion Fortune, were familiar with the published work on psychic research, as well as traditional spiritualism. Ironically,

Fortune really *was* also a mental health care professional, but had no problem whatsoever in the literal existence of spirits. One of my abiding gripes from day one of my association with occult groups, is that, aside from, say, the Edgar Cayce people, their ignorance of 130 years of scientific research into the paranormal is as vast as the Arabian desert so, as with the Bible, any opinion is of equal worth. And speaking of the Bible, the major desire of the current crop of "magicians" is religion. They twist the definitions of magic in any direction required to accommodate this need, while still referring to themselves as magicians. The ultimately ridiculous example of this has occurred in the Crowley groups where a *church service*—the "Gnostic Mass"—is now referred to as a "magical ritual." Well, Crowley always wanted to be a Bishop.

So perhaps now is the time for a basic definition. *Magic is the manipulation of hidden forces or intelligences to produce a desired result.* A church service produces no results except for, at best, hypnosis, and more usually, boredom. My morning tarot reading is more magic than twenty years of this kind of nonsense. It is expected to forecast the immediate future, and before the day is over, I will know if it worked.

The tarot example aside, magic is frequently hard work. While there are enough lazy people in the occult who want to avoid this outright, still, over the years, I have known many involved in the sort of thing I have just criticized who were adept at both the martial arts and some of the more demanding forms of yoga; and indeed, the Rites of Eleusis that I mentioned above can take days of physical preparation. Yet, most of these same people wouldn't lift a finger to draw a magic circle, while still wanting to be called magicians. One wonders what the problem is.

I think the answer is twofold. To begin with, people become deeply and emotionally attached to dogmas that give them personal status. If a person is inducted into a group or tradition that says spirit evocation is creative visualization, they can practice in that vein, and call themselves "initiated magicians." If presented with the data that such is not the case, but "spirits" literally exist, then they are just another failure.

Once, some years ago, just after Falcon published either *Pacts With the Devil* or *Aleister Crowley's Illustrated Goetia*, I had the chance to overhear a conversation about the book (which one, I don't remember, and it isn't important) where an obviously Protestant Christian man was reading an account of drawing a magic circle, and calling up a spirit. In an almost panicked voice he kept repeating, "I'd *never* do that! I'd *never* do that!" As the conversation progressed, it became clear that the man's religious orientation was not the only factor in his reaction. It was also the notion of direct, individual contact with the supernatural. If confronted, the man might even have claimed not to believe in it, but the tone of his voice said otherwise. I suspect that most "neo-pagans" of one kind or another, having been raised in white, Protestant environments, have the same deep-down reaction. They are willing to do anything, so long as it doesn't work. The reasons for justifying such inaction are also ingenious. Many are the initiates that I have met over the years who do no practice—and are damned proud of it.

The main solution to this problem is disciplined antinomianism, which is more difficult than it sounds, and has little place in a book on the evocation of spirits, except for the fact that the successful practice of this Art requires the acceptance on a gut level of the falsity of the accepted reality that our culture teaches us—which is no easy thing. So difficult is it, that persons who start as sincere students of magic art often feel compelled to adapt that art to middle-class suburban views of the universe...

Floating Lights and Exploding Toilets

One of my earliest experiences in evocation occurred around 1979. I had moved to Southern California from the Midwest, and was living alone, so I could experiment fully for the first time without fear of interruption.

I constructed a circle (from a design in Francis Barrett's *The Magus*) from a painter's drop cloth that could be folded up and put away when not in use. I had decided on a ritual from one of the Grimoires (it was either *The Key of Solomon,* or *Goetia,* I no longer remember which) and began to do a full evocation around five nights a week. What I *do* remember is that it was connected with the Sun. Early on, perhaps the third or fourth night, I was in the middle of the conjuration when I was stopped cold by a physical sensation emanating from the (outside) doorway. There was a buzzing sensation on the surface of my skin, probably what the spiritualists used to call "vibrations," and an overpowering feeling of something physically bigger than myself in the room with me. It was the middle of the night, the windows in the room faced away from the street and were covered with blackout shades and drapes. No streetlight, no passing headlights could enter the room. There was only candlelight, and yet, in the area of the triangle, a coherent ball of orange light had formed on the floor. A *ball* of light, not a *spot* of light. I could see it from all angles but the back, and believe me I looked. It rose slowly into the air to the level of three, or four feet and disappeared. Boom. Just like that. I don't remember if I got what I asked for—and it may well be that I didn't ask for anything, only performed an experiment. In any case, that was not only the first visible manifestation that I produced in a ritual, but probably only the second evocation that I attempted. At that time, I was so ignorant that I didn't "know" that it was all psychology, so, not knowing that the instructions were all blinds, I followed them.

Some years later I was living in Hollywood, in one of the few roommate situations I have been in, when she announced she wanted to get a job elsewhere and leave. This, I thought, would leave me with the entirety of the rent for the remainder of the lease on the apartment. Consulting yet a different grimoire, I created a talisman to prevent her from getting another job and then leaving. The creation of the talisman involved the evocation of the arch-demon Beelzebub and the extensive repetition of the spell. In fact, since I considered myself in rather desperate straits, I repeated it whenever she was gone, and placed the talisman under her bedroom carpet. It worked. Over almost two months she repeatedly failed to get jobs she was qualified for. In fact, knowing of my interest in magic, she once asked me if I had cast a spell on her. In any event, I eventually tired of this, and two or three days after I ceased and destroyed the talisman, she, of course, got a job.

The success in material terms of the working aside, a curious thing happened sometime during the first week. I awakened one morning, a bright summer California morning, to the sight of a tall figure, swathed in Byzantine-style robes standing in the corner of my room. He had pearl-gray skin, slanted eyes, and was holding what appeared to be an ivory baton in one hand. He stared at me for a moment, and vanished.

More recently, I performed an evocation according to the *Grimoirium Verum*. After the ritual, I was in another room. making notes, when I looked up, and saw in the hallway, what appeared to be a large smear of white paint hanging in mid-air. Once again, this was in broad daylight. A second after I saw it, it turned the corner into a room. I, of course followed it, but nothing was there. This is the closest thing to classic ectoplasm that I have ever seen.

Finally, there is the common occurrence of poltergeist phenomena accompanying such experiments. Apart from the classic crockery-slinging, there are sourceless and unpleasant odors; raps (which do not sound like ordinary raps, and have been analyzed in the laboratory and determined to have originated *inside* the wall or furniture, not outside as an ordinary blow); doorbells ringing with no one at the door, or indeed (as I have experienced) no bell, and no door. Things—large, heavy things—tend to break of their own accord. Once, after an extensive working in the Santeria system, Dr. Hyatt and I experienced some very odd peripheral stuff. He awakened one night, hearing voices and movement in the living room of his home. He went out, gun in hand, and found nothing. I, also experienced something similar, and not long after we received many thousands of dollars in totally unexpected funds for our joint Falcon work. Soon after, I had dinner with him . Just before leaving, I used the toilet. The next morning, I was informed of a small disaster after I left. They heard a loud concussion from the restroom and, upon checking, discovered that the toilet tank had exploded.

It wasn't my fault.

So, with all of this said, *Ceremonial Magic* is the best, clearest, book on the subject that I have read, and you don't have to worry about "blinds." There aren't any.

— S. Jason Black
June 2004

Chapter One

The Purpose of this Book

This book you now hold in your hands is like no other in the darkly compelling realm of magic known as "Evocation to Physical Manifestation." It is designed to serve as a manual of *serious*, **practical** magic. To accomplish this, I have given it a unique structural arrangement and content, as you will soon see. This is meant to guide the earnest Practitioner in a way that is not new in and of itself. But this particular presentation is new principally because of the content, magical discussions, axioms, instructions, commentaries and annotations contained in its pages. As far as I am aware, they are not given in any other text on the subject, and they will truly lead the earnest student of our Art and Science to successfully experience one of the ultimate aims of magic: the evocation of a spiritual entity (in this case, demonic) to physical manifestation. While this text is targeted to the advanced Practitioner, those relatively new to magic and who have done some earnest preliminary study and basic ritual work will most certainly benefit from it as well.

Arm-chair critics and self-proclaimed authorities of Medieval and Renaissance Magic in general, and of this book in particular, will assuredly describe this working manual as being one of those magical 'recipe' books so readily found on today's New Age mass market: "Do A and B" with the *promise* of getting result "C." If you study and practice what is laid down here however, you will find that nothing could be further from the truth. Why? Simply put, you *will* get results. By diligently *applying* the counsel given, and carefully *integrating* it into your *personal* magical system *in the way recommended*, you *will* behold one of the most fascinating, terrifying, spiritually exalting, and very possibly **materially** gratifying realms that magic has to offer—the High Ceremonial Evocation of spirit beings.

Although much has been written about ceremonial magic in general and of the evocation of spirit entities in particular over the past eight hundred years, all of those original texts or Grimoires (Grammars of Magic) combined do not equal the smallest fraction of the new books that have appeared on this subject over the last forty years. As one who began studying and practicing magic all those years ago, I not only saw the confusion, frustration and disappointment so many of the newly emerging books on the subject caused other sincere students whom I knew, but I experienced those agonizing states of bewilderment and disappointment myself.

I was extremely fortunate however to have Israel Regardie take me under his wing in this matter of magic, from September 1971 until his death in March of 1985. It was through his direct guidance and tutelage that I came to see much of this material available on bookstore shelves is either one of two things. Either it is simply a reprint of one of the Grimoires with a modern commentary added (usually by some author of this-or-that magical current), or it is a piecemeal presentation of original grimoiric material in terms of someone's own personal system of magic, which the aspirant is to follow blindly and practice religiously if he or she is to experience the results the author's methods *promise*.

As Regardie pointed out, such attempts by individual authors or a particular magical order or group are simply blends of their own *a priori* system of chosen doctrine and dogma placed within the contents of a specific Grimoire. That august writer or magical group then solemnly promises the desirous student of Magical Art that he or she will have their fill of spiritual treasures. This is the exact *opposite* of what the original Grimoire states! Such a

text contradicts the Grammar of Magic directly by promising the opposite, while only *alluding* to a bountiful
harvest of material benedictions that will (somehow)
follow not far behind the exalted spiritual treasure! To be
sure, they have their reasons for doing this.

It never ceases to amaze me to see even the most experienced student of magic accept this dichotomy and
struggle on, attempting to apply those spiritual forces,
whose very *nature* is to bestow material gain and power,
to some nebulous, undefined, quasi-spiritual end, while
secretly hoping this spiritual benediction will turn into the
hard core physical reality he or she needs. Why does the
ardent student persist in this bizarre pastime? If truth be
known, it is because the student does not really believe
magic works, at least, not to fulfill material aims. "It can't
because ...well...it just can't!" are the secret sentences that
run through their heads. By consciously accepting and
working with this firmly entrenched attitude and the mass
of books out there that support this spiritual or psycho-
logically-based magical quagmire instead of the material
treasures upheld by the grammars, they are right—it just
can't work!

This is not the case here. Not with this Grammar.
Within these pages you will find not only a system of
hard-core magical practice that will enable you to succeed
in evocation, but an eclectic and very effective philosophy
that can be used to build your *own* system of general
magic, just like all of those successful magicians out
there—both known and unknown—have forged for themselves, and which some even write about. Systems that
work for *them*. And now *you* can do the same with this
text. (We'll also address this problem of belief in magic as
well, and show you that you already possess more than
enough belief to succeed. You just have to redirect it so it
can do the most good.)

It is very important that you understand my exact
usage of the word grimoire. As the term is typically used,
it refers to one of the Medieval or Renaissance texts that
deal solely with the summoning or calling forth of an intel-

ligent, disembodied entity generally referred to as a spirit. Such classical grimoires include *The Sworn Book of Honourius the Magician, The Greater Key of Solomon, The Lemegeton* (or Little Key) and its most famous component, the *Goetia,* the *Grimoire Verum,* the *Grimoire of Armadel,* the *Secret Grimoire of Turiel,* the *Grand Grimoire,* and the *Sixth* and *Seventh Book of Moses.* All are examples of typical Grammars of Magic.

However, such compiled texts as *The Magus, The Book of Ceremonial Magic,* or even the *Secret Lore of Magic,* also qualify as grimoires in the broad sense, simply because they aim to clarify the theory and practice of *systems* of magic; and always *practical* magic. Despite their authors' long-winded Christian stance and admonitions—a socially proper and politically correct carry-over from the days of church punishment if the grammar fell into the hands of an Inquisition tribunal—such texts have their practical use.

Throughout this broad-based grimoiric class, you will find the same essential theme running throughout their pages. They solemnly avow that if the Practitioner or Operator simply holds fast in obedience to their holy writ, and during the Operation the Operators find within themselves the fortitude to face and command the spirits when they appear without the Circle of Art, then the secret desires nurtured in the depths of the magician's heart will be fulfilled. While not explicitly stated in the grammar, the implication is that the fulfillment will occur in the twinkling of an eye. In other words, in a very short period of time. Rest assured, it most certainly will, if the above conditions of evocation are fulfilled. A case in point is the now popular *Goetia,* though a terribly misunderstood, misused, and abused example of such a grimoire.

You may well ask, "Well, what about the really good books out there today that deal with evocation, different systems, and currents of magic? I'm confused! You seem to be saying they are based upon someone's personal system of magic that works for them only, and that even the current grammars can't be relied upon because they talk one way or another about spiritual rewards and power first, and then mayybbeee somehow the material desires come along as an after-effect. Are you against all of them?"

Certainly not. The fact is they are as I described them, and you, the reader, know this. They have their place in the grand scheme of things, and in your personal development as a human being. In fact, it is your responsibility as a human being to be the best you can be, eventually discovering what your 'True Will' is as is exhaustively treated in the writings of Israel Regardie (1907–1985) and Aleister Crowley (1875–1947), to name two contemporary authors.

But in fulfilling this responsibility, you are going to need...plain and simple...those material goods, be they money, better health, a healthier environment, a suitable mate, or any of the myriad of other physical pleasures that will *allow* you to progress spiritually and attain full development. Throughout my forty years of magical involvement, I have all too often seen such scenes of human tragedy; people living in the most appalling squalor and filth, yet firm in their 'belief' that they were developing spiritually and 'rising on the planes.' This is my bone of contention if you will, with many (but not all) of the modern books on the subject. They preach salvation through spiritual attainment in a diseased host whose life conditions mandate that at best they struggle for their daily bread. This is utter nonsense.

The magical propositions and axioms presented in this book will allow you to develop your *own* magical system of personal development in a holistic way; attaining spiritual development as both a cause *and* an effect of having used your latent divinity to satisfy those material needs and wants that are now blocking your full concentration. You can and must sweep away those million minutia that are consuming your daily life. And with this text, you can!

It was necessary to take the time to explain these finer points to you and to answer your inner arguments against what you have read thus far. Throughout the years I have seen these same concerns arise in the minds of all students of our Art and Science. They may seem theoretical to you now. You will come to realize just how pragmatic they are as you progress through these pages.

Our concern here is with one and only one Grimoire— the *Heptameron*. This is the oldest, most useable, most misunderstood and neglected document of its kind, despite the utter simplicity of its philosophy and use. Yet the commentaries and discussions provided as annotations in the actual *Heptameron* itself which I have reproduced in this book, can be applied successfully to working with any grimoire, just as the propositions and axioms will allow you to design and construct your own system of magic. Taken together, you have all you need to become who you already are, and achieve that which you so deeply desire.

Throughout this presentation you will find I make reference to various other books. In each case, I highly recommend you obtain them while they are still in print. No one book can do it all as you are aware, and with those appearing in the Suggested Reading List provided at the back of this book, you will have a working research resource at your disposal that will take you far down the Path.

A final word before concluding this chapter. You will notice that I use repetition freely throughout this volume. It is done intentionally. There is no more fundamental key to successful learning than repetition. But the typical process of repetition we were all taught, going back and re-reading the material, is not the most effective use of this process. Rather, the most effective type of repetition is that used to remind the reader of key points and ideas throughout a presentation, in addition to it being used to tie concepts together. This is what I have done here, I have employed the latter two modes of recapitulation to impress upon you what you need to know. If you actually work from this book, you'll thank me for it!

Chapter Two

History of the Grimoires for the Practitioner

History is not the static study of events frozen in time. It is a dynamic mental exercise in learning the cause-effect relationships of forces that have shaped any given area of investigation. Without an understanding of these forces, regardless of the historical subject being investigated, there can be no concrete grasp of the overall state of that subject, or of the underlying intricacies that provide the intellectual shape needed to productively direct and use those forces.

Yet regardless of the subject, the study of history bothers most people. Typically, the mental effort required to understand the underlying background of any subject is, by and large, labeled as wasted time. Yet these same people will, every once in a while, watch some historical television presentation, read a magazine article with an historical slant, or even take to a book that deals with an historical perspective of some issue of interest. Usually however, this is when they have nothing better to do.

In today's society, people try to make time only for those matters that fill some specific need, and that, quickly. This is understandable to a certain degree when it comes to routine, daily life concerns. But there could be no greater single mistake in learning and effectively applying hidden, occult techniques of magic such as are presented in this book. By understanding the basic cause-effect relationships that motivated the writing of the grimoires, and the forces of human need that refined them, you will be in a much better position to understand and intelligently interpret not only the grammars of the past, but the more contemporary broad-based magical texts as well. These are the reasons for this brief historical rendition.

You will learn where the grimoires came from, how they were originally composed, the pertinent religious and social factors that influenced their creation and content, and how the summoning of these spirits evolved over the past twenty-three hundred years. Yes, that's right, over a period of approximately two-plus millennium. Indeed, it might surprise you to find out that the ancient Egyptians had rituals designed for a type of evocation that would not be recognized as such by today's standards. By gaining a glimpse into such historical perspectives, you will come to understand the foundation of magic in general through its structure. In turn, this foundation will serve as a spiritual platform upon which you can build a magical edifice that becomes your own personal system of magic. One that works for **you,** and works **consistently.**

Thus, you would do well not to pass this chapter up or rush through it in order to get to the meat material. If you do, that same meat will turn rancid very quickly, and thrust you head-long into a physically, mentally, emotionally, and spiritually sickening experience. Remember. The intelligent forces underlying all genuine currents of magic are as real as any of the forces that operate our physical universe. They have nothing whatsoever to do with your beliefs, at least, not as you probably understand it at this moment. Jump off any roof and you will quickly come to an appreciation, understanding, and experience of the force of gravity. In the same way, if you toy or dabble with the forces of magic, you will quickly gain a hard appreciation of their reality as well.

As a physicist, I am deeply concerned with *structure* and *causation* in my scientific research. Why? Because structure provides a framework for seemingly disconnected bits of data, much like the frame of a picture puzzle provides glimpses of the scene being work on. It also gives insight into *patterns* that are not easily seen; hidden clues as to the physical forces behind the phenomena being studied. Causation allows for an understanding of the forces that mold structure itself, and shape the patterns being studied. These are the same essential ingredients needed to understand the history of any subject, magic included: structure and causation. In understanding the structure and causation behind the history of magic, you find two powerful tools needed to understand magic itself. Once you have these tools, your intuitive faculties will automatically teach you how to use them effectively in your daily and special magical workings, so that you proceed with confidence in your secret work.

In synthesizing my own personal magical system throughout the past four decades, I applied the above reasoning and ideas of structure and causation to it as well. I soon found it helpful to divide the history and practice of magic in general, and of Ceremonial and Ritual Magic in particular (which encompasses Evocation), into seven distinct systems or currents, each of which has a fairly clear historical timeline. The reason for these divisions is that they introduce further structure into the problem. Once we have structure, we can look for patterns. Patterns lead to a deeper understanding of the subject. This understanding then becomes a tool which the intuitive faculties begin to direct through the performance of the actual ceremonial or ritual action. In turn, the intuitively-based ritual action confers a confidence which is reflected back to the Practitioner in the real-world results obtained from the magical workings. With these concepts in mind, we can now explore the basis of magic intelligently.

The seven Systems of Magic are:
1. Hermetic Era Magic
2. Dark Ages Era Magic
3. Medieval Era Magic
4. Renaissance Era Magic
5. Transition Era Magic
6. Gothic Revival Era Magic

7. Modern Era Magic

We will take each in turn and investigate the forces involved in shaping magic in general, and evocation in particular.

1. Hermetic Era Magic—332 B.C.E. to 500 C.E.

Hermetic Magic encompasses a complete system of theoretical, theological, philosophical, and practical magic. If magic can be said to truly have a starting point or an origin in the classical sense of the word, then it lies here; in the original magic derived from Graeco-Egyptian sources. As Dr. Stephen Edred Flowers points out in his landmark contribution, *Hermetic Magic—The Postmodern Magical Papyrus of Abaris*, the magic given in the papyri is the first known attempt to merge the then varied forms of magical traditions from many different Mediterranean and Eastern countries into one integrated system of magic. A rigorous analysis of Dr. Flowers' book reveals that the resulting Graeco-Egyptian eclectic system still retained significant traces of its original component parts; keys used to extend this magical system into yet other magical systems over time. Not only are the ritual actions found in the Graeco-Egyptian system strongly reflected in the later six magical systems cited above, but their patterns of thought and philosophy are more or less imaged in these latter day schools of magic.

Dr. Flowers illustrates this point perfectly in his construction and interpretation of a Hellenistic "Cosmographic Tree." This is a pagan version of the much later Hebrew Qabalistic glyph of the Tree of Life so well know in today's magical community, and upon which many of the contemporary currents of magic are built. Yet this particular glyph has its origins in Neo-Platonic Cosmology.

Like its Hebrew counterpart which was used as a template to construct it, it too has ten spheres of pure or "Intelligible" qualities, and 22 Paths or "Sensible" projections of those qualities into the world of mind and matter. Like the Western Qabalah, which is based upon the original Hebrew Kabbalah, this pagan glyph has Path attributions and connections between its ten spheres or "Sephiroths." More importantly, even a casual study of this early pagan glyph reveals several different connections of Paths between the spheres than those used in the Western version. This immediately suggests other forces or spirit-interactions, thereby possibly extending the range of the Qabalistic Tree of Life into new ritual and ceremonial constructions beyond what is known today even in the most contemporary magical societies.

Another tract of vital importance in understanding the practical side of Hermetic Magic is that entitled *The Greek Magical Papyri in Translation,* by Professor Hans Dieter Betz. It is mentioned in Flowers' book for all those who seriously consider experimenting with Hermetic Magic. This is a very scholarly work in the purest sense of the word, being an in-depth presentation of a large number of magical spells and formulae derived directly from original Graeco-Egyptian papyri. As such, it is an invaluable workbook for the Practitioner of magic today, even though it was meant primarily to influence scholars working in the field of the history of religions.

The hard and cold fact is that the magical currents of today that append the word Hermetic to their name are, for the most part, woefully lacking any substantial basis of Hermeticism. The reason for this is the magical formulas and spells given in the papyri, which were not discovered and imported into Western Europe until the earliest years of the 19th century, required extensive examination by authorities in the field over the last eight or nine decades before they yielded their fruit, as Flowers points out. Hence their Hermetic influence on the developing magical systems of the time were minimal at best.

In terms of the Golden Dawn material, this is mentioned by the brilliant esoteric scholar, R.A. Gilbert, in his 1997 introduction to the important work *Collectanea Hermetica.* In this single volume of ten papers, compiled from a series of classic alchemical, Gnostic, and other related texts by none other than W.W. Westcott, the co-founder of the Hermetic Order of the Golden Dawn, Gilbert writes of one of these papers: "Similarly we can, with hindsight, see the weaknesses of Florence Farr's *Egyptian Magic*, but in 1896 it was a pioneering study. There was nothing at all then available to the general public on Gnostic Magic, and little enough of any value on the *Egyptian Book of the Dead.*"[1]

Yet Farr's paper, and the other nine of the *Collectanea*, laid down the intellectual basis for that system of magic, as Gilbert goes on to explain. Surely Westcott, a medical doctor, scholar, and thorough researcher, was aware of the discovery of the Graeco-Egyptian papyri. He must also have been aware that this discovery was less than a hundred years old at the time of the formation of the Golden Dawn, and realized that their content would require generations for translation and study.

This comes through in studying Westcott's several Prefaces to different sections of the *Hermetica*. In them, one gets the feeling of hesitancy in his writings; that he suspected the incompleteness of the *Collectanea* because of this missing material. Yet he had the courage to intimate this shortcoming in the very documents that served as the intellectual underpinnings of the magical order he created. But his caution, as with his famous foundational tome, was and still remains largely ignored, when one examines a number of the ritual and ceremonial documents of the Golden Dawn or any other current society that bears the word Hermetic in its name.

From ritual construction to the names of the Gods and their hermetic pronunciation, many are either skewed, contain errors to varying degrees, or are simply incorrect. It only takes the most casual study of Flowers' and Betz's texts to see this clearly. The question remains. What forces were brought to bear upon the Egyptians and their magic that eventually produced the synthesis we call Hermetic?

---

[1] Westcott, William Wynn (1848–1925). *Collectanea Hermetica Parts 1–10*. Introduction by R.A. Gilbert. Samuel Weiser, Inc., York Beach, Maine. 1998. page xiii.

Remember, this is a system of magic which would indirectly influence the creation and development of the other six different systems of magic previously listed.

The magic of the original papyri is, arguably, completely Egyptian in composition, content, and structure. This is extremely important to remember because it is from this point onward that we find the beginnings of the synthesis of Hermetic Magic—that body of work which would covertly inspire and serve as base material for the other six systems. As early as the 7th century B.C.E., war between Egypt and Greece brought about one of the earliest and most pronounced Greek influences on Egyptian culture, its magic included.

But this influence did not escalate until 332 B.C.E, when Alexander the Great conquered this magically-based country. It was from that time forward that Egyptian thought, theology, and philosophy provided the raw material for the Greeks, who then applied their logic and analytical rigor to create the magic we call Hermetic today. In fact, an examination of early Greek writings will show that Greek philosophers credited the Egyptians for much of their own magic, theology, and philosophy, and this influence can be found within the writings of Plotinus, Porphyry, Pythagoras, and Ptolemy.

Over the ensuing centuries, the magical papyri that resulted from this synthesis of Egyptian Magic with Greek self discipline and analytical thinking were produced. In fact, the papyri manuscripts that serve as the foundation and structure of Hermetic Magic is actually dated from circa 100–400 C.E., although their contents date back to a much earlier time.

An example of how Hermetic Magic influenced the development of these other systems can be seen when we look at the use of magical "tools." In and of itself, the use of tools or "instruments" in rituals and ceremonies of other cultures was a matter of course, and so was not unique. For example, the earlier flourishing civilizations of the Babylon, Persian, Syria and Phoenicia used various devices in their formal public religious ceremonies, and in their individual private devotional practices.

The concepts behind their use, and the manner in which they used them, contain such strong elements that we would designate them today as ritual instruments used in what we term the Magic of Invocation. But the first use of such instruments in a cohesive, balanced, and personal ritualistic manner that is defined by a complex, ordered approach to a god or demon, became clearly integrated and refined only in the Hermetic Tradition. Such items as the lamp, altar, incense, robe, ring, and even the circle, combined with words of power and formal rules of working, did not arise until the Greek influence of logic, analytical and mathematical thought blended with Egyptian Magic. When this synthesis was achieved, these instruments became the active components through which the magician impressed his Will and desire upon the universe, always in keeping with the philosophy and theology of Hermetic Tradition that also arose through this synthesis.

It is true that the earliest Egyptian magicians did use simple tools and in a more meaningfully ordered way than those that were employed in other earlier cultures and those that existed during the time when Egypt was at its zenith. But not even here did the thoughtful, intelligent design of ritual and ceremonial actions take place until the Graeco-Egyptian papyri manuscripts came into being through the Greek effort. And while the magical weapons or instruments used in Hermetic Magic as it exists today are the simplest of all, they are in no way to be confused with the simplicity of tools used in the earth religions. The theory underlying the rituals of this Hermetic Current, and the practice of this type of magic, creates as great a strain on the mental structure, psychic nature and very real spiritual faculties of the Operator, as much as any of the High Ceremonial Magic rituals in our contemporary Western System of Magic do. And here, Evocation is one such example.

Unlike some of the pop, convenient, instant gratification so-called rituals of some elements of the Modern Era Magic that we find ourselves in today, this original Hermetic Magic does not demand a slavish repetition of ancient rituals. Rather, just as it did fifteen hundred to two thousand years ago when Hermetic Magic was being forged by the Greeks, this unusual form of magic even now not simply encourages, but demands a *modern synthesis* of the ancient theory, theology, and philosophy of the rituals within the life of the contemporary magician. This can only be accomplished through experiencing the rituals in actual practice.

When such a synthesis is achieved, a new, *personal system of magic* arises for the individual Practitioner. In this case, a Hermetic System of Magic, as strange and as different from the Hebraic-based Western System we have today, as can possibly be imagined. In keeping with such a desire, to those individuals who decide to study the underlying theory and theology of this system of magic, and who wish to practice it, I highly recommend the books by Flowers and Betz cited earlier and detailed in the Suggested Reading List. Those who do so, will find that Hermetic Magic is magic in its purest and finest form.

2. Dark Ages Era Magic—476 C.E. to 1000 C.E.

Most academic sources include the Dark Ages as a part of the Medieval or Middle Ages era, and cite the time-line for this period as being between 476 C.E. and 1453. Others narrow the era of the Dark Ages between 476 C.E. to 1000 C.E. For our purposes, I have adopted the latter convention. With the fall of Rome, civilization as the world knew it ended. Roman law and justice, enforced through its military might, came to a sudden and abrupt end.

For over five hundred years, the glory that was Rome, itself an eclectic synthesis of the Greek and earlier cultures, disappeared from the face of the earth. Its art, political structure, philosophy, and education in the classics, ceased in the twinkling of an eye. When the Roman sun set, the western world entered a time of extreme social repression and all intellectual growth was extinguished. Raiders from the north—the Northmen—burned, raped and pillaged hamlets, villages, and towns at will. There was no protective force to stop them.

There is a prayer from this era of the Dark Ages that sums up very well the desperation of the people of that time. "Oh Lord, save us from the fury of the men of the north." In addition to these coastal raiders, bandits and criminals of every sort roamed the highways, forests, and inland villages, destroying, killing, and stealing as they pleased. Life shifted from the cities to rural areas, as the seat of government and the orderly regulation of the daily affairs of life faded away.

With that shift and the migration it generated, came a time of personal contraction. At best, life was a horrible daily struggle. To live from sunrise to sunset and see the return of the sun again was a feat that required all of one's resources: mental and physical, for the spiritual sun had set along with the Roman one. It was in the shadows of this nightmare world that, not coincidentally, Christianity arose and entrenched itself firmly in the individual psyche for the next fifteen hundred years. Ironically, the meteoric rise of this religion began under the Roman Emperor Constantine in 325 C.E.

Imagine yourself living in this time. While wrestling with the earth to grow enough food if you were lucky enough to have a hovel in the forest and access to a small piece of land, or doing menial work for those a little better off than you, there would be death and destruction constantly pulling at your ragged clothing from every side. Is it any wonder that your attention moved away from living a long and happy life in this world, to the acceptance of a creed that promised you eternal joy around the throne of God if you sought salvation and only salvation while in this life?

Of course such salvation could only be obtained by complete and blind acceptance of the Christian church in its entirety. Its dogma and doctrine replaced all dreams and aspirations. Attendance and participation in its first creation, the synthetic ritual called "The Celebration of the Mass," was an absolute, mandatory requirement. The minimum participation demanded at least once a week attendance to the Sunday Sabbath; more often, if your wretched life condition permitted it.

The new authority of your world of the living dead—the Priests—became the keepers of the keys to the Gates of Heaven by which you were to enter. Rigid and absolute obedience to their word as preached from the Gospels, and to their own personal whims, was now the guiding light in your life. The complex, highly successful societal structure of Roman civilization was thus greatly simplified. They were the masters, the givers of daily as well as spiritual law. You were now a single element in that pathetic body they termed the faithful, or willing slave if you prefer. You were not fit to understand and interpret the Bible, if indeed, you were fortunate enough to have been taught to read by someone who had learned from another, and if you had a copy of that rare document of salvation. Only the priests, those ordained by Holy Mother Church and the 'true' representatives of Christ on earth, could do this. And so you obeyed.

If you were somehow 'blessed by the grace of God,' you were recruited by the local priest at an early age, and entered the only common organization of the church that provided a substantial measure of physical protection and sustenance. This would be the monastery, where you became a Brother. There, you were taught to read and write, but only such approved works as the Gospels and writings of the early saints. After awhile, you came to learn from the hushed whisperings of older Brothers, of the collections of heretical works kept under lock and key by the Head Abbot in massive reserves in forbidden areas of the monastery.

Such horrific manuscripts presented the details of Roman law and justice, pagan literature, damnable art treasures that portrayed the naked human body, and yes, even those disgusting writings of the Greeks that dared to teach the principles of logic, mathematics, and the workings of the human mind and soul, all of which portrayed the world around you as something worth studying and understanding, in an attempt to provide some control over it. All were there, but only for the eyes of high-ranking, privileged church hierarchy. They were not for you. They could study them in order to teach you what was best for you. But certainly, you were unfit for such "works of the devil." Your superiors were better than you, because God, in his infinite wisdom, saw them as fit dispensers of His law, as they determined was proper for you, a mere Brother, to know.

But the early church took this continually evolving hierarchal structure much further. Even if you were exceptional and were later 'educated' as a priest, yet you were allowed only those approved works determined by someone in the next tier above you. Whether you had a tiny, poorly constructed church in the middle of some forest that your peasant faithful worshiped in, or if you were called to fulfill the duties of a scribbler, as the term of the day was used to denote a scribe, your life was severely limited.

This church structure was purposely designed by the higher ups in the church, both to maintain their political positions of power and their offices, in order to pass them down to their sons, as was the tradition of the early church. So even if you were one of the chosen, your life was by all standards, only a couple of cuts above the peasants that labored in your church every Sunday for the inspiration and succor they needed to somehow inch through yet another week of 'living.'

These were the life situations you were born into during this era. If you were like the herd of the faithful—whether you administered the Word of God or were one of those administered to—your only relief and way of escape was that which still terrifies all men and women today: the cold and silence of the grave. Imagine being born into such a world.

Put mildly, discontent was everywhere. Members of the church were not exempt from the natural, human longings to have and be more in this life; to accomplish feats of wonder in any field of human endeavor, and be remembered for their work after living long, healthy, happy, and prosperous lives in the here and now. To the average peasant, this was impossible of course. But to a member of the clergy with a moderate or even rudimentary education, the good life was not an impossibility. After all, he heard of those forbidden books kept tucked away by the Abbot.

Books of Roman and Greek origin, also reputed to be Hermetic in nature, yielding power and prize to those who could study them and work their wonders. I can only speculate here, as there are no records to confirm or deny this. But based upon the scenario given above, much of which has been documented in historical tracts of the Dark Ages and the Christian church of the time, it is reasonable to think it was only a small leap for discontented clerics of every garb and station to realize that the basis of their own religion surely must offer the means and ways to the better life the higher ups in their own church were enjoying on a daily basis. Power, prestige, love, fame, all were there for the taking. If only...

Gradually, over the first few centuries, bits and pieces of the few Hermetic texts available leaked out. A trusted scribbler here and there made an extra copy of the forbidden text his Abbot or Bishop ordered him to copy, while another copied sections of other tracts he was commissioned by his superior to adorn with the latest approved church art deco. Slowly but surely, by couriered letters and word of mouth, discontented clerics began comparing notes, holding secret meetings, and spreading the word and content of the practice of magic to their tightly knit brethren of like mind. That this scenario is accurate is based on the private letters that have survived to this day, and which are still contained in such repositories as the Bibliothèque de l'Arsenal in Paris, and in the British Museum.

But as we also know, the great bulk of genuine, original Hermetic texts were sealed away in the secret cloisters of Hermetic magicians in the Mediterranean, only to be discovered centuries later by Western archeologists and then exported to Western Europe in the early years of the first decade of the 19th century, a historical perspective mentioned in a number of scholarly works, including *Fragment of a Graeco-Egyptian Work Upon Magic,* produced by Charles Wycliffe Goodwin for the Cambridge Antiquarian Society in 1853.

Nevertheless, the Hermetic influence spread by those few manuscripts and excerpts of early discontented clerics and genuine church scholars of the day, and it had an impact on the developing Christian church and the church fathers. Think not? Read the 4th century C.E. treatise by Didymus the Blind. There you will find direct quotes from hermetic texts of the day. And yet his treatise was a scholarly though dogmatic rendition of the principles behind the concept of God as being three persons in one, the very foundation of Christianity!

Flowers points out that both Lactantius in the 3rd century C.E., and Cyril of Alexandria in the 5th century C.E., literally praised Hermês Trismegistus, the "Father of Hermetic Magic" as a "prophet of Christ!" As you can imagine, with such church authority extolling the virtues of Hermetic magic, early clerics began fashioning their own system of magical thought, all with the approval of the church. These texts were then re-discovered by later clerics of the Dark Ages, and the synthesis of the grimoires began.

As mentioned previously, and as the study of medieval history reveals, the Christian church became firmly established with the fall of Rome. People had nowhere else to turn for the authority they needed to govern their daily lives. With its ever-increasing stranglehold upon the lives of the people, the Christian church quickly recognized its own doctrines had to be strictly enforced. First, among its own clergy, and through them, to the faithful. Of paramount importance was the absolute public elimination of anything pagan.

Anything connected with the worship of many gods was ruthlessly suppressed, if not outright destroyed. Even though the Christian Doctrine of Philoque, which holds to the theme of three persons in one God, and the concept of saints (a minor-god corollary to the polytheistic basis of paganism), contradicted its stand against the matter of many gods, pagan polytheistic concepts were nevertheless rooted-out and eliminated. Such exalted matters as the Doctrine of Philoque and the concept of Sainthood were theologically separated from daily church matters early in the church's history, and closely guarded. These concerns were only to be interpreted by the highest elect of Holy Mother Church. This was (and still is) the attitude directed by the Vatican not only toward its common members, but toward the average cleric as well. Any texts other than its own were abolished and forbidden under pain of damnation.

Chief among the prohibited works was the scarce body of hermetic texts, ironically used by the earliest church scholars to pound out their own theology! No doubt it was due to this scarcity, as well as the human need to fashion a new creation, that the earliest grimoires arose. However, the same disgruntled clerics, also convinced of the sanctity of the church and heavenly power, turned from trying to produce grammars of magic from the few hermetic manuscripts available, to generating their own magical texts, based primarily on church liturgy and extracts from the performance of the catholic Mass.

Such a text as *The Sworn Book of Honourius the Magician,* reputed to have been written by Pope Honourius, is a case in point. This grimoire may be the earliest grammar of a Christian-based system of magic known. In it, the use of prayers and the employment of canonical hours for their recitation certainly indicate that the book, as it appears today, was probably produced during the early 13th or 14th century. However, of the two original manuscripts extant—Sloane MS. 313 and Royal

MS. 17A xlii, the older of the two—Sloane 313, indicates (at least to me) that of its division into three parts or books, Book 1, *Concerning the Seal of God and the Attainment of the Beatific Vision,* is clearly of Dark Ages origin in its language, speech, content and purpose, when compared to the more familiar contents of Books 2 and 3.

Additionally, in my opinion, Book 1 contains a heavy Augustinian influence, while the other two books are more pragmatic in aim; the type of pragmatism that is seen to clearly govern the writing in later grimoires, as in the case of *Clavicula Salomonis* or *The Greater Key of Solomon the King.* While touted by 'modern authorities' as being unusable in a practical sense, two things must be remembered.

First, there is a terribly fragmented work (not to be confused with *The Sworn Book*) bearing the title *The Book of Honourius,* also referred to as, or appearing under its other title of, *The Book of Honourius the Magician.* This is a true hodgepodge of excerpts taken from several grimoires along with purely unintelligible material. It may very well be a relatively recent attempt at producing a new grimoire, although I personally feel it is a botched attempt to either confuse this already unclear area of magic, or to simply lead gullible individuals looking for a quick solution to their problems astray. In its own right then, it is useless as a manual of practical magical evocation.

Secondly, it must be remembered that *any* of the grimoires, of whatever period of history, are themselves the synthesis of numerous hands, as *The Sworn Book* itself may very well have been. Given this, it is my opinion there is nothing in the edition of *The Sworn Book of Honourius the Magician* referred to here to stop the ambitious *and* knowledgeable but cautious Practitioner from attempting to operate from it.

I say cautious because *The Sworn Book* is essentially a *framework* of evocation. It does not, for example, give directions for the preparation and consecration of weapons and materials to be used in the ritual. Rather, as Daniel J. Driscoll points out in the most literate and workable edition of this text with which I am familiar, the

Practitioner using it was assumed to have taken some degree of ecclesiastical training, and hence would know how to prepare the various impedimenta required. Again, this is an indication of the Christian basis of the magic that evolved from the Hermetic stream.

The Sworn Book of Honourius the Magician is probably the oldest existing text of this Dark Ages era. I might add that Waite refers to another version of this work, entitled *The Grimoire of Honourius the Great,* otherwise referred to as "Honourius the Third." Waite describes it at some length in his *Book of Ceremonial Magic.* While Eliphas Levi also commented upon this text as having some importance for the student, I have not seen a complete copy of this particular version of the work, but only excerpts of it. Essentially it is the same in composition and style as *The Sworn Book.*

Likewise, *The Enchiridion of Pope Leo,* which is believed to have first appeared in print in Rome in 1523, gives "...a collection of prayers, to which wonderful virtues were attributed."[2] These were allegedly given to Charlemagne by Pope Leo III in the year 800 C.E., as Arthur Edward Waite, writing in his important work, *The Book of Ceremonial Magic,* states. But by comparing the content, structure, style, and especially the language employed in these prayers with missals of the time, it is clear that this collection—the very basis of the magical text—predates 1,000 C.E., even if their being made a gift to Charlemagne is accepted as a fable. Thus, the very basis of this grimoire has its birth in the era of the Dark Ages. Yet these prayers find their final use in the latter magical tract, which as pointed out, is of much later origin. Such conclusions are important, in that they serve to show the evolution of essential magical material that would be fashioned into magical thought proper during the Renaissance period.

Another unusual manuscript of interest is *The Sword of Moses,* an ancient Hebrew or possibly Aramaic book of

---

[2] Waite, Arthur Edward. *The Book of Ceremonial Magic. A Complete Grimoire.* University Books, Inc., NY. 1961. page 40.

magic believed to date back to the 10th century C.E. This text, translated by M. Gaster in 1896, deals with the use of a magical sword reigned over by angels who were to "attach" themselves to the magician who properly pronounced a special conjuration over the sword, after the appropriate personal preparation and summoning the angels who governed the magical weapon. The names of the angels are completely unintelligible, although the randomness of their spelling is similar to the Barbarous Words of Evocation or Words of Power. They also bear an uncanny resemblance to Enochian names and words that would come into use centuries later due to the work of Dr. John Dee and Edward Kelly. It is interesting to note that even in this 10th century manuscript, there is a distinctive Hermetic style as far as the structure of the manuscript is concerned. Yet, possibly due to its Aramaic or Hebraic influence, it was all but lost or rejected by the early Christian cleric-magicians, who opted to devise their own grimoiric system based upon their religious church doctrines and rituals.

In the end then, the grimoires as we know them today are chiefly of Christian origin, based upon church ceremonial and spiritual ideas, although later secular influences would import the Hebraic Kabbalah into these texts, and expand upon them in ways more familiar to the Western European mind.

3. Middle Ages or Medieval Era Magic—1000 C.E. to 1453 C.E.

Due to the relatively few known magical texts that have survived from this period, we have to begin at the end of this time period and work our way backward. For it was at the end of this period that Heinrich Cornelius Agrippa von Nettesheim was born in Cologne, Germany, in 1486. The works of Albertus Magnus, which were produced from circa 1220 to his death in 1280, served as fuel for Agrippa's intense interest in hidden, or occult, matters. This we know from a letter he wrote to Theodoricus, the bishop of Cyrene.

In that letter, Agrippa states that one of the first books on magic that he ever studied was Albertus' *Speculum.* No doubt, other now lost occult, magical writings and even grimoires from the Dark Ages were also at his disposal during that time. In addition, that Agrippa's writings also reflect much of the earlier Pagan and Neoplatonic magical work of the Hermetic period is obvious, as anyone with even a modest background in Hermetics will quickly note when studying the *Three Books.*

After attending Agrippa's style, along with the works of Albertus Magnus that have survived, I think it is fair to conclude that it was Agrippa who rescued *some* of those early, primarily unknown Dark Ages grammars which are the subject of concern here, and combined them into his now famous *Three Books of Occult Philosophy,* the texts that literally serve as the foundation matter for both the Renaissance Era magic and that of the contemporary Western Magical Tradition.

Another reason Agrippa is credited with carrying over the magic of the Dark Ages can also be presumed from the heavy influence of his senior, Johannes Trithemius (1462–1516). The close, mentor-student relationship between this German abbot and Agrippa is well documented. Owing to Trithemius' own mystical writings, it is almost certain that the abbot had a pronounced effect upon the young Agrippa.

Donald Tyson, writing in his splendidly edited and annotated edition of the *Three Books,* states that it may be that the abbot was not simply Agrippa's counselor and friend, but his master and teacher—particularly in the area of magical evocation. This view is most certainly correct, as the evidence points in that direction, not the least of which is that contributed by Henry Morley in his classic work, *The Life of Henry Cornelius Agrippa.*

But there is another matter to be considered here in terms of the abbot having more than a mild interest and effect on the young Agrippa. The *Three Books* were written by Agrippa in 1509 and the early part of 1510. To me, it is a far reach indeed to conclude that a youth of twenty-three years could have amassed such vast amounts of knowledge and experience even with the help of his master Trithemius, especially given Agrippa's constant wanderings and perpetually meager financial resources. Theory is one thing. Writing from experience, as Agrippa's *Three Books* certainly illustrate, is quite another. Yet he does write with authority, and it is an authority that, in my opinion, surpasses his age at the time this was written.

Additionally, if Trithemius' most famous and notorious work, the three books of his *Steganographia* or Secret Writing are examined, the depth of the man's knowledge and mystical insight becomes abundantly clear. At first glance, the *Steganographia* seems to describe a system of angelic magic. But within it is a highly sophisticated system of cryptography; one that claims to house a synthesis of the mechanics of memory, the science of knowledge, a unique language learning system, practical magic, and a method of transmitting messages without the use of symbols.

In private circulation, the *Steganographia* produced such panic and dread among those who managed to acquire a private copy of it, that Trithemius decided it should never be published. As such, it continued to circulate in manuscript form quietly, until it was finally published in 1606, long after the abbot's death. Comparing its content with that of the *Three Books*, we find similar material as appearing in the *Three Books*, in addition to new material derived from the former's earlier wisdom.

Given this and my suspicions that a young Agrippa would not have the knowledge to pen them from his own experience, it seems very probable that while the *Three Books of Occult Philosophy* were actually written down by Agrippa, they were in fact the result of a lifetime of mental, spiritual, and experimental labor of his master, the abbot Trithemius. However, owing to the latter's clerical position, it is reasonable to speculate that Trithemius wisely chose Agrippa as a vehicle in order to preserve the particular knowledge given in the *Three Books of Occult Philosophy*.

Thus, it may be that it was actually Trithemius who rescued much Dark Ages material and passed it down throughout the generations. In like manner, the magical grimoire the *Heptameron* or "Magical Elements" which is the foundation of this present book, and which is attributed to Peter de Abano, was produced. It was later appended to the so-called *Fourth Book of Occult Philosophy*, which, like the *Three Books*, was said to have been written by Agrippa himself. We know today that this claim is fraudulent, and it will be discussed in some detail in Chapter Four. Nevertheless, in Abano's text, a carryover of Dark Ages and early Christian church material can be clearly found.

Whoever was the true author of the *Three Books* may never be known, if the suspicions presented above are entertained. What is important however, is that this text was produced, and that the authoritative, well-annotated edition of Mr. Tyson's is readily available to us today.

4. Renaissance Era Magic—1460 C.E. to 1600 C.E.

This period in history was a time of rebirth. It was the era of the Renaissance—a resurrection of classical art, architecture, literature and learning. Its first glimmerings blazed across the screen of men's minds in Italy during the latter part of the 14th century. This timeline can be thought of as marking the transition from the Middle Ages to modern times. Thus, the *Three Books of Occult Philosophy* not only support a carry-over of magic from the Dark Ages period, but they also serve as a bridge between the Medieval Era and the Age of the Renaissance.

This transition to the modern world began, strangely, in the very country that became the seat of Christendom. It was marked by the rejection of medieval church teachings and a turn toward reason and empirical knowledge that could be verified through experimentation. Yet, the hold of the church was not to be cut short during this era. Rather, the early objectivists of this period still saw themselves as Christian men, for the most part upholding the values and sanctity of Holy Mother Church.

How did they reconcile this contradiction of faith and
fact? In the same way that most people of religious
conviction do today. They saw their Christian values
reflected in the forbidden, occult and magical works of the
day, or took prohibited teachings of earlier philosophies
and integrated them into their own theology. This very
human need to rationalize uncomfortable and conflicting
conditions is exemplified by an inscription that adorns the
cathedral at Siena, Italy, which was built in the latter part
of the 15th century. The Latin inscription reads: "Hermês-
Mercury the Thrice-Greatest, a contemporary of Moses."
Using such rationalizations then, it is easy to understand
how the Renaissance mind could balance its need for new
knowledge with its Christian-doctrine-based faith in God.
Once again, the effect of early Hermetic Magic on newly
forming occult ideas is apparent. But the matter goes
much further than this.

In this era when such Christian (really, Roman
Catholic-based) magical texts as *The Enchiridion of Pope
Leo*, the *Steganographia, The Sworn Book of Honourius the
Magician* and others, were beginning to enjoy a restricted
circulation, and other grimoires such as the *Grimoirium
Verum*, the *Grand Grimoire,* and the *Arbatel of Magic* were
being produced, (the latter around 1575 according to
Waite), an original Greek document, the *Corpus
Hermeticum* ("Body of Hermetics") was discovered and
translated. This document contains the complete philoso-
phical basis of Hermetics. Its counterpart, the Graeco-
Egyptian papyri, represent the practical magical application of that philosophy.

That the *Corpus* came into such demand during this
period by secular and Christian scholars is understandable, since it was believed that this ancient body of writing
was the true basis of all religions, including Christianity. It
was seen as containing the actual seed material that
would later germinate into Christianity itself. To the
magicians of the time, it represented a sourcebook of great
power, elements of which could be, and were, woven into
their developing grimoires.

The *Arbatel of Magic* especially marks a resurgence of the Hermetic influence. Writing in the introduction to *The Grimoire of Armadel*, a similar-sounding but different grimoire that S.L. MacGregor Mathers would translate centuries later, William Keith states, "The name Arbatel probably derives from Gnostic sources. Arbatiao occurs in the Greek magical papyri, e.g., London papyrus, and the name, APBA£EI, is inscribed on an ancient medal in the Bibliothèque Nationale."[3]

It seems obvious that if it was not for the monumental writings of Dr. Flowers and Professor Betz, our modern understanding of the importance of the true Hermetic Tradition and its effects on the Western Magical development in general, and of grimoire composition in particular, would be as incomplete today as it was in the late 19th century when the Golden Dawn was founded. Nevertheless, human nature being what it is, I believe this shift away from the Hermetic basis of magic occurred due to the lack of Graeco-Egyptian magical papyri. If the magicians of the Renaissance had access to that vast cache of magical papyri that would only find their way to Western Europe in the very early years of the 19th century, I have no doubt that the grimoires we use today would be of an entirely different kind. But the human need to covet and change what exists at any moment in time willed out, and the grimoires as we know them today are the result.

This time period gave rise to a split in the developing magical literature of the times, primarily due to the still prevailing Christian culture. As we have seen, while many of the theories, modes of interpretation, ritual structure, invocations, conjurations, and understanding written down in the *Corpus Hermeticum* were skillfully integrated into the developing magical documents of the era, by and by the Renaissance magicians shifted their focus of atten-

---

[3] Mathers, S.L. MacGregor, translator and editor. *The Grimoire of Armadel*. Introduction by William Keith. Samuel Weiser, Inc. York Beach, Maine. 1998. page 10 footnote.

tion away from the *Corpus Hermeticum,* and toward the compilation of their own magical tracts.

An example of this shift in focus can be found in such strange works as *The Secret Grimoire of Turiel,* dated by its discoverer Marius Malchus as being obtained from an original bearing the date of 1518. This is an early example of a completely Christian-based grimoire using the Hebraic Names of God and early Kabbalistic spirits, messengers, and angels. And while the original manuscripts from which Mathers produced the famous *Clavicula Salomonis* or *The Key of Solomon the King* have their origins in the 17th century, there is also a related 16th century manuscript in the British Museum, in addition to several medieval references to a *Clavicula Salomonis* and *Sigillium Salomonis* ("Seal of Solomon") described in a pamphlet dated 1456, as Richard Cavendish mentions in his introduction to this important grimoire.

Additionally, as early as 1531, Agrippa mentions three of the five books of the famous *Lemegeton Clavicula Salomonis,* commonly called *The Lesser Key of Solomon.* For as Joseph A. Peterson, editor, writes in the most lucid edition of *The Lesser Key* I have seen to date, "In a 1531 list of magical texts, Heinrich Cornelius Agrippa mentioned three of the books of the *Lemegeton* in the same breath, *Ars Almadel, Ars Notoria,* and *Ars Paulina.*"[4]

The other two books of this important grimoire, the *Goetia* and *Theurgia Goetia,* are also mentioned by Agrippa in this list, indicating that most of that magical material was known during the Medieval Magic Era, if not earlier. *The Grimoirium Verum,* another very important magical tract, also appeared during this time. This grimoire is alleged to have originally been published in the year 1517 by Alibeck the Egyptian at Memphis, another clear reference to the Graeco-Egyptian influence.

---

[4] *The Lesser Key of Solomon or Lemegeton Clavicula Salomonis. Detailing the Ceremonial Art of Commanding Spirits Both Good and Evil.* Joseph H. Peterson, ed. Weiser Books, York Beach, Maine. 2001. page xi.

Once again, we also find another example of the Christian need to incorporate such knowledge into their own grimoire production while sharing the credit for it. This can be seen in the attempt to give it Hermetic legitimacy and yet also its own distinctive Judeo-Christian flavor simply by looking at its title page: "Translated from the Hebrew by Plangierè, Jesuite Dominicaine." There are other less known works of this period to be sure, such as *Theosophia Pneumatica* and *The Sword of Moses*. But those presented here seem to be the most important in providing the reader with an introductory understanding of the ideas and social forces that brought these magical texts, and their successors, into being.

Aside from this mainstream magical activity, the basis of which was the betterment of the individual Practitioner's life in the here-and-now, it would be improper to end this time period of magical history without at least mentioning the separate, powerful, magical influence which would be born out of the intense, almost schizophrenic work of Dr. John Dee and Edward Kelly.

Dee was an advisor, confident, and perhaps even spy for Queen Elizabeth of England, who referred to him as "My Noble Intelligencer." Together with Edward Kelly, an eternal romantic dreamer, and sometimes rogue, they formed perhaps the most unusual alliance in all of magical history—but it was one that worked. It was through Kelly's scrying ability that Dee was able to explore and chart the world of the Enochian Angels, eventually synthesizing what is termed Enochian Magic today.

From 1582 through 1587 these two men worked together on a daily basis. As Kelly scryed, Dee took copious notes, applying his tremendous intellectual ability to give structure to the knowledge the angels of the Tablets imparted to Kelly during their crystal gazing sessions. In a microcosmic way, the interaction of Dee and Kelly is metaphorically comparable to the Greek influence on the Egyptian magical papyri; for it took the magical or scrying ability of Kelly, made understandable and ordered by the intellectual struggles of Dee, to evolve this particular system of magic. Yet it was not until the advent of the Order of the Golden Dawn that this strange system of magic would become popularly known to the world. Like the *Corpus Hermeticum*, it would remain submerged for centuries to come.

5. Transition Era Magic—1600 C.E. to 1800 C.E.

I have labeled this period of history as such because it seems that during this time further efforts to develop what would come to be known as the Western Magical Tradition, fell to a great extent to the individual, lone Practitioner here and there. Those efforts to refine or produce additional grimoires from existing source material were conducted privately, and the grimoires eventually found their way into such collections as the British Museum in London and the Bibliothèque de l'Arsenal in Paris.

Such works as the *Lemegeton,* and its most popular tract, the *Goetia,* as they are known from the 17th century onwards, were composites of earlier works as we have seen. They were synthesized or put together into the workable form we now recognize during this period. The same is true for such others as the *Clavicula Salomonis,* a 1655 Latin edition which exists as Waite cites in his work, and the *Grimoire of Armadel.*

This was also the time period in which many of the Sloane manuscripts were produced, used to integrate the works in question and which we fortunately still have access to today. Examples of these are Sloane 2383, Sloane 2731, Sloane 3825, Sloane 3648, Harley 6483, and additional MS 10862, among many others. Granted, it was through the later efforts of such translators as S.L. MacGregor Mathers, A.E. Waite, Aleister Crowley and others that the grimoires we have use of today actually came into being. But it was the efforts made during this era—from 1600 to 1800—that gave them the basis for translation and construction. What then were the forces that produced this period of grimoiric refinement and synthesis of the magical tracts as we recognize them today?

The forces at work are clear enough. First, a continuation of the Renaissance influence which was then, secondly, accelerated by the Industrial Revolution. For it was the Renaissance or Period of Enlightenment that produced a movement away from the dictates of the Christian church toward logic, reason, and the scientific method. In turn, these intellectual stirrings eventually loosened the stranglehold of the Christian church, even upon the average individual.

But with that loosening evolved a shift away from all things magical over these following two centuries, principally because during this time people sought to exercise direct control over their daily, personal lives. Rather than supplicating to a Christian god believed to be in the clouds, people began to explore not only the realm of Nature, but their own inner world of self-determination and thought during this transitional era. Reason, Aristotelian logic, and the Scientific Method were the means by which those explorations were made, and as is so often the case with individuals, the entire European and Western culture countered the centuries of religious influence by swinging to the opposite extreme.

Of course, as in the Renaissance, the average man and woman still could not yet fully extricate themselves from the church's influence. But unlike the Period of Enlightenment, rather than find Christianity in pagan symbols or blend other, more ancient philosophical ideas and magical systems into their own religious beliefs, people simply choose to all but ignore both the daily demands of the church, and discard anything that had the term 'magicalism' attached to it. This quickly became a popular and derogatory word during the 18th century, and referred to anything supernatural that laid outside of the church.

It was during the later years of this era, the Age of the Industrial Revolution, 1760–1830, that Western society as a whole eventually responded in such a way. The mass of people now looked toward structured governments—ever increasing in their complexity—and to the world at large for their daily sustenance, comfort, and intellectual growth. In short, science was 'in,' the church was a convenient 'there' when it was needed, and magic was 'out.' As a result, those individuals who, as in all eras, were interested in matters occult or hidden, continued to work with the material they had, evolving the grimoires and producing synthetic, integrated magical tracts which many of them then refined further through private experimentation or practice. It is to these individuals that—in effect—we owe as much today as we do to those later translators who were to popularize and perhaps even fine tune the work of this era.

6. Gothic Revival Era Magic—1800 C.E. to 1900 C.E.

In the early years of the 19th century, three very important events in the history of magic occurred. First, in July, 1801, a rather young man, Francis Barrett, successfully published his magical tract *The Magus—A Complete System of Occult Philosophy* through the firm Lackington, Allen, of London, England, as reported by Timothy d'Arch Smith in his introduction to the 1967 edition. What is not generally known is that this system of magic is actually the *Three Books of Occult Philosophy* penned by Agrippa, although in considerably modified form.

Barrett's publication is important for several reasons. But before we look at them, it is necessary to understand a bit more of the history of his work. Although *The Three Books of Occult Philosophy* were penned by Agrippa in 1509–1510, they were not published until 1531, and the edition itself was not complete. Rather, while it contained the entire index for all three volumes, it ended with Book One and a note to the reader. In that note Agrippa explains that personal problems prohibited him from releasing the other two volumes, yet he assured the reader they would soon be released after being edited. It was not until 1533 however, that the first complete edition of *The Three Books* was published in Cologne, Germany.

Two years later, Agrippa died in France, penniless and among strangers. His work would appear in the Latin *Opera* not long after his death. The English edition with which modern day occultists are so familiar, was translated and published in 1651 in London. It is, even for its errors, the best of the English translations as Henry Morley, the biographer of Agrippa, wrote in the 1856 edition of his important contribution *The Life of Henry Cornelius Agrippa.*

The English translation of the *Opera* contains all three volumes of Agrippa's writings. Barrett plagiarized large sections of *The Three Books* in his publication of *The Magus, or Celestial Intelligencer,* without giving any credit to Agrippa. This is held as absolutely contemptuous by many modern day writers, and they are most certainly correct. But I think the reader should also know—plagiarism aside, but not excused—that if it were not for Barrett, large sections of *The Three Books* would probably have been lost to antiquity.

For nowhere during the period extending from 1533 to 1801 do we find any mention of *The Three Books* in any magical writings, save for its translation into English in 1651, and in Henry Morley's book. There is no doubt that the 1651 English edition had a powerful impact upon the production of later grimoires, although not credited by them. Traces of this influence can be seen in such 17th century grimoires as the *Grimoire of Armadel,* especially in the wording and style of the conjurations, and in what appears to be derivations of several sigils of the spirits. Additionally, as I view them, several of the Sloane manuscripts of the time also show evidence of Agrippa's influence.

Thus, whether by omission or commission, other writers neglected to cite their Agrippa source material as well. Without adequate reference to such material, the student of magic is, regardless of the period of history, left to fend for himself in a field already muddied with distortions and confused by errors at the very outset. This can and does increase the student's chances for partial, incomplete, negative, or worst of all, disastrous results.

There are also two other strange twists regarding the importance of Agrippa's books and Barrett's pirating. These are other examples of how human and social forces were instrumental in forming the grimoires and methods of magic that we see today. First, because *The Three Books* were not plagiarized earlier reveals the depth of obscurity into which they had fallen. Plagiarism is a difficult task to accomplish, at least with publications generally known. But with obscure or forgotten texts, little skill is required, and this is another indication of the ambiguous state into which *The Three Books* had fallen.

Secondly, that Barrett's book succeeded in effecting to such an extent what would become the most famous magical order in history, the Hermetic Order of the Golden Dawn, is remarkable, and can only serve to further illustrate Agrippa's anonymity. For as Tyson so accurately points out in his edited and annotated edition of *The Three Books*, this magical order based much of its very root material on Barrett's plagiarized publication, along with all of the errors and omissions that *The Magus or Celestial Intelligencer* contains.

One has only to compare, side by side, Barrett's writings with the original Order material of the Golden Dawn itself, to see this clearly. Hence the Hermetic Order of the Golden Dawn did *not* base the names of its spirits, their sigils, the structure and configuration of the planetary kameas, or their Qabalistic techniques upon the original 1651 English translation of *The Three Books*; but rather upon the dubious work of Francis Barrett. As history has shown, Aleister Crowley, in turn, based his entire system of magic and subsequent magical orders directly on the Golden Dawn, of which he was an early member. In the end, Barrett's character flaws and their role in pirating massive sections of Agrippa's writing cannot be overlooked or condoned. But his unintentional contribution of rescuing *The Three Books*, and the impact his one book had on Western Magic, must be recognized for what it was: a bittersweet fruit that provided the seed material for the development of later structured magical systems—a phenomenon unknown up to that time.

What I consider to be the second major event that occurred during this era was the arrival of a large cache of magical papyri, purchased by an Armenian, Jean d'Anastasi. As Dr. Flowers explains: "He [Anastasi] bought the bulk of the known magical papyri in a single purchase in Thebes and had the entire lot shipped to Europe where they were auctioned off to a variety of European museums..."[5] But still, the papyri were largely ignored until the *Fragment of a Graeco-Egyptian Work Upon Magic* was produced by Charles Wycliffe Goodwin for the Cambridge Antiquarian Society in 1853; a mere thirty-four years before the founding of the Golden Dawn by Westcott and Mathers.

Doubtless this and other Hermetic documents from that cache were used in the synthesis of the Golden Dawn material. From Egyptian Names of the Gods and Goddesses, to Words of Power, ritual structure, the construction and use of magical alphabets, and mental visualizations, the Golden Dawn system exemplifies the use of original Hermetic material found in the papyri. But even so, it must be remembered that the science of translating and understanding the papyri had only begun when the Golden Dawn used what was available to form its own structure and practice. As such, errors, omissions, and a lack of understanding that plagued the early years of the field of papyri translation found their way into the formation of the Golden Dawn, as did the genuine Hermetic kernels of power.

It might also be interesting for the reader to know that Goodwin's paper contains the basis of what would become known as The Bornless Ritual, the very heart and core of the magical system that would be expanded and

---

[5] Flowers, Stephen Edred, PhD., ed. *Hermetic Magic. The Postmodern Magical Papyrus of Abaris.* Samuel Weiser, Inc. York Beach, Maine. 1995. page 15.

popularized by Crowley in the next magical era to follow. Yet here too, the base information derived from Goodwin's work contained many errors and omissions. Although a number of them have been corrected by authors after Crowley, the actual ritual as contained in the papyri in question remains vastly different from that which is still found in books being published on the subject.

The third major event that occurred during this period was the magical work and detailed writing of Alphonse Louis Constant (1810–1875), known by his magical motto or name of Eliphas Levi. Levi's works are deeply steeped in Christianity, which is apparent from their theology. Yet he misses nothing as far as Qabalah and Practical Qabalah or Applied Magic is concerned.

It is my view that Levi's life and writings constitute the first significant attempt to achieve a synthesis of Christian doctrine with Esoteric philosophy and magical principles. He was occupied with the synthesis of those three great subjects that run as a continuous thread throughout all the eras of magic: the nature of Man, the Universe, God, and the intersection of the three. His many books reflect some of the earlier Qabalistic principles of Agrippa, although he also borrows from such strictly Jewish texts as Simeon Ben-Jochal's *Siphra Dzeniuta,* and Johann Reuchlin's classic text *De Arte Cabalistics* (The Art of Kabbalah), along with Reuchlin's *De Verbo Mirifico* (The Mirific Word).

It is interesting to note that Levi, like Agrippa, was so influenced by Reuchlin. A strict follower of Jewish mysticism, Reuchlin refused to join with his Christian contemporaries of the time, believing them to harbor intents of destroying the Hebrew Kabbalah and the Talmud. Ruchelin so spoke out against this Christian arrogance as he perceived it, that he insisted it was only possible for Christians to have meaningful intellectual exchanges with Jews unless they first acquired a deep knowledge of the Jewish philosophers and their doctrines.

Yet in Levi's case, his gentle nature and penetrating, formidable intellectual ability were able to override even these dogmatic attitudes as well as those of his own Christian church, enabling him to nurture the information he found in the Qabalistic treasures of these Jewish sources. Even his expulsion from the seminary after first taking minor orders and later becoming a Deacon, did not decrease his love for the church. This expulsion, due to holding views contrary to the Roman Catholic Church, may have fanned his already deep interest in matters occult, and may have been the very source of his radical views that brought an end to the clerical life designed for him by his family and parish priest.

Yet Levi did not borrow from *The Three Books* or the earlier Hebrew Kabbalistic sources so extensively that his own writings failed to achieve their own unique identity. Rather, these earlier writings served as base material which he would transform through his own genius and magical practice into a powerful and viable system of magic that is all but disregarded by today's New Age movement and its magical currents. Moreover, his writings produced what I consider to be the first true eclectic synthesis of Medieval, Renaissance, and Transition Era Magic.

The interested reader might take note that his works of special importance are: *Dogme Et Rituel De La Haute Magie* (Transcendental Magic—Its Doctrine and Ritual), *The History of Magic*, *The Paradoxes of the Highest Science*, *The Book of Splendours*, *The Mysteries of the Qabalah*, *The Great Secret*, (the latter three are a trilogy), and the *Magical Ritual of Sanctum Regnum*. Two interesting short papers, *The Conjuration of the Four Elements* and *The Science of Hermes*, are also noteworthy. More of Levi's magical work became integrated into the foundation of the Golden Dawn and through it, into Crowley's own Order than is admitted to or even known by the proponents of these two schools of magic to this day.

A fourth and final major event that occurred during this time period was the formation of the magical society upon which most of today's Western Occultism is based: the Hermetic Order of the Golden Dawn. So much has been written about the history, theory, and ritual procedures of this society however, that another extensive rehash here of the known facts would not serve to give the seasoned reader further insights into this magical Order. I have however, provided some references in the Suggested Reading List that may prove to be of value to newer students wishing to learn more about this group.

For our present purposes, what might prove helpful to all readers is a summary of those key points regarding the Golden Dawn that have been discussed throughout this chapter, and to flesh them out a bit with some small amount of additional material. These issues are admittedly not popular. Some are personal interpretations of the writings of Westcott. Others are simply factual. Together they are meant to be used in tempering the grandiose and oft times spectacular claims made about the Order work by numerous authors and different factions claiming to have 'direct apostolic descend' from the original Golden Dawn society.

As in the study and practice of any subject, grand, sweeping emotional claims inevitably lead to unrealistic expectations that eventually culminate in disappointment, frustration, and anger. The result is the disappointed student, who scraps all of the information or the entire system itself, since he or she cannot prove all they were told is inevitable or even possible by "holding to the letter of the instructions and Teachings." The key points worth remembering are:

✧ — Hermetic manuscripts were used in the construction of the Hermetic Order of the Golden Dawn system of magic. Yet the original Hermetic Order did not possess the substantial Hermetic basis to which it laid claim. The reason for this is that the magical formulas and spells given in the Graeco-Egyptian papyri, which were said to have served as the basis of the Order Teachings, required extensive translation and study by authorities in the then emerging field of Papyriology. This study required the last eight or nine decades before those ancient writings finally began to yield their magical fruit. Whether this was suspected by W.W. Westcott, a co-founder of the Golden Dawn, can only be surmised. But his *Collectanea Hermetica* seems to suggest this.

Additionally, it must be remembered that it was actually Westcott who established the Order, and it was he who wrote the Knowledge Lectures and laid the foundation upon which it was built. His co-founder, S.L. MacGregor Mathers, confined his contribution to producing the Grade ceremonies from the famous Golden Dawn Cipher Manuscript. Nevertheless, even though Westcott was a part of the Gothic Revival Era Magic owing simply to his time in history, he appears to have had the vision to at least intimate that a broad-based Hermetic quality was lacking in the very Order documents that served the basis for the magical order which he—for all practical purposes—created single-handedly.

It is my contention that Westcott's public claim to Hermeticism was not an act of deception meant to mislead the aspirant. Rather, one gets the impression he was simply aware that the Hermetic material to which he had access was very sparse. It is likely his scholarly nature and academic training as a physician lent him a more rational view of life, although he could not resist claiming to a certain Hermetic basis according to the ancient tracts available at the time. But apparently his caution, as detected in the *Collectanea*, was largely ignored, as can be found by examining many of the ritual and ceremonial documents of the Golden Dawn, or the material of most other contemporary societies that bear the word Hermetic in their names. In short, it is my view that from the beginning of the Golden Dawn to this very day, the word Hermetic is used incorrectly, and that in place of it, another term more closely describes the content of such magical teachings. Such a word would be Arcane.

✧ — A powerful example of this Hermetic deficiency can be seen in the poorly translated manuscript that served as the *summum bonum* of both the Golden Dawn, and Crowley's later magical order which was built upon the Golden Dawn structure: the *Fragment of a Graeco-*

Egyptian Work Upon Magic. As mentioned before, this was produced by Charles Wycliffe Goodwin in 1853, just thirty-four years before the founding of the Golden Dawn by Westcott and Mathers, and its errors, omissions, and the lack of Hermetic understanding that plagued the early years of papyri translation found their way into the formation of the Golden Dawn. This particular paper of Goodwin's served as the basis of what would become known as The Bornless Ritual, the very heart and core of the magical system that would be expanded upon greatly and popularized by Crowley in the next magical era to follow.

✧ — It was Francis Barrett's 1801 publication of *The Magus Or Celestial Intelligencer*—a plagiarized and butchered version of Agrippa's lost *The Three Books of Occult Philosophy*—which served as the source book from which most of the Golden Dawn's root material was derived. Owing to this, the errors and omissions in that Hermetic, Qabalistic, and arcane material also entered into the structure of the Golden Dawn. As a result, the Golden Dawn did not base the names of its spiritual hosts, their sigils, the structure and configuration of the planetary kameas, or their Qabalistic techniques upon the original, most complete 1651 English translation of *The Three Books*; but rather upon the dubious work of Francis Barrett. And as history later shows, Aleister Crowley, in turn, based his entire system of magic and subsequent magical orders directly on the Golden Dawn, of which he was an early member.

7. Modern Era Magic—1900 C.E. to Present Day
From 1900 onward, after the dissolution of the Hermetic Order of the Golden Dawn, the original members went off on their own to pursue further magical or occult work. Mathers founded his own magical society, the Order of the Alpha et Omega. A.E. Waite, his own school of Tarot, while yet others took to Eastern philosophies and went so far as to take up residences in far off eastern lands, practicing various forms of Yoga and Buddhism.

Accounts of these individuals and their post-Golden Dawn activities can be found throughout the literature of the field. In the case of the Golden Dawn, I have provided a few references in the Suggested Reading list at the end of this book for those interested in such details.

The three most notable events arising out of this breakup will now be dealt with briefly. Selected material is provided in the reading list that will enable interested readers to pursue these matters further.

First, there is the life and magical activities of Aleister Crowley. He translated the famous grimoire, the *Goetia*, for Mathers; he published his famous *Equinox*; he founded his own magical order, the A∴A∴ (Argentum Astrum); he made contact with his spiritual guide, Aiwa, which resulted in the *Book of the Law*, which is supposed to lay the groundwork for a new way of living; he engaged in many episodes with drugs, sex, and intrigues; and he pounded out a system of magic and spelled it Magick to differentiate it from the earlier forms he considered vulgar.

His magical system is eagerly followed by thousands of people to this day. His impact on magic in general and on the Attainment of the Knowledge and Conversation of the Holy Guardian Angel in particular through his intense ritual—which serves as the very heart of his system—cannot be denied. Opinions of him are as varied as are his voluminous writings on poetry, science, religion and magic, all of which are integrated at different points in his career. He insisted his religion of Thelema is not for everyone, but as with any area of magic, it is up to the individual to determine the worthiness of his writings and methods for use in the synthesis of their personal system. Perhaps the most fitting description of this man is that he was an oddity wrapped in an enigma. His greatest impact on magic began around 1900 and ended with his death in 1947.

Born Israel Regardie, he later took the name Francis after Saint Francis, for personal reasons besides those that appear in print. While working as a secretary for Crowley, the very little magic he actually learned from his employer coupled with his already intense interest in occult matters, skyrocketed his influence in providing the psychological framework of Western Magic which underlies the popular conceptions of the field as it is known today. But in doing so, he still retained the purity of earlier Medieval, Renaissance, and Transition Era magic material—at least in his early writings.

A good example of this retention can be found in what is still considered his most valuable contribution, *The Tree of Life*. That Regardie would forever be tied to Crowley may have been inevitable, seeing the influence "The Beast," as the older man called himself, had upon the younger man. Regardie would spend his entire life defending his former employer and sometime friend, publishing books and papers, always trying to explain the bohemian who was Aleister Crowley.

At the same time, Regardie remained dedicated to the Golden Dawn. From publishing the original Order material which brought him both fame and infamy, to his attempts to relate that material to both known and suspected psychological functions, to his efforts to integrate those explanations into expanded and refined material as can be seen in his book *The Art of True Healing*—Regardie's life was dedicated to the exploration of the unconscious: the very working realm of magic.

Despite this public image, during one of our conversations in 1978 he admitted to me, "If the truth be known, I am still of the old system of magic, just as you are!" Such was the complexity of the man. Since my final views on magic differ considerably from those of Regardie's, my former Teacher and friend, I recommend caution when studying his works. It is not because they are wrong or inaccurate. Rather, their turgid psychological conjecture and explanation require an extensive knowledge of both psychology and psychoanalysis in order to effectively understand them. In addition, the psycho-babble diatribe that now defines what has come to be known as the New Age, and which I place as beginning in 1965 and continuing on to this present day, has muddied those already thick psychological waters even further. The other reasons for giving the reader this general caution when dealing with such 'new' material will become more apparent as he or she continues to study this book. Certainly psychological principles are involved in *any* form of magical practice. But one must ask whether they are *practical, verifiable* principles, or artificial, unverifiable constructs used to give structure to explanations of magic where none exists.

The third and final event of this era of magic is the arrival of the so-called New Age. Around 1965 there was a new, fresh feeling in the air. The restraints of Christian and other fixed, dogmatic, doctrinally- driven religions became all but completely severed from the minds and lives of everyday people. An expanding economy, higher wages, experimental television, an explosion of printed media ranging from magazines and tabloids to newspapers and books, loosened the puritanical and provincial codes of conduct and thought generated and maintained by the religious status quo for over two millennium.

Along with the change rode an honest, pure desire on the part of many people to explore new personal vistas and ideas. But as is so often the case with radical change, something else hitched a ride with this double-edged sword of new and plenty. Something no one at the time could have predicted. The human need to explore and improve, quickly became overtaken by the shiftless, lazy, irresponsible, instant gratification, quick-fix minorities. It was they who made the news, a media attitude that entrenched itself deeply into the public psyche. In keeping with this self-serving motive, the 'oppressed' were handed a wide audience by the media and press.

For over a decade, it seemed that this vocal minority and the objects of their disagreements were all that existed, and so public opinion was swayed. After all, it was the Dawning of the Age of Aquarius, the time of the hippie, free love, dropping out and tuning in, flower children, make love, not war, and love everyone. All of this was instantaneously discarded by these same free thinkers when their own pleasures were challenged or their views questioned. It was not a time of reaction. It was a time of action, unleashed by the infantile in people. A time to allow the child within to have free and blameless reign over everything without.

Upon the heels of these 'rights' to 'do your own thing,' came the writers of a type of occultism that perfectly reflected the prevailing social chaos. Books slid off the presses by the thousands, all advocating the occult equivalent of the new social norm. Golden Dawn, Crowley's system of magic, Medieval, Transition and Gothic Revival Era rituals could be done with whatever sort of implements ('weapons') one could make in a few minutes or buy at the nearest head shop.

And the grimoires? "Man, I want all that power!" was the rallying cry of those drawn toward the "New Occult." It was summed up in the attitude, "Hey, man, do I really have to do all those weird and impossible things, like draw some crazy seal with the blood of a black rooster and draw all those complicated circles on the floor with some so-called Holy Name I don't understand? Man, it's gotta be easier than this! Nothin' can be this hard, 'cause I got **rights**!" And all too often the answer he or she wanted to hear came back to the budding aspirant on the New Path to spiritual advancement and worldly power.

"Of course not!" was (and still is) the resounding counsel given by some latter day, self-styled 'authority' of this New Occult phenomenon. "It is enough that you have the 'intent' in mind. It's enough you can visualize the circle—you only need one you know, not three like those musty old magic books say—and all those divine names? Ha! They can be dispensed with! In these 'modern times' we *know* better! 'Blood of a black rooster?' Come on, give me a break!" the new authority would continue. "Everyone *knows* that those 'requirements' in those old musty books were traps for the gullible. They don't apply to cool dudes like us! And who says you can't perform all the magic you want in your dingy little apartment right here in the middle of Squalor City, USA? Man, I'm telling ya, it's better to do a little magic than none at all!"

Rationalization, laziness, lack of Will, absence of self discipline, greed, mental instability, emotional immaturity, all prevailed in the written presentations that dared to call themselves magical texts. It is my opinion—and I warn the reader, only *my* opinion—that these expediencies and human deficiencies were and still are at the root of most of the so-called New Age material available today. In the main, I consider that material utter rubbish, to be disregarded and despised both for what it is and for what it is not, but claims to be.

This hippie era transitioned into the next period of disgrace, that of the yuppie generation. Those years, peopled by the occult-minded members of the former drop out and tune in crowd who were disillusioned by the New Age expediencies, saw the rise of a new banner. The new battle cry of anything for the God-almighty dollar, symbol-over-substance, prevailed from the early 1980's through the 1990's. Today, their successors have no banners or rallying cries at all. Rather, their teckie mentalities aim to improve upon nature without understanding their own, and it has reduced the world of intellectual and spiritual stages to a mock play with lines of a resurging dialectical materialism that are read over and over again, day after day. In their shadow are the popular New Age teachings spouting their own band of dogmas, replacing those of the former Holy Mother Church.

In concluding this chapter, I would like to make one final distinction in the eras of magic that I trust will help to fine tune the reader's awareness of the material to follow. The following divisions of magic will prove helpful—

Hermetic Magic is considered here to be a *separate,* distinct era when core magical material was developed. It is not dealt with in this present book.

Dark Ages, Medieval, Renaissance, and Transition Era magic constitutes a developmental and application period which will hereafter be referred to as the **Old System of Magic** or simply as the **Old System.**

The **Gothic Revival** and **Modern Era** magic will be made reference to by what I have already termed **New Age Magic** or simply the **New System of Magic** or **New System.** Yes, this is correct. I place the Golden Dawn, its numerous spin offs—for example, the works of W.E. Butler, W.G. Gray, and Dion Fortune, as well as Crowley's system of magic in with this lot—because once again, in my opinion, while these magical systems are ultimately viable and workable, they are so only in a purely theoretical sense.

This conclusion, a consequence of what has been given in this chapter concerning these systems of magic, is that in their present form, their eclectic nature is fragmented. That is, the pieces which compose their systems do not fit well together. They do not support either the whole, or the specific rituals whose framework they are supposed to support. This inadequacy leads the Practitioner into states of severe personality imbalance, self-delusion, reality distortion, and extreme rationalization that requires the use of selective attention in order to prove the magic works, or more correctly, in the end: "Well, it works— sometimes. Sort of. You know. That's just how it is." And the Practitioner of these systems is right—that's just how it is.

Our concern throughout the rest of this book will deal exclusively with **Old System Magic.** Certainly this earlier type of magic is difficult. But its material will be empty of the double-talk, interpretations, hypocrisy, empty promises, and monumental distortions that define the so-called New Age.

Chapter Three

Magical Propositions and Axioms for Success and Survival

By now you must be saying to yourself, "Well, you've condemned the Golden Dawn and Crowley's system of magic, so what do *you* have to offer that's so much better?" So I will answer.

From this point on, the reader will be given Magical Principles—not speculations or conjectures—that will enable him or her to do two things other books have not been able to. Why am I so sure of this? Because otherwise the reader would not have gotten to this point in the text. The principles to follow will enable the Practitioner to:

1. Perform the magic of evocation the way it was designed to be performed by the ancient magicians, and to do so with the expectation of success while yet *thriving* on such a mentally and emotionally harrowing experience.

2. Design, perfect, and polish the only type of magical system that will work consistently and reliably. And the only system that will do this is *your own system*. There are none others. There are no recipe books in this field. There is no single magical book that will enable you to achieve all that you want to achieve, do all that you want to do, and become all that you want to be. Instead, there are Magical Principles that will enable you to accomplish all of the above, but they are to be used or discarded, as the intelligent or foolish nature of the Practitioner dictates. It is as simple and as hard a fact as that.

Gothic and Modern Era Magic aside, it is nevertheless necessary to state that in the past forty years of personal magical practice, I have seen very few of the grimoire-based, material gain promises fulfilled—at least to the full extent promised. I am speaking here of those operations taken from any of the classical grimoires I so obviously favor, namely, the grimoires of Old System Magic. More importantly, even when partial results were achieved, those results were *always* accompanied by a series of events that took some material asset away from the Practitioner as if in payment for the paltry results achieved, while in addition causing him or her some serious personal problems. Yet, I am sure the reader who has experimented with evocation from texts of Old System Magic knows this all too well.

Why the silence of the ancient magicians on these key points of evocation? It can only be surmised, but it is a reasonable guess, based upon a study of the Old System grimoires, that they are literally ceremonial workbooks, much like a laboratory manual the reader might remember from a high school or college chemistry or physics course. The instructions are given as to how to produce the result, but the theory and interpretation behind those results are left to the course textbook, in this case, the private magical journals of the Old System magicians. And to date, none of those magical course textbooks of the early Western magicians have surfaced.

To be sure, there are many reasons for the partial results achieved, and the evocation aftermath as I call the personal problems that also arise. As it was in times past when each magician had to find his own way through the perils of magical practice, so it remains today. The difference is, what I am about to give the reader here are the insights which I have worked out throughout the past four decades of practice, and which were confirmed time after time by my contemporaries who tested them out in their own practice of magical evocation to physical manifestation.

The long and the short of it is that they *work*, as the reader will find for him or herself if they put this 'grimoire' of mine into practice. In short, what is written here is the equivalent of what every magician from the Hermetic Era of Magic through the Gothic Revival Era of Magic had to work out individually. Group working in this case did no good. Each individual has a unique set of mental, emotional, psychic and spiritual variables which must be dealt with by the individual Practitioner.

But there is even more to the matter. The serious Student of the Mysteries will find that if the magical propositions and axioms to follow are used to design, test, refine and polish their own integrated system of magical practice—one in which evocation is but a very important component—they will be able to devise a life philosophy that will enable them to grown mentally, emotionally, psychically, and in the end, spiritually, but in a true sense. A new human being will be produced. One who will have discovered his or her own True Will or the Will of God for them in their present life. Such an individual will receive all of the divine and material aid they need to accomplish this Will *easily*, and perfectly. The ancient promise set down in the Old System grimoire *The Book of the Sacred Magic of Abramelin the Mage* will be fulfilled. Such an individual will become one of the elect of the earth, and one of the greatest beings to have walked upon it. Their influence will endure throughout the ages, and will emerge unblemished. The attempts of the inferiors to decry, ridicule, and rationalize away the work of such a one who has attained, will disappear as quickly and completely as a mist in the morning sun, as will they.

Evocation, like any branch of magic, is a *tool* to be used in accomplishing this final end; this Great Work. As a tool, it is not to be worshiped. It is not to be used to give you dominion over others, or to interfere in their life paths, unless you are attacked by them unjustly. It is not a method of exalting your own weak ego, so you fancy yourself something you are not, and increase the suffering in this world. Nor is it license to allow your infantile hates,

self adulation and whims of desire to run wild, turning
you into another tragic case of Dr. Jekyll and Mr. Hyde, or
another Dr. Faustus. Yet this act of evocation is to be
respected. Such respect comes only through understanding the Act of Summoning, the nature of the beings you
will be dealing with, the mechanics behind the rituals, and
the forces involved in the ceremony. The magical propositions and axioms which follow will enable you to lay the
foundation for this understanding. The respect will flow
from it.

You have probably hear the statements "Physics is
nothing but mathematics" or "The Great Mathematician
geometrized and created the universe and everything in
it." Both are true, for mathematics is the very language of
nature. It is a process by which formerly unknown relationships existing between components in a physical system are expressed in quantitative terms. In turn, such
mathematical terms then allow for prediction and independent verification of the physical system; the very basis
of scientific thought and here, of magic.

Of course, it is not possible to quantify the objective
and subjective experience of any magical act, ritual, or
ceremony, due to the human element. Nevertheless, it is
possible to use the principles of mathematics to establish
the relationships that exist between the components of the
magical system. I am not using the mathematical model
here in a metaphorical sense, but rather as an *application* to
the experience of magic. Let us begin with fundamental
units and later apply them to the practice of evocation as
set down in this book.

There are two basic ideas upon which all branches of
mathematics are constructed, evolved, and applied. The
concept of the *proposition* and the *axiom*. A proposition is
simply a sentence or formula used in a logical argument.
It has a 'truth value.' That is, it can either be true or false,
but not both. Any argument then consists of a series of
propositions that lead to a conclusion, which itself is
another proposition. The propositions of the argument are
themselves linked by logical Operators or devices which

indicate relationships between the statements (propositions).

An axiom is an *initial* proposition (statement) *that is accepted without proof, and from which further propositions are then derived.* So a logical argument can begin with a proposition that is an axiom, and from which other propositions follow, and which lead to a conclusion. The idea behind all of this is then a *proof,* or formal way to insure that the entire argument—from initial axiom (proposition) to conclusion (proposition) is true. It is not hard to apply these general concepts to magic, remembering that the human element cannot be quantified in the process.

Now we can look for the structure and causation behind magic, just as we did in coming to an understanding of the structure and causation behind the history of the grimoires in Chapter Two. It is up to the Practitioner to *"Do the proof"* of these arguments as it is called in mathematics. And this can only be done by performing the evocation itself, as I did throughout the four decades spent in (re)discovering and ironing out these principles of magical working.

The reader will notice that while the axioms presented are exactly as defined above, some propositions of the arguments are presented in the form of what are called negative propositions. These are statements whose nature are the opposite of the axiom, and which are an allowed style in logical argument. I have used them here in order to make a more powerful impact on the reader's mind. Do not fear. The conclusion of each argument will be found to be inevitable as a result of both the negative and standard form propositions, and will support the original axiom.

Axiom 1—Different systems of magic as previously defined; or components and requirements of different systems of magic, must never be mixed. Neither must grimoires or other magical texts within a given system itself be mixed.

Argument 1—The New Age, that period spanning the years from 1965 to the present, not only introduced the idea of expediency in magical working as explained in Chapter Two, it expanded upon and mandated it as an obvious necessity during the decade of the 1990's. It became 'reasonable' to use the ritual implements from one system of magic in another system of magic. For example, everyone knew (and most New Agers still do!) that it was perfectly acceptable to use the magical weapons from the Golden Dawn, for example, in evoking a demonic entity from the *Goetia*.

The logic for this freewheeling permission? It would follow something like this: "Well, this author says so. After all, he's an *authority*! He's got a book published, so he must *know* what he's talking about! Besides, there's a picture of the author on the back cover of the book, standing next to this world renowned magician! He even has his arm around him! Surely this is more *proof* that this author is an *authority*! So I can do what I want—oops, that is—what he says I can do! And it's soooo easy now! What a relief! World of power, fame and riches, here I come!" Or worse yet, "Spiritual development and power, here I come!"

An author's authority to write and effect the life of his reader does not come from such pictures on the back cover of his book. Nor does it come from the benedictions granted his work by other 'authorities' in the field, or from reviewers' opinions, whether good or ill. The authority the Practitioner seeks will be found in the author's words themselves. They will speak with an experience to a level of the reader's mind that is beyond the conscious realm. The reader will know the author has arrived in the work being read, and that the particular book being studied is there to guide the Practitioner along his or her own *individual* Path. There is no more 'authority' to be sought than this.

By contrast, another expediency developed was to change the requirements set down in the ancient grimoires. As an example. Another individual desires to work from the same *Goetia*. But the directions for preparing the weapons are—well, you know—just too 'weird.' They are unreasonable. "The 'blood of a black cock that never trode hen' needed to make the Secret Seal of Solomon? This is ridiculous! Where do I get a black rooster from? This is obviously one of those traps for fools I read about in that other book. Sure. That's what it is! There's gotta be an easier way!" And the easier way is taken. Then the experiment in evocation is conducted—after it has been butchered by the "true Practitioner of the magical art" so as to be unrecognizable from the original. The result of the evocation? Now look who the fool is!

Yet another false permission devised by the trite and trendy attitudes of the New Age was that of mixing the Words of Power from the grimoire being used with "more powerful" Words of Power or "Barbarous Words of Evocation" from another grimoire, or importing and mixing magical languages together. Another example using the *Goetia* will make this clear. In the last years of the 1990s, books appeared advocating that the pronunciation of the conjurations given in the *Goetia* were not uttered in their given tongue, but in the Enochian, or the language of the angels as it is also called.

The result? An established set of words, set side by side in order to produce a desired physical effect, were distorted beyond recognition. It is no different than trying to tune the FM dial of a stereo to your favorite radio station after adding more elements to the tuner. What you will get is a distorted signal, mixed with more overlapping frequencies and harmonics, with more distortions above and below the desired frequency than you could count. There is no difference in magic in general, or in evocation in particular. And as to the so-called results produced by such an effort, and the backlash or slingshot effect we will discuss later? Your guess is as good as mine.

Just to make certain you get the point being made here, let me mention two more final liberties given by the peddlers of the New Age. The first is the perfume of Art as it is called in many grimoires, which refers to the incense that is to be used in the ceremony. Many times more than one is required. For instance, one perfume must correspond to the nature of the spirit being evoked, and is to be compounded *by the Practitioner.* It is in this perfume's rising swirls of smoke that the spirit will take form. Yet a second perfume will be used to consecrate the Circle of Art, while a third will be held in readiness in case threats, enforcement, and the "Curse of Chains" or similar drastic measures are required to force the spirit to manifest without the circle.

In many cases, the grimoire does not mention how the perfumes are to be compounded or where they are to come from. In other cases, they specifically mention a few ingredients and warn the Practitioner he or she must 'divine' or 'Kabbalistically' determine the others required. Yet in other instances, instructions are given to "compound the perfumes of Art thyself." Yet the prevailing trend is: "Oh well, it is enough that I get something like this scent or that one. Heck, that's good enough!" Is it really?

The second instance is the magic circle. "What? I have to draw three circles on the floor? The first one nine feet in diameter, and the other two a hands breadth apart, and then fill up the spaces between them with an endless string of divine names, and all in those hard-to-draw Hebrew characters yet?" is the general mutter of our New Age Practitioner. "This is nuts!" they go on. "This other *authority* says I don't even need one circle on the floor! All I need to do is visualize one and I'll be protected to high heavens! Why, after all, it's the 'intent' that really counts. Not all that hard work! So what if those three physical circles add to my intent and establish physical boundaries that define the area of the work in the world of Malkuth! All that is just not needed and I know it! It's too much work! Yep, visualization is enough!" My reply to such a 'Practitioner' of our Art? "Talk to me after you do your so-called 'evocation.' I'll be looking forward to hearing about all the marvelous results you got—or not—as the case may be!"

Conclusion 1—The content of the grimoires, that is, their requirements for the production of the implements, the languages used in the conjurations, the circle design and construction, the perfumes, in short, *any* of their instructions are not to be meddled with. They do not allow—and the results from working with them do not tolerate—flippant, expedient, haphazard substitution, mixing, or changes of *any* kind beyond what each allows in its actual instructions. Just because one or more requirements are not convenient or palatable to the Practitioner, does not give them any license whatsoever to change those requirements. It is as simple as that.

As Dr. Flowers correctly states in his classic *Hermetic Magic,* "When one of the old spells called for the 'blood of a black ass,' it was really no more a rare ingredient than, let's say, the crank case oil of a black Chevy pickup truck would be today."[6] This is exactly the point. The requirements are what they are. Whatever the particular grammar of magic, those materials and requirement needed for its proper performance were as normal and readily available as the crankcase oil in the example given above. I cannot prove this conclusively. But from my own experience, I strongly suspect that the actions of preparing the magical implements according to strange requirements powerfully effects the mind of the Practitioner, placing it in a twilight world where magic makes all things not simply possible, but highly probable. It may even be that such preparations and rites actually produce a temporary physical change in the brain matrix, which hurls the Operator back to a time of belief when magic ruled, and its effects were as expected and common as the change of seasons.

In the end, if the Practitioner wants his or her desires fulfilled through evocation, he or she can either work with the demands laid down in a specific grimoire and produce what must be produced according to the writ, or they must look for another grimoire that is easier or more

---

[6] Flowers, Stephen Edred, PhD., ed. *Hermetic Magic. The Postmodern Magical Papyrus of Abaris.* Samuel Weiser, Inc. York Beach, Maine. 1995. page xviii.

convenient for them. There is no other way to attain the full results, and have them manifest without the slingshot effect.

Axiom 2—Every aspect of any magical ritual, ceremony, or rite, including evocation, must be consciously and thoroughly understood.

Argument 2—Another strange attitude toward magic in general arose out of the New Age. It translates into the magical act as "What you *don't* know *can't* hurt you." You can pronounce all of the Enochian words that you want, or all of the Barbarous Words of Evocation that delight you so much, and not bother with understanding their meaning, Qabalistic significance, or their root ideas. These prophets of the New Age tell the would-be Practitioner the very strangeness of the sound made by pronouncing such words—which of course no two New Age so-called authorities agree upon to begin with—will magnify the altered state of consciousness which all magical actions create.

And somewhere in this state of blissful ignorance, not only will the Practitioner automatically be able to tap into this secret reservoir of power, but they will be able to control and direct it as well. "Gee, magic is so easy and effortless! I can't wait to get all of those goodies this book says—well, sort of says, you know, kinda means I guess—that I'm bound to get!" And with this 'initiated' attitude, results will be produced, but not the kind desired.

As the reader will learn in Axiom 3, an altered state of consciousness is indeed a part of the magical state of awareness. However, it is utter nonsense to think this state is somehow magnified by human ignorance and laziness. Rather, this alteration in conscious perception is one of the effects—not the cause—of a process I term *subjective synthesis*. This is the practical psychological component of all magical practice.

Understanding this synthesis does not require you to take a postgraduate degree in psychology or seek a license in psychoanalysis after completing your residency as a medical doctor. It does require studying a few textbooks in the field of psychology, so you can understand the principles involved, and gain a working knowledge of general psychological terms and concepts. This will not only enable you to develop a basic understanding of the workings of your own mind, but will provide a stop gap measure against deluding yourself as to the why, how, and if of any positive or negative results you *think* flowed from your magical practices.

Perhaps more importantly, by objectively evaluating such results, you will be able to reproduce them at will, instead of blindly repeating rituals that you 'feel' gave you positive results. The reader will find that a conscientious study will equip one with the necessary tools to work in magic intelligently, thoughtfully, and *willfully*. This is essential in order to bring about a state of subjective synthesis, the details of which will be given in Axiom Three. One book I highly recommend is Charles Brenner's *An Elementary Textbook of Psychoanalysis*. Others books listed in the suggested reading list at the end of this book are by the authors Roberto Assagioli, Dr. A.A. Brill, Sigmund Freud, Karen Horney, William James, and Carl G. Jung.

Conclusion 2—Each aspect of any magical action, be it of a daily invocation, divinatory practice, or evocation of a spiritual entity to physical manifestation, must be studied and thoroughly understood. It is both foolish and reckless to think a lack of such understanding increases or deepens the altered state of consciousness resulting from the practice of magical rituals, ceremonies, or rites of any kind.

Axiom 3—A state of *Subjective Synthesis* is produced *through* the *conscious* study, understanding, comprehension, and *acceptance* of the theory of all elements that compose a given magical act. As a result of this synthesis, an integrated belief system is taken up in the Practitioner's subconscious mind. This

allows the individual to perform the magic and obtain the results desired from the magical act.

Argument 3—I define this state of *subjective synthesis* as a mental process which leads to an *integrated belief system*. In this case, it is the Practitioner's belief system in the power of magic and in how the magic works. This belief system is held in the part of the mind below the level of conscious perception, known as the subconscious (or unconscious) mind. These ordered set of beliefs are then used by the subconscious (or unconscious) mind during the magical act.

Since these beliefs have been *consciously* accepted by the Practitioner as being true, the limitless power of the non-discriminating, deductively reasoning, subconscious mind produces the physical phenomenon associated with magical acts through ways and means as yet unknown to modern science. By the same process, the purpose for which the magical act—in this case evocation—is performed, also manifests itself as a reality in the outer world of the Practitioner. Additionally, if the result desired is for some inner change or the addition of some quality to the mentality or psychic nature of the Practitioner, that change will be manifested within the individual as well.

What is not generally understood about the process of subjective synthesis, is that its *first and foremost* requirement is the *conscious acquisition and acceptance* of the beliefs held by the Practitioner. Further, this acquisition (through planned study), and acceptance as part of the process can literally be used by the Practitioner to *purposely* design his or her own desired system of beliefs. This is done through a *conscious understanding* and *full acceptance* of the conditions behind the ritual, the meaning of the weapons, Words of Power, the Conjurations, the nature of the beings summoned, and indeed all aspects of the rite.

It is therefore the systematic, conscious understanding of the theory behind the rite, along with the comprehension of the theoretical underpinnings of all aspects of the ceremony, and the conscious acceptance that this understanding and comprehension is true, which eventually produces a corresponding subconscious (unconscious) subjective synthesis within the Practitioner. *By turning inward and considering the theory carefully, sublime realizations result, uniting higher aspects of the mind with the material being contemplated.* This is *how* it is done. In turn, this synthesis allows the magical act to succeed—on the magician's terms. In other words, a complete picture of the material being worked with is necessary so the magician's mind operates in *harmony* with the *process* of evocation, not against it, as occurs when the subconscious 'picture' of the evocation is *fragmentary.*

I can hear some reader now. "Well, if this subjective synthesis is so important, and if it's true, then why can't it work for New Age or Gothic Revival Era Magic too? I mean, if I can get myself to fully believe and accept all of the elements of, for example, the Golden Dawn, then it should work just as well for it as it's is supposed to work for those old grimoires of the Middle Ages, right?" Wrong!

The Gothic Revival and New Age Era material in general, and the Golden Dawn material in particular—from which most if not all New Age material has been fabricated in one way or another—is based upon operational principles that are incomplete, filled with errors, and therefore misleading. Remember, the sourcebook for the Golden Dawn's essential core material came from Barrett's *The Magus, or Celestial Intelligencer,* which is the butchered version of Agrippa's *Three Books of Occult Philosophy.* Hence the belief system you would be constructing would operate along those same incomplete principles.

While you can force yourself to believe anything, the subconscious will—in all cases—operate from those principles consistent with the actual working. You may not be able to detect anything wrong with them, but when the subconscious executes its instructions and finds them inoperable, it will continue to do its best to carry them out. Consequently, your altered state of consciousness will be greatly effected at the worst possible time—during the performance of the magical act. The result achieved from the magic will be the incomplete results already spoken of and of the slingshot effect, to be dealt with later. Both effects will be experienced with full force.

Am I saying the grimoires of the Old System of Magic are so complete, so thorough, so perfect, that they cannot possibly cause any problems once their theory and principles are comprehended and accepted? Not quite. What I do attest to here, based upon my own forty years of experience and those of my contemporaries who have also worked according to these axioms, is that these Old System grimoires are sufficiently structured so that they do operate to give full results *when the axioms are used*.

As to their slingshot effects? These effects will be produced as well, unless the Practitioner follows *all* of the axioms laid down here. In the collection of propositions laid down here lies a unique, integrated code which the subconscious mind recognizes and applies automatically, not only to evocations, but to all magical practices whatsoever. A big claim? Try it out for yourself, and then write me!

There is also the matter of the Practitioner's general psychological state. It must be understood it too has direct bearing upon the process of subjective synthesis. Indeed, the general psychological state determines to a significant degree just how well the individual is able to genuinely accept the various 'truths' of the grimoire intended to be worked. This in turn effects the altered state of consciousness produced which, while so crucial in any magical act, is of paramount importance in evocation.

No one can assess, let alone accurately determine anything they lack knowledge of. This is the reason I cited the general books on psychology and psychoanalysis. By studying those books and applying their principles to the workings of your own mind, you—the Practitioner—will be able to exercise a more or less stable control over your general psychological health. This being done, the manifestations of your desires from your magical practices will improve, as will the overall balance of your daily life.

Conclusion 3—A state of subjective synthesis is produced in the subconscious mind of the Practitioner by the study, understanding, comprehension, and acceptance of the theoretical material underlying any magical act. This is especially crucial in the evocation to physical manifestation of a spiritual entity. It is this subjective synthesis which enables the subconscious mind to produce the physical effects associated with magical rituals, strengthen the altered state of consciousness, and enable the spiritual entity to manifest. It is also important to understand the subconscious does not create the manifesting spiritual entity, unless it is the belief of the Practitioner that the nature of the spirit is purely psychological. This issue with be dealt with thoroughly in Axiom 4.

Axiom 4—**The nature of the spiritual entity summoned during evocation to physical manifestation, is either objective or subjective according to the subconscious belief system resulting from the process of subjective synthesis.**

Argument 4—The most important views of evocation or any magical act are those internal views held by the Practitioner. As pointed out in Axiom 3, the resulting belief system, the very product of the subconscious process of subjective synthesis, actually enables the magic to take place. Since this integrated belief system is held within the subconscious mind that also produced the subjective synthesis, the reader might now begin to grasp just how important such beliefs are.

If, for example, the Practitioner insists upon operating from the still-reigning nineteenth and twentieth century psychological view of general magical practice set down by the Golden Dawn and expanded upon by Aleister Crowley, his or her belief system, moral and ethical values (or lack of them), as well as his or her general psychological state and the altered state of consciousness achieved during the operation, will work together and have direct bearing on the 'fullness' of the results achieved. That is, taken together, these variables, as they exist within the subconscious and conscious mind of the Magician, will all have a direct bearing on the magnitude of the results obtained.

I want to be very specific and clear here, which is why I have detailed the role of the conscious mind in magical matters. It must be understood that while the process of subjective synthesis takes place in the subconscious mind which then houses and acts upon the resulting belief system in a deductive way to take the beliefs to their logical conclusion through the rite, it was the conscious mind that did the work of understanding, comprehending, and accepting the 'truths' that were then turned over to the subconscious mind. As such, there will exist a constant interaction between the conscious and unconscious levels of the mind during the magical act. To put this more simply, the *unconscious beliefs* and the *conscious expectations* of the Practitioner will combine to have a direct bearing on the extent to which the promises of the Grimoire being worked from are fulfilled.

In general, these variables must be *thoroughly* understood, if *complete* success in the evocation is to be achieved. In the case of our Golden Dawn or New Age Practitioner who insists the demonic entities—the spiritual beings largely dealt with in the grimoires—are simply psychological projections of the subconscious complexes and chaotic mental processes, that is exactly what will result in the evocation. To be more specific, such Practitioners will *only* receive the signs of evocation that echo throughout the New Age literature. There will be the sense of a presence outside the circle, or a feeling of something in the room, or a partial formation of the spirit in the incense smoke, or some other vague, ill-defined manifestation that 'proves' the spirit was actually present, and has or is about to grant them their wish.

In my opinion, the very setting and circumstances of an evocation are scary enough so as to enable the Practitioner to imagine anything he or she wants to. Proclaiming some imaginary or spooky feeling as the being the real thing, however, is self-defeating. I will *guarantee* you this. When you do get the real thing in an evocation, long before the entity actually does materialize in the smoke of the incense, you won't have to listen for noises in the room, check on your feelings, or try to see something in the smoke to find out if the spirit is really there. You will know it beyond a shadow of a doubt. Then all of your straining to detect the spooky feelings will be the least of your problems because you will have plenty to worry about as you will find out when you proceed through these axioms. Therefore it is the Practitioner who holds to the exclusive belief that spiritual beings are nothing more than psychological phenomena who will receive, at the very best, only partial results, along with no end of problems stemming from the slingshot effect.

Am I saying there are no psychological bases to spiritual entities? Am I also saying such bases cannot be projected from the Practitioner into a triangle of manifestation by the process of commanding such a spirit, and upon re-assimilating it into the corresponding complex of the Practitioner, it is removed from the psyche? In other words, is it possible that the entire process of evocation can become a type of instant psychoanalysis to restore mental and psychic health to the individual? Frankly, *I don't know!*

This was a sore point of contention between Regardie and myself throughout the years. I favored—and do so now more than I did twenty-five years ago when he and I first disagreed over this point—viewing spiritual entities as purely *objective beings,* with a life, will, consciousness, and an independent existence of their own. Regardie was uncertain. He favored both views at times, but then one view over the other at different times. In the end however, he always seemed to lean toward the modern position that such entities were psychological projections. It is safe to say he and I disagreed on this one point until the day he died.

Does this mean it will be easier for the Practitioner if his or her subjective synthesis and resulting belief system are designed only to view spiritual entities as being objective in nature? This is not a question of ease. It is purely a matter of pragmatism. It is a matter of what you want. The issue here is, does the Practitioner want a full manifestation of his or her desires and results, or not? The beings I have dealt with throughout the years have been found to be—through my personal subjective synthesis and subconscious belief system—completely objective. It is the type of phenomena they produce, along with results, that leads me to that conclusion. It is not the other way around.

When outside of the circle during an evocation to physical manifestation: winds begin to stir in a sealed, windowless cellar room and blow objects around; green mists and blinking, multicolored lights of various sizes and shapes appear floating through the air; candles are extinguished and knocked over; moans and screams rip through the darkness; shafts of golden or different colored lights appear out of nowhere and streak across the cement walls and through the air; these same walls are pounded on so violently by something that (at first) is invisible, and which causes the walls to begin to crack; in the rooms above there is the horrifying sound of something huge smashing against the floor over your head as if trying to get at you from above; and finally, an unmistakable form appears in the smoke of the Perfume of Art (incense) and begins to cry and wail; it is then that the you, the Practitioner, will become grimly aware of the objective nature of the being summoned forth.

Finally, when the desire requested from this being manifests from what can only be described as 'out of the blue,' in some dramatic fashion, and *fully*, for all to see, it is then that the Practitioner or Operator must struggle to accept the reality of this Magic which he or she did not *really, really,* believe at first. And mark me in this. You *will* struggle to accept a world of existence beyond the one you have known throughout your life. It is not as easy as it seems. The psychological impact is second to none, for you have journeyed to the outer limits of human experi-

ence, and have returned to tell the tale. Then and *only* then
will you begin to comprehend the magical adage, 'The
student of the Mysteries lives in a vast spiritual universe
in which he lives, moves, and has his being.' So wrote
Eliphas Levi over a hundred and fifty years ago.
If you choose to accept the nature of these beings as
being objective, you should also know this. Much has been
touted by the New Age prophets that these beings are
partial intelligences or chaotic, irrational beings, or are
semi-conscious, or deceitful, or a hundred other themes
along these lines. I suppose if you evoke psychological
projections from your psyche they very well could be all of
these things. But as objective entities, they are not. They
are willful, thinking entities which enter into our four-
dimensional universe of matter without physical form.
They are fully conscious of their own existence. They
mean you no harm. They seek neither your sanity nor your
life. But yet, they are bound by their ancient natures to be
contrary to the will of *any*, including *your* will. They will
use this willfulness against you. If you think of them this
way, you will find they are not much different from the
people who live next door to you. The best way for the
Operator to understand their nature is to view them as
highly charged thoughts, in that they have enormous
power, but no tangible form. Yet, as with thought, they
can change the world—*your* world, specifically—for good
or ill. Know too they use the mind of the Operator, which
is so in tune with their objective reality, to cross into the
Operator's world. And when they do, they will use anything to clothe themselves so as to take a temporary form,
since this stabilizes them in our universe.
While such a being will instantly seize upon particles
of a perfume congruent with its nature, it will lock onto
anything it can. It will even use water vapor or carbon
particles rising from candle flames if it has to in order to
assume a shape. It is my suspicion this is the reason
behind much but not all of the physical phenomena
produced before final manifestation occurs. When the
entity first comes through into our world, it is panicked,

and it tries to latch onto whatever it can in order to create its own body. Remember this, and be certain to provide enough incense in the room, prior to beginning the first conjuration. Otherwise, the physical phenomena the entity produces upon first entering our space-time continuum can become very, very violent.

Conclusion 4—The nature of the spiritual beings evoked to physical manifestation by High Ceremonial Magic are either objective or subjective, according to the subjective synthesis and resulting integrated subconscious belief system of the Operator. If subjective, they are psychological projections of the Practitioner's own psyche, to be dealt with according to the dictates of the New Age belief system.

If their nature is accepted as objective, then the rules of the ancient grimoires must apply. Viewing these beings as objective does not in the least run contrary to the establishment of the state of subjective synthesis and the integrated belief system resulting from it. Rather, acceptance of the objective view tunes the psychic mechanisms of the Operator to provide a *physical channel* through which the entity being summoned enters our physical universe. That channel is the mind of the Operator. It is the tunnel through which the entity crosses the threshold from its universe into ours.

Axiom 5—Every magical action, every evocation to physical manifestation, produces a complex field of energy. This field is composed of different frequencies each at their own energy level. This complex field results from a combination of the subjective synthesis; subconscious integrated belief system; physical movement during, and internal images of the rite; as well as the thoughts, sounds, emotional anticipations, consecrations and natures of the magical instruments.

Argument 5—Forced visualizations and artificial, strained emotional states of exaltation so demanded by modern magic are absolutely unnecessary. They are the fabrications of a weak school of magical thought. They do not aid either the magical act, or the results obtained from it. At best, they hinder the entire magical process. At worst, they destroy it completely.

The aim of all magical action, be it a daily invocation or a High Ceremonial evocation of a spiritual entity to physical manifestation, is a *singly* focused, psychically integrated, willfully directed field of complex energy produced by all of the components of the ritual, channeled toward the attainment of one given end. The enormous psychic energy resulting from the process of subjective synthesis, and the subconscious, integrated belief system that results from it, is added to the other energy frequencies generated by the magical implements and the conscious states of the Operator. The state of physical, mental, emotional, and psychic tensions builds in crescendos throughout the rite, and are propelled into the *physical* universe of the Practitioner, to effect the results desired.

In the case of evocation to physical manifestation, it is the convergence of all these factors at one supreme instant that initiates the manifestation of the entity. At no time during this critical performance is there any room for the artificial, emotionally strained states of exaltation and visualizations advocated by the New Age system of magic. Rather, it is through a careful *conscious* effort leading to the development of subjective synthesis and the integrated belief system arising from it, that the subconscious foundation needed for successful magic is laid. Then psychic development rises *naturally* within the Practitioner, stimulating and heightening the supporting internal images of the rite built through the conscious study of the material.

This produces a corresponding altered state of consciousness, guides the body gracefully in its physical movements throughout the magical act, focuses thought, and yields a sound intonation of a complementary pitch during the conjurations. These conditions accelerate emotional anticipation, acting through duly consecrated magical implements, which bring about a successful and fruitful magical act. Such are the workings of the complex field of energy produced.

Although I will have more to say on this matter in Axiom 8, it will help you to understand at this point, daily exercises in visualization and concentration are useless. It is the nature of the human mind to use mental imagery automatically. When imagery is of something intensely desired, there is never any problem seeing it clearly in the mind's eye. Remember preparing for your first date with that special someone? I'm willing to bet you had no problems with mental imagery here! Likewise, the faculty of concentration that supports and breathes the life of anticipation and expectation into the image, becomes as intense and natural as is the image formation when it embodies that same desire. Hence, all enforced daily routines are simply contrivances, designed by modern 'authorities' as crutches to explain away the failure of their magical writings to their audience. You know what I am talking about. You have experienced it yourself, countless times.

At this point, the reader has probably guessed that the intensity of the magical act—be it evocation to physical manifestation or a daily rite of secret communion with the divine part of one's own nature—demands all prayers or conjurations, as the case may be, are *completely* committed to memory. Reading such critical material off a card or from a book while in a heightened altered state of consciousness, coupled to the beyond-fever pitch of *naturally* occurring emotion exaltation, will thoroughly and completely destroy the psychic state necessary for the desired results to manifest.

This is why strict adherence to every aspect of the rite is *absolutely necessary*. From the conscious effort behind subjective synthesis, to the understanding of the nature of the entity being summoned, to the details of the circle's construction, the types of robes, prayers, conjurations, construction and consecration of the implements, all are separate steps, connected through the magical act itself, in an exacting process designed to bring you, the Operator, the object of your heart's desire.

Conclusion 5—Every magical act produces a complex field of energy. The components of the ritual, each possessing their own characteristic energy frequency, merge through the ritual performance into a highly focused action that transmits the complex energy outward into the *physical* universe of the Operator. As is one of the fundamental laws of physics, "For every action there is an equal and opposite reaction," the projection of this energy into the strata of the Operator's world causes an equal and opposite reaction here, which is the full manifestation of the desired result.

Axiom 6—In every evocation to physical manifestation, you *must* have full manifestation before you can control, and you must have control before you can command. Unless these three critical conditions are clearly established, the operation will end in a partial result with serious "Slingshot Effects," or produce no result whatsoever. To the best of my knowledge, these conditions have never been set down in print before. It is *absolutely* imperative they be fulfilled to the letter.

Argument 6—By now the reader has noticed that I have been very specific in my description of evocation. Time and time again I used the phrase, 'evocation to physical manifestation,' rather than just the word 'evocation.' There was a reason for this. First, I want to instill in the reader the *absolute necessity* of the phrase, since there is no evocation without the physical manifestation. This was pointed out by discussing what the New Age considers to be evocation, but which I do not, owing to the endless self illusion and delusion this school of magical thought produces. This is in addition to the resulting trouble such evocations also cause the Practitioner.

Second, it was my intent to lay the foundation in the reader's mind for the *imperativeness* of the *three critical conditions* discussed here that *must* prevail in every such magical operation. These three conditions are so important that by rights, they should be considered *operational magical laws*, and not simply axioms. Having warned the reader of the importance of these three conditions, it is now necessary to discuss them thoroughly.

After the subjective synthesis and resulting subconscious belief system has been established in the Operator; after the mechanics of the grimoire being worked from have been dealt with; after the preparations of the Operator have been executed; after the conjurations have been repeated from a fire deep in the belly, and an intensity that has sent the altered state of consciousness to heights undreamed of by the Practitioner; after the physical phenomena has subsided and a form begins to take on a shape in the rising, now swirling-around-the-circle smoke of the Perfume of Art; after all of these efforts and their effects have propelled the very core of the Operator to the furthermost boundaries of human experience, then and only then has the task just begun.

For it is at this juncture that the Operator must allow—not make—the connection between his finite consciousness and the divinity within him to occur. And it will automatically, by virtue of the rigors of preparation and execution he or she has endured up to this point. The New Age need to fake this connection or try to induce it will be seen for what it is: a lie. But at the same time, the Practitioner must maintain control over his or her own consciousness, because a strange type of intoxication arises within the Operator.

In this state, one will feel changed. They are not who they were before. The Operator will feel a more-ness, and will literally perceive a brilliant light in what was the mind. This state evolves quickly into a state of exaltation, then into an ecstasy, next, into a bliss, and then rapidly into something beyond the bliss—something the reader may have read about in magical literature. Finally, the name to be attached to this advanced state of existence that lies beyond bliss will be found: *Divine Love.* It is not the love you are normally familiar with, even in your most selfless moments. Nothing can compare to it. It is Divine Love for all things, including the entity appearing in the incense smoke.

At that moment, you will understand you do not need to force the being to do anything for you. Rather, you know you will have to force *yourself* to maintain some conscious control over *yourself* so *you* can complete the rite. It cannot be said any simpler than this. It is a state that must be experienced, and once it is, its descriptions will lie beyond all words. It will be a *feeling realization* that will forever abide in the deepest recesses of your own heart. Nor can instructions in how to do it be given, as the New Age pretends to do.

It will, as I have said, occur automatically, as a consequence of all you have done. When this state of Divine Love is at its zenith, the spirit will fully manifest in the smoke of the incense. It will all happen in a microsecond of time. You should also know when this divine connection occurs, it will last throughout the remainder of the rite, and in fact, will take three to four days to fade away. It is this connection to the divine within you and the Love that results, that brings about the full manifestation of spirit in the smoke.

If, however, for some reason you have not obtained full manifestation, *abort the operation immediately!* Under no circumstances continue! If a partial manifestation of the spirit appears in the smoke of the incense, or a feeling of something in the room or some physical phenomena is all you achieve at this point, something has gone wrong. Most likely the problem lies in the lack of attaining a solid subjective synthesis, or in the mechanical preparations of the weapons, such as some short cut taken in their construction or consecration. As I warned before, such expediencies *will* show up in the rite!

If this happens, *immediately* give the License to Depart from the grimoire you are working with, and follow through with its recommended prayers as well! Under *no* circumstances use *any* New Age techniques of banishing pentagram rituals or any of their other recommended devises! Remember, *you must not mix magical systems of any kind!* After giving the License to Depart several times, and praying as the grimoire recommends, and when you feel it is safe, make certain all incense is extinguished, leave the circle, and shut up the room in which the evocation to physical manifestation was attempted. *Do not enter it again for the space of one month.*

You must also understand that failed attempts will bring about negative effects due to the slingshot effect. Generally, these negativities will not be too extreme *if the rite is ended at this point.* Nevertheless, these undesirable events will tax your patience for awhile. Their nature includes things going wrong with your life in general and with human relationships. In short, these will be milder versions of the effects you *could* experience from a *seemingly* successful rite, which will be addressed fully in Axiom 7. Assuming you have produced full manifestation however, and after this event has stabilized—and it will do so in between the ticks of a clock—then the second condition must be established by *you,* the Operator.

At first, the spirit will appear in whatever classical form its nature demands, which has been written in the grimoire being worked from. It will either be hideous to look upon, or else it will mesmerize you. So you must struggle within yourself to maintain a conscious awareness of the process, while the divine intoxication automatically continues to course through your very being. You cannot yet command anything, regardless of what you have been told in pop, modern books on the subject, much less order the being to 'assume a more pleasing form.' Rather, it is at this moment that the willfulness of the evoked spirit will assert itself. It will intensify its appearance to terrify or mesmerize the Operator even more, or throw up new physical phenomena in the room, or both. It may even begin to speak, threatening and cursing, or begin to move around the circle, if a constraint such as a Triangle of Manifestation is not called for in the grimoire being used.

Remember when such events occur, you have nothing to fear. It cannot break through your defense of the physical circle set down on the floor, or carved into the earth. Besides the magical weapons (implements) with which you will be armed, the divine state you are in will provide more protection than you could imagine in your wildest dreams. Hence it would not dare to try such an action. It is as a child throwing a temper tantrum, trying to coerce an adult to do what it wants.

In the middle of this drama, you will feel tugging going on between you and the spirit. It is as if both of you are pulling at the ends of a cord invisibly connected to your solar plexus or belly mind, the seat of emotions within you. This is the second of the three conditions. It is this process which enables you to establish control over the entire rite, your state of rapture, and to *extend* that *control* to the entity's *will*. This is the hidden, or occult modus operandi of the rite.

You do it *not* by forcing, *not* by trying to establish control, but by *maintaining a conscious hold over your rapture, and by simply watching the tug-of-war feeling continue between you and the entity.* In short, it is your *passive resistance* which forces the entity to surrender its attempts to control the situation and to surrender its own *will*. You are now a divine being, and it is subject to *your* will. It will relent, which is the exact opposite of what you have been told in all those modern books on magic.

When control has been established, there will be an immediate cessation of any physical phenomena in the room, curses or threats from the spirit, or whatever actions along these lines it has thrown up to wrest control away from you. The tugging feeling will not disappear immediately, but will fade slowly throughout the rite, and will last until you give the being the License to Depart. The reason for this is that even though you are now in complete control of the ceremony, the spirit will still attempt to raise objections to do your bidding, and will continue to entertain thoughts of gaining control of the rite. At this point it knows it cannot do so. But as a spoiled child, it will nevertheless make weak attempts, and grudgingly object. This is simply the nature of these entities so do not be afraid. After you gain control, the final part of the drama commences.

Having attained control, you are now ready to command. Your first command must be to tell the entity to take on a more pleasing appearance, as the one it usually first shows can be quite upsetting to human sensibilities. You will show it the Seals of Power according to the text you are working from, be they the Pentagram, Hexagram, or Secret Seal of Solomon or variations according to your working text. They must be unveiled now and shown to the spirit, while repeating the appropriate words of constraint you learned from your text. After a few seconds, it will comply. But remember, it will do so grudgingly.

Holding steadfast to your position within the circle, you begin to give it your command or 'Charge' as it is called in the grimoires. While the reader may think this is the easy part, I assure you, it competes with the process of establishing control as the most difficult part of the rite to accomplish. Why? For three reasons.

First, you will still be struggling with the state of rapture within, trying desperately (unnoticeable to the spirit) to maintain some conscious control over the rapture. Second, you must also maintain the control you have established over the spirit so you can proceed with the rite. Third, you must be able to speak your Charge completely and succinctly, yet with such *perfect clarity of meaning that there is no ambiguity the spirit can use to turn your own Charge against you.*

Mind you, the spirit's willful nature will still be at work. If there is anything unclear in the wording of your demand, anything with a double meaning or with an interpretation that in some way the entity can use to give you the opposite of what you seek or use the vagueness hidden in your words or phrases to get out of doing it altogether, it will. You *must* understand this. This requires extensive, brain-wracking work on your part, both in composing such a Charge prior to the rite, and in retaining it so perfectly during the ceremonial performance, that even while in your state of rapture and control you can nevertheless deliver it almost without consciously thinking about it. If this sounds like a big order, it is. But a few suggestions here will show you that it is not as impossible as it seems.

Several precautions are in order before I give you the framework of the Charge I evolved throughout the years in my own evocations to physical manifestation. First, *never* use *generalities*. Don't ask for wealth or power or love. If you do, you will receive their opposites. Second, do not be so specific that you leave your words open to misinterpretation. I will use an example from an event that occurred to a colleague of mine who did not follow my advice on this issue.

He sought a large amount of money for a very worthwhile end, but he got carried away when issuing the Charge. His Charge, as he told me, was "I want one million American dollars free, that I don't have to pay back to the source I get it from, and without taxes, that I can spend as I please, on whatever I want." Three days later he received a letter from the American Internal Revenue Service stating their computer had uncovered his account as a target for auditing. They had gone back twelve years into his records, and he wound up paying thousands of dollars in back taxes, late charges, and fines. As to his desire? Needless to say, it did not manifest.

Why? He used the words free, American, and taxes, all of which opened up a new interpretation to the spirit that he successfully brought to full manifestation, and over which he did establish control. The reader should also know that amazingly, these spirits of the various grimoires loathe helping the Operator whom they see as trying to get away with something or pull a fast one on someone, as occurred in this example in which the word 'free' was used. Finally, do not specify what you are going to use your fulfilled desire for. That is no one's—especially the spirit's—business but your own.

I have used the following illustration as a general Charge framework which is adapted according to the grimoire being used and the desire sought. It works. But the reader should also devise his or her own over time. Nothing sticks in the memory as something individually created for one's use. It is the same here.

"I salute and greet thee, O Thou spirit (given spirit's name here), and require that thou aid me and my cause by performing the duties of thy office according to the dictates of my words, and always in agreement with my conscious will. I therefore charge thee to bring unto me (name your desire here), that it pleaseth and serveth me in all respects according to my word and will, and remain with me so long as it pleaseth me to have it in my life.

"Further, that thou shall perform this which have I charged thee to do, all without any interference, harm *or* destruction, or without any interference, harm *and* destruction to me, those whom I call mine and whom I love, and to those whom I call 'friend.' Nor shall any beast be subject to any effects from thee whatsoever. Further, thou shall faithfully and completely fulfill my words of Charge given here within the space of thirty days from this moment, and all without trickery, deceit, or guile of any kind.

"In addition, as part of my Charge to thee here, give me some word or words or a sign, by which I can summon thee at my will and as I please, safely, without the Circle of Art, thou being ever ready to fulfill my future Charges to thee as I see fit, while being yet bound by my words and my will that giveth me thy obedience and harmlessness in this, my original Charge to thee."

Such a Charge is not general, it is specific in critical ways, and it does not mention what use I, the Operator, will make of the fulfilled desire. It is clean and to the point. The reader will do well to heed this counsel in composing his or her own Charges.

Conclusion 6—Full manifestation of the spirit, control of the rite and strict command of the spirit must all be established completely and fully as laid down in this axiom if the Practitioner is to experience the success being sought without the slingshot effect. Such an effect is produced by incomplete manifestation, improper control, and the delivery of an imperfect Charge to the entity summoned. The entire process—from full manifestation to sustained control through delivery of a precise Charge—occurs so quickly in actual practice, as to be deceptive to the ordinary senses of the Operator. Practice and experience alone will enable the Operator to gain and eventually master this inner sense of the ceremonial process.

If full manifestation of the spiritual being cannot be manifested, the rite must be abandoned immediately, with the License to Depart and prayers given in the text being worked from used without any hesitation. All burning incense in the room is to be extinguished, and the room sealed off for a minimum period of thirty days. During this time it is up to the Operator to diligently study his or her internal preparations, the material and mechanical constructions of the weapons and their consecrations, as well as the process of the ceremonial performance as it was conducted, in order to determine what went wrong before trying again. It is during this thirty-day period of time that the Operator can expect strange events to occur in his or her life, ranging from personal issues to relationship problems, owing to the slingshot effect which will now be discussed in Axiom 7.

Axiom 7—In the process of evocation to physical manifestation, there exists the possibility of what I term the Slingshot Effect. While this effect is most severe in the evocational act, it is a distinct possibility in any magical act, including that of simple invocation. In general, it results from an improper subjective synthesis and the resulting subconscious belief system. In evocation to physical manifestation, the effect is compounded by the magnitude of the altered state of consciousness achieved, the rapture produced during the early phases of the rite, the necessity of

establishing and maintaining control, and the problem of delivering a perfect Charge. As an effect from an evocation to physical manifestation that has gone awry, five very distinct, *major* conditions are produced in the Operator's life, and always in the order given.

Argument 7—During my early years of magical practice, I had quite a number of evocations to physical manifestation turn out very badly. It took more than twenty years of what seemed like constant practice, the recording of copious notes, and more nights spent in analyzing those notes to determine what went wrong, than I care to remember. They were far, far, from happy years. But in the end, they revealed the very undesirable condition I came to call the Slingshot Effect. Really, it can proceed from any magical ritual. Something as mundane as the New Age recommended daily invocation can also produce variations of the five conditions that strangely arise in the life of the Practitioner.

In typical magical practices, they usually do not cause any significant harm other than varying degrees of frustration. But in High Ceremonial Evocation to Physical Manifestation, these conditions can become very severe. In my own case, my first evocation, which did bring about an enormous amount of physical phenomena and only a partial manifestation of the spirit, threw my solid, stable, financial affairs into utter ruin within four days. This was immediately followed by an inexplicable deterioration of my usual excellent physical health to such an extent I wound up with a collapsed left lung and a massive infection which very nearly cost me my life.

For exactly one year, until the anniversary of that first High Ceremonial Magical act, my life was literally hell on this earth. No statistician could possibly argue away the multitude of bizarre events as being coincidental, regardless of the short intervals of time chosen to look at my life's events during that year. Nevertheless, I continued to experiment with the various forms of magic, and did indeed receive untold benefits from the practices.

However, it was the magical act of evocation to physical manifestation that captivated me, despite the harsh effects I experienced from its first performance. Consequently, as the years went by, I continued this work beyond all else. I was finally able to establish with certainty that the ten Axioms presented here, and the slingshot effect, were indeed real, and I was able to define their characteristics. The following are the properties of the slingshot effect which the wise Practitioner would do well to study carefully, prior to performing the ceremonial act.

It is important for the reader to understand, that regardless of the benefit sought through the evocation, whether it be for some material object or inner quality, the five conditions are *always* produced when the rite falls apart. To date, I still cannot explain *why* this is the case. But I can tell you, that it *is* the case. I can also tell you, that if you abort the operation *immediately* if a full manifestation does not occur, the five conditions will still occur but not as severe as those stated below.

However, if you persist and rationalize away the lack of full manifestation or complete establishment of control, or if you fail to deliver a tight, efficient, clean Charge and proceed with the rite anyway, the *major* five conditions discussed below *will* occur, and they will have monumental negative effects upon your life. To be sure, there are additional minor conditions that arise at the same time, and they will be dealt with at the end of this section. Please note that I include the financial ruin and serious health problems I experienced nearly forty years ago in with the class of minor problems. It is rare these conditions occur, as other colleagues of mine have confirmed. But they *can* happen, and hence I included them as possibilities in this minor class.

In order to make my point crystal clear, I will state the five *major* conditions as they occur to an Operator who does not abort the rite, but instead, having convinced oneself that everything is going alright, proceeds with the ceremony anyway. This should make it clear to the reader just how these conditions surface. Also please note that these five major conditions *always occur in the order given.* They do *not* occur out of phase, or in any other way. Forewarned is forearmed.

1. Money comes to the Operator—For some unknown reason, within a week at the most, money comes to the Operator. It ranges from several hundred to several thousands of dollars. It will literally come out of the blue. Some relative will call offering to share some windfall with you. Or you will just happen to buy a lottery ticket that turns out to be a (small) winner. Or you will receive a notice from one of your credit card companies that they have added a thousand dollars to your available credit, or offer you a cash outlay in payment of some class action. The list of possible avenues for this manifestation goes on and on. But it will happen.

2. An event occurs that takes some of the recently acquired money away from the Operator. Within a few days of receiving the unexpected windfall, something will happen to take away some of the money received, usually about one-quarter to one-half of the assets that came to you. The condition causing the removal of money will also be one that causes the Operator a great deal of mental anxiety. Perhaps you become involved in a minor traffic accident, and have to pay an insurance deductible to have your auto repaired. In the meantime, you find out your insurance does not cover car rental even though you were sure you had it, which means laying out even more money to rent a car for the week yours is being repaired. Or you go to your mailbox and find a letter telling you an old, unjust debt that cost you thousands of dollars in legal fees to stop has now been sold to a new parasite who wants his money—and now. So, it's back to the lawyer's office, where you find out it will take another $300 to settle the matter permanently. In the meantime, you will have no end of nightmares as to the possibilities of what the situation will wind up costing you until it is finally done and over with. There is the mental anxiety I spoke of. It can be anything, coming out of any corner you least expect. But one thing is for certain: it *will* occur.

3. A long held, life-sustaining relationship is suddenly broken. This is the worst of the events to occur. Someone you know and trusted; someone you confided in and shared the most personal, intimate details of your life with up to that point, will betray you. Seriously. What is more, you find out about it, and a confrontation occurs. In the best case scenario, there will be a period of separation between you and this other person. Typically it will last anywhere from one week to one month. Worst case, the break will be permanent and immediate. The other person could be a dear friend of many, many years, an employer you thought you knew, a child, a fiancé, a brother, sister, or a wife or husband. It could also turn out to be an aunt or uncle who you looked upon as a parent. In any event, the betrayal will be so complete and so all encompassing, you will never be the same again. And even if the bridges are mended, neither you nor that person will ever be able to fully trust the other again. Of course, where there is no trust, there can be neither friendship nor love. Hence, even after a reconciliation, over time the relationship will fade. When it does, the end will be amicable but sad, and that sadness will remain with you both for the rest of your lives. As your author, I truly wish I had better news for you on this point, but I don't. Evocation to physical manifestation is nothing to fool with as you can see. It is a grim business, to be undertaken only by the those willing to pay such a high price in order to *experience* and *learn* those things hidden from the eyes of the masses. My words to you here are not meant to be self serving, nor to suggest that you attempt evocation to physical manifestation in order to prove yourself better than the masses. Such attitudes are detrimental to you and will only aid failure in this work. Rather, these hard facts are provided so you might question your own deepest motivations for going into this particularly hazardous and extreme realm of magic. For you will find, in the end, the desires you *think* you so desperately seek are also attainable through other means, including the normal ways of the world. They are the *effects* of your work. Your *motivations* are the *causes*. Think deeply on what I have said here.

4. In the case where a relationship is ended immediately and permanently, either a new relationship is created, or an old one is reestablished. But this relationship will not endure. It is as if the powers that be give the Practitioner who has suffered a permanent break in a relationship some relief by creating a new and promising one, or else it reestablishes an old one. This amazing situation enables the Operator to get past the very painful, permanent breakup. As with the other conditions discussed above, this new relationship or the resurrected former one comes out of nowhere. It happens by a chance meeting, a telephone call one lonely night, an old picture that brings back memories of a lost love, or through any one of the myriad possibilities the human mind can conceive. Somehow, at least for awhile, new light enters the Operator's life, giving him or her a vision of new possibilities and even hope for the future. Curiously, this lasts as long as the Practitioner needs to recover from the original, permanently failed relationship. As soon as recovery is complete however, the new person either leaves the life of the Operator quietly, or the Operator loses interest, and goes upon their own way. In doing so, the Practitioner has been healed of the trauma, and their emotional state heals as well after the new relationship disappears. It is a very curious situation, but it does occur.

5. The fifth and final major condition to manifest is that more money comes to the Operator. This marks the end of the cycle of major negative conditions that occur after an evocation to physical manifestation has gone badly awry. In this case, the additional amount of money comes once again out of the blue. Usually, it is on the order of one to two hundred dollars. By this time the Operator has passed through so much, even this modest amount is welcome, and it serves to put a slight smile on the face of the now beleaguered Operator. Most of the Operators I have known who made it through this harrowing time realized what they passed through was the result of the evocation going bad and they never attempted evocation to physical manifestation again. I don't blame them in the slightest. For myself, I had to find out what was happening, and so continued until these principles were ironed out so I could formally state them. I trust you, the reader, will benefit from them in your work.

Finally, there are the numerous minor effects that will plague both the Practitioner who rationalized away his or her lack of results and continued through with the evocation, to the hapless Operator who rightly aborted the evocation when full manifestation did not occur. These annoyances creep up, also unexpectedly, in everyday life. Anything and everything from lost wallets and keys, to keys that break off in locks, illegal charges made to credit cards, or legitimate but duplicate charges made, deposits made at the bank that were not recorded resulting in an overdrawn account, a rash of unexpected repair bills for home and office, to broken bones, rapid weight gain or loss, nightmares, animal attacks, feelings of extreme anxiety, panic attacks, disciplinary reprimands from an employer, aberrant behavior of children, to a general feeling of doom—all and more are within the realms of possibility of the types of minor effects that will occur.

Conclusion 7—In all magical work, but especially in the process of evocation to physical manifestation, there exists the possibility of what I have come to call the slingshot effect. In the main, it is caused by an improper subjective synthesis and the subconscious belief system that flows from such erroneous synthesis. In the High Ceremonial act of evocation to physical manifestation, this effect is intensified by the magnitude of the altered state of consciousness achieved, the rapture produced during the rite, the necessity of establishing and maintaining firm control, and of delivering a imperfect Charge to the spirit so summoned.

In an evocation to physical manifestation that has gone awry, this effect produces five very distinct *major* conditions in the Operator's life, and always in the order described. In addition, minor negative effects will also occur which is to be understood and accepted by the Practitioner as being inevitable. But in the main, these minor ones will simply bring about frustration, with no lasting harm being done to either the Operator, his or her life, or affairs.

Axiom 8—Daily 'magical exercises', the product of New Age charlatans and well meaning dilatants which supposedly are designed to bring about the Practitioner's spiritual development, are unnecessary. These extraneous fabrications confuse the issues of 'spirituality' and 'psychicism,' genuine personality development and its attainment of accelerated human qualities with ego weakness, while creating an artificial dependency upon a divine father figure in the clouds meant to rescue the Practitioner from his or her self-made plights of unease and distress.

Argument 8—During my early years in magic, I too bought the going line of the New Age that daily spiritual practices were going to elevate me to a position of near godhood, enabling me to cure all of my life's situation ills. It was inevitable that then I would ride out into the sunset, a magnanimous being, shedding blessings from my glowing, holy hands, to all who ask for them. It did not take me very long to realize there was something drastically wrong with the thesis behind this rosy, spiritual picture of goodness, light, and love.

My readings in psychology—old psychology mind you, the psychology of James, Freud, Jung and Assagioli—soon made me realize that the idea of spirituality was really the ideas behind psychicism blown all out of proportion. In my opinion, the supposition that there is (somehow) a separate source behind the psychic forces that gives rise to genuine intuition, astral sight, divination, evocation to physical manifestation, and virtually every type of phenomena that is dubbed as 'spiritual' by modern magic, is without any foundation whatsoever.

This apparent need for a secret source led the Gothic Revival Era and later New Age magicians to postulate this separate, unreachable source as being, *in its essence*, the 'father figure in the clouds' image. No one in the New Age today will admit to this openly. If you pointed it out to them they would deny it. How could they not? They are not even aware of their own inner views, other than what some modern magical authority tells them! But if you question them persistently, you will find that their entire magical or occult philosophy is based upon a watered-down version of the Judaic or Judaic-Christian religious-ethic, which does indeed have an unreachable father figure at the center of their secret source.

It was not enough for the Gothic Revival and New Age magicians to accept this psychic source as the outer cloak of the divinity within the individual. Instead, these latter day occultists felt the need to generate an entire cult-concept of a secret source from which some mere psychic abilities flowed. And it was to this unreachable secret source and the spiritual nature within them, that their literature was written. Instead of psychic qualities that made the magic happen stemming directly from the center of their own divinity within, it now had to come from the secret source which was unreachable, yet which could somehow be reached if they could only develop themselves spiritually.

This state of disconnection from their own psychic natures in favor of a more elaborate construct, produced the waywardness in modern magic that is so prevalent today. Consider this. You cannot experience this spiritual nature of yours, but you can experience flashes of intuitive insight. You cannot experience the soul, but you can experience the qualities of mercy, caring, and forgiveness—all traits of an advanced psychic *personality*, whose favorable traits can be further developed. But frame those qualities into some nebulous idea of a spiritual nature, and you are lost at once. That is, unless you begin your daily modern magic practices that will lead you toward spiritual growth.

This would be the very spiritual growth you have experienced as psychic power, and which you can develop further through, for instance, attaining a rock-solid subjective synthesis. At once, the problem disappears. You are now in your own hands, capable of developing your own talents and qualities. You are no longer at the mercy of some father figure or daily practices designed to developed you further along some way leading you to 'his glory for you.'

Make no mistake about this. The qualities of mercy, kindness, tolerance, understanding, and caring are personality traits. They do not stem from your divine nature within. The divine part of you may very well encourage you to develop these qualities for many reasons, but it—your divine nature—is as far removed from being the source of them, as you are able to stand on the surface of the sun. They are life-enhancing manifestations stemming from a well developed psychic nature. And that nature does not lie concealed in some secret source you must work toward daily through some special practices set down by some modern day guru. No.

By understanding the workings of your own mind, and working equally hard at attaining a stable, firm subjective synthesis while taking responsibility for your own life and for your own actions and the lack of them in any given situation, and while developing clarity of thought and your great gift of logic and reason, you—the Practitioner of our Art of Magic—will, through the proper employment of magic, become and achieve more than you could possibly believe or dream of at this moment.

Do I favor any daily psychic practices? If you consider seeking a twenty-to-thirty minute period of silence at the beginning and end of each day, in which you turn your attention inward and simply watch the movements of your own mind while detaching yourself from it as psychic practices, then yes, I suppose I do. But even here, these practices are not what you might think. If you will but study and implement the works C.S. Hyatt and Roberto Assagioli as given in the Suggested Reading List, I think you will find the most balanced of all psychic exercises, that will magnify what you can do in magic, and give you the most profound insights into what and who you truly are—a holy being, capable of creating and manifesting whatever it is in your life and world that will give it added meaning, direction, and peace, while helping those around you. Pretty words and big promises? You bet! Are they really, I mean, really, really true and possible? Try them for yourself. You'll find out I am right!

Conclusion 8—Remember, the book you are now reading was written not only to help you with evocation to physical manifestation, but to enable you to develop a magical system that works for you. To effect this end, I am trying to give you as much as I can in these pages. In the case of daily magical exercises supposedly designed to bring about spiritual growth, such practices are absurd. They confuse the issue of psychic development with some netherworld spiritual qualities which, properly speaking, are simply desirable human personality characteristics raised to a high level. Yes, such terms as the Higher Self may have application here, but only as a mental construct designed by the New Age to erect yet another barrier between you and your achievements in your personality and psychic development.

Why not give the credit to the one who struggles to improve? Why not credit yourself instead of some quasi-imagined, ill defined construct? Do you turn down your paycheck and tell your employer to give it to the charity of his choice, or do you accept it and do with it what you will? Don't be so eager to throw away the self-earned accolades of your hard work on some concept meant to prove someone else's belief system.

As to your own psychic development, one or two twenty-minute-or-so periods a day spent in quiet reflection and working with the concepts laid down in the books written by Assagioli and Hyatt, are all you need, along with your daily effort to attain a rock-solid subjective synthesis in magic, of course. If you follow this counsel you *will* grow in all of the important ways that count, and you will have no one to give the fame or the blame to but yourself. That is the only way for a man or woman of Principle, Honor, and Integrity to act. Forget the rest.

Axiom 9—Do not reject the religious tradition in which you were raised, nor the commonsense found in what religionists call the Commandments of God. The use of these precepts is crucial in devising an effective subjective synthesis and producing a corresponding coherent, integrated subconscious belief system. It is also the one fundamental axiom every Practitioner of magic rigorously avoids, which accounts for more magical failure than is realized.

Argument 9—I can imagine there are readers who will object strenuously at this point. "Whhaatt? This guy has been badmouthing organized religion of all kinds from page one, and now he tells me I have to go back to my church or synagogue or temple and get involved in their worship services? Me?! Is he crazy?! He must be! I've had enough!"

Before the reader discards this book once and for all (?), hear me out. No greater genuine authority than Abraham the Jew, writing to his son Lamech in his 1458 C.E. Old System of Magic masterpiece, *The Book of the Sacred Magic of Abramelin* the Mage stated, "...and never have I failed in attaining mine end, I have always been obeyed (by the Spirits), and everything hath succeeded with me because I have myself obeyed the Commandments of God."[7] Abraham further states "...and [obtain] the actual assistance of His Holy Angels, who take an incredible pleasure...that you intend to follow out the Command-

---

[7] Mathers, S.L. MacGregor, translator. *The Book of the Sacred Magic of Abramelin the Mage as delivered by Abraham the Jew unto his son Lamech A.D. 1458.* Dover Publications, Inc., NY. 1975. page 34.

ments of God..."[8] This Jewish writer then brings it all together when he admonishes, "For it is an indubitable and evident thing that he who is born Christian, Jew, Pagan, Turk, Infidel, or whatever religion it may be, can arrive at the perfection of this Work or Art and become a Master, but he who hath abandoned his natural Law, and embraced another religion opposed to his own, can never arrive at the summit of this Sacred Science"[9]

Although the book in question deals with the Attainment of the Knowledge and Conversation of the Holy Guardian Angel, the principles it lays down are extremely accurate and apply to all branches of magic. Furthermore, their conscious use leads the Practitioner to attainment of the *full* results across the entire spectrum of magic, and without any slingshot effects. The reason for this is that the Abramelin principles in general, and the two being discussed here, are crucial in forming an effective subjective synthesis. Beside these magical reasons, they are also just downright practical.

Consider the Ten Commandments. As in no other age, we are besieged with more laws and codes of social conduct than any of us may realize. It was recently stated in a television documentary that the average American citizen breaks at least three laws everyday that are punishable by fine or imprisonment, and commits at least four major felonies in his or her lifetime. Imagine that! If the so-called Ten Commandments are viewed from this perspective, it makes sense to observe them if for no other reason than to preserve your liberty and allow you to live your life the way you desire. Either this, or live behind bars, literally fighting for your life in the insane jungles of perversion and death those places have become.

The Practitioner who follows Abraham's advice will also discover a quieter, calmer life. Why? Simply because these so-called Commandments are so instilled into the human psyche by society, that they can be found in all

---

[8] Ibid. page 36.

[9] Ibid. page 24.

religions and all societies from time immemorial. They are not the invention of Jews, Christians, or any given sect. Rather, they are the province of all. They have enabled society to develop, and the individual to grow in many important ways. So carefully consider adherence to these Commandments.

What do I recommend here? It's more a matter of what I found out the hard way. Put bluntly, I strongly urge the Practitioner to follow out the Commandments of God, as Abramelin phrased it, and I don't mean when it's convenient. The construction and development of your subjective synthesis and the subconscious belief system that results from it, is hard work. Period. It's not something that will be created and perfected overnight, or whenever you feel like working on it. It requires conscious attention as I have said so many times, along with deep reflective thought at any and all times you are not occupied with the daily duties of life. It is *serious business*, and keeping the so-called Commandments is part of it. As such, Practitioners owe it to themselves to keep the commandments as if their lives depended upon it, because in a very real way, this is true. Your life will either be built and perfected through magic, or destroyed by it. I can't make it any simpler than this.

As to maintaining a connection to the religion in which you were born? Oh, yes. This is of paramount importance as well. In today's society, rights are everything. They are all around you. They are yours for the taking, until you unknowingly or otherwise break one of the tens of thousands of laws designed to modify these rights so others are respected. So everyone is, to some significant degree, free-wheeling.

You have the right to become a Wiccan, break with your religious upbringing, hate the church or the synagogue or the temple in which you were raised, and form your own philosophy of life, and you most certainly can do all of these things. But if you do not maintain some basic, ever-so-modest link with that original religion, I guarantee you, you will never manifest the full results of your 'philosophy,' no matter what kind it may be, including those individuals who are trying to form their own magical philosophy or system. How do you do this? It's really very simple.

If you are a Catholic, you don't have to go back to Holy Mother Church, involve yourself in the Mass, receive Holy Communion or become a staunch member of the Sacred Heart Society—unless you feel so moved, of course. Nor am I advocating you return to the protestant sect you came from and become a deacon. If you were reared as a Jew, you don't have to put on your yarmulke, take out your sacred scrolls, and begin praying, or sit in a synagogue listening to the rabbi rattle off what you can no longer accept. The same applies to those raised along other religious trains of thought.

Instead, the Christian can spend some quiet time reading the New Testament while the Jew occupies himself with the Old Testament, or both delve more deeply into the beauty and power of the Psalms. If so moved, the Practitioner of whatever faith could steal into an orthodox house of worship when services are not being performed, and simply sit and think, and offer up some small prayer to the god of his or her childhood. This is all that is required. Those Practitioners who follow these simple and easy suggestions will find that they feel better inside, and for longer periods of time. Why is this? Because to deny the faith in which you were raised sets up hostilities with those regions of your subconscious where such thoughts and religious inclinations are still going on, even now as you read these words. You are at war with a vital, vibrant part of your own nature, and it is a war you cannot win.

Conclusion 9—For the sake of the Practitioner developing an effective subjective synthesis and a solid subconscious belief system that results from it, keeping the Commandments of God and maintaining a link with the religious tradition in which the Practitioner was born is not simply a convenience, it is a necessity. Owing to the state of society today, the wise individual who follows this advice will also find themselves among the most truly free individuals of all, able to grow and develop in their own self-determined ways, without the unnecessary interference from societal laws, and the machinations of those who have created and maintain those legal dictates.

Axiom 10—All evocation to physical manifestation *must* occur directly on the ground, either in the outdoors (preferably in a secret wooded area), or in a house equipped with a cellar or basement with a dirt or concrete floor.

Argument 10—I have read of many so-called evocations to physical manifestation being conducted in apartments, somewhere high up in the clouds, a few dozen or hundred feet away from the ground. Besides the New Age problems already pointed out, the practice of any of the powerful forms of magic—and especially evocation proper—in such a setting will prevent the full manifestation. This of course, will magnify the problems of control and command all out of proportion, so that in the end, the Practitioner will achieve anything but the full results they were working for.

Such an attempt must never be made, regardless of the inconvenience it costs the Operator. Remember, magic is not a trite contrivance. It is not an activity to be engaged in because you suddenly feel like it, or—believe it or not, I have heard it countless times before—because the so-called Operator had nothing better to do. The practice of *all* magic is unstable at best. At worst, it is the equivalent of playing Russian Roulette with all chambers loaded. I'm not joking here. So if you find yourself living in a city, or in an apartment, or even a house without a dirt or concrete floor, you will simply have to make other arrangements if you truly want to do evocation to physical manifestation, getting the full results you are so desperate for, without serious, deleterious effects.

I struggled with this hidden problem of where to conduct an evocation for many, many years, until enough evocations were done, and the variables in them eliminated. I was left with this conclusion. Evocation to physical manifestation must be conducted directly upon the earth. I employed this conclusion many times. It not only eliminated the problems of obtaining a full manifestation, but the physical phenomena produced from the evocation and the results achieved, were utterly astounding in comparison to operating on the upper floors of some building.

It is important the reader understand a very difficult point here. Manifestation, like all phenomena in magic, is a matter of *degree*. You may indeed get what you *think* is a full manifestation by operating on an upper floor in some building. But when you see the results of full manifestation that occur when the operation occurs directly upon the earth or on a concrete floor laid directly upon the earth, you will see the difference immediately. In the latter case, the image that appears in the smoke of the Perfume of Art will be so real, you will think it is another physical being you are conversing with.

It is this *difference* that jars the mind into a new state of recognizing the reality of the entity, which then allows *complete* control and command to occur. Experience is the best and *only* teacher here. To put it into more concrete terms, the difference here is the same as to how you think and act when you are thinking of someone, as compared to when you are actually in their presence. Your entire demeanor, actions, voice, and attitude toward the person change dramatically when you are with them. Prior to meeting them, in your imagination you may see yourself saying and doing all manner of things in a very arrogant or loving way. But when you are with them, what you say and do are *completely governed by being in their presence*. You know what I mean. This difference applies in evocation to physical manifestation, and in a very powerful way.

Why is this so? I have only been able to come up with one theoretical construct to explain this. The earth itself *stabilizes* the *entire* operation. This stabilization is comparable to electricity. If a circuit is not grounded, that is, not connected to some part of the metal chassis it is built into, and that chassis is not connected to an earth ground either through a separate connection or through a grounded electrical cord, the signal floats. Even if the circuit is connected to the metal chassis but the chassis itself is not connected to an earth ground, the fundamental frequency of the signal you are after still floats, or fades in and out. This is because there are other distorting frequencies (harmonics) that lie above and below the fundamental frequency. It is their *natural presence* that destroys the pure, clean signal you are after.

But when you ground the circuit, the harmonics are removed *because of their unstable nature*. In other words, *their very instability operates against them*. The same phenomenon happens in evocation to physical manifestation. Can you imagine all of the other entities—the other spiritual harmonics—your rite will be attracting as you proceed with the conjurations? You see my point. So when preparing for your evocations, make them evocations to full manifestation, and not the clap-traps of futile convenience, eventual disappointment and slingshot interference. If you conduct just one—just one, mind you—evocation in the manner recommended here, I promise you will never be able to even think of doing a evocation in any other way. The difference between the mechanics and process of the rite, and the full results attained without any consequential negative effects, are greater than the difference between night and day.

Conclusion 10—The only way a true evocation to physical manifestation can be conducted is by performing the entire rite—from the construction of the Circle of Art to the conjurations and through the License to Depart—is by conducting the rite directly upon the earth, or in a basement or cellar that is equipped with a concrete floor that rests directly upon the ground. To attempt any form of high magic otherwise, is to not simply look for, but to ask for very serious trouble.

It is all up to the reader whether to follow the Ten Axioms presented here. The important thing is that they have been stated for the first time in any book, and they have been thoroughly explained. In closing this chapter, I leave the reader with this parting thought. Play around with Magic, and you're going to get burned. Play around with this particular branch of Magic, and you are going to get burned *very severely*. There is an ancient alchemical axiom the Practitioner of magic would do well to remember and apply to his or her would-be magical work at all times. *"Know the Theory before attempting the Praxis!"*

Chapter Four

The Fourth Book of Occult Philosophy and the Heptameron — Their History, Purpose, and Power

I take my hat off to the reader who has made it this far. I am well aware of the inner turmoil Chapter Three must have caused you. I too had to endure much anguish when I finally realized the facts underlying the art and meaning of what I term the Science behind the Art of Magic. The gloss and glitter of 'modern magic' faded for me as quickly as a cheap paint job on an old jalopy. I wish I could apologize to you for the anguish you have and no doubt still are enduring. But the cold hard fact is that I cannot. This is the only way evocation to physical manifestation can be brought about, and the only way genuine magic can be operated, as described, and as confirmed countless times by my colleagues and myself. That being said, perhaps I can make it up to you—at least to a point—by getting on with the business at hand.

Thus far, you have been instructed in the history of the grammars of magic, and in the 'thou shalts' and 'thou shalt nots.' But how to apply those restrictions and directions has been held back until you were grounded in the underlying theory and warnings. Remember, they will go far in aiding you to construct your own effective subjective synthesis, and the subconscious belief system that results from it. In this and the succeeding chapters we will get down to business of just how to apply what you have learned thus far. But first, by obeying the injunction

"Know the Theory before attempting the Praxis," we have some (more) preliminary work.

What never ceases to amaze me is the reaction to the grimoire you will be using in this work of application. It is so little known. Yet why, I have no idea, because there are few Practitioners or occult writers who are not well acquainted with its presumed author. Even while writing this book, I was introduced to a well known writer in the occult who, when I mentioned I was writing this book and the grimoire it is based upon said, "Whhaatt? I never heard of that grammar! Where did you find it!" His response is the rule, not the exception to it.

The relatively unknown grammar you will be using is entitled *Heptameron or Magical Elements*,[10] supposedly written by one Peter de Abano in the late thirteenth to early fourteenth century C.E. This grimoire is by far the simplest, but perhaps not the easiest grammar of magic to work from. It is simple, because it is very straightforward in ceremonial mechanics. It also has very few weapons or implements, none of which demand the blood of a black cock that never trode hen or the like in their preparation, nor any of the other 'vulgarities' you will hear your New Age counterparts label whatever is too difficult or inconvenient.

It is not so easy so as to fail to introduce you to the *objective* existence of a world of beings you only speculated about up to now, or viewed solely as psychological projections. This magical grimoire will require you to begin to build your subjective synthesis immediately, and without the fanfare and cuddly levels of grandiosity that saturate New Age preparations for whatever it is they do that they call evocation. This will require hard and meticulous research on your part. There is no effect without cause, and no cause without the energy of work.

---

[10] Agrippa, Henry Cornelius. *Fourth Book of Occult Philosophy.* Kessinger Publishing Company, Montana. Heptameron starts on page 73.

Even though everything you need for performing an evocation to physical manifestation with as little of the slingshot effect as possible is given here, there will be innumerable questions that will arise. However, you must answer them yourself. Neither I nor anyone else can do that for you. Please don't waste your precious time looking for a Master or other such guru or worse yet, try joining some magical group in order to let them do the work for you or to lessen your burden. I assure you, no such individual or group exists, or ever existed. Do the work *yourself.*

This curious grimoire, the *Heptameron,* was popularized in recent times by A.E. Waite. Actually, the history and purpose of this grammar of magic is inextricably connected to another book in which it first appeared. Writing in his famous 1911 edition of *The Book of Ceremonial Magic,* Waite tells us that the *Heptameron* first appeared in *The Fourth Book of Occult Philosophy* which, as with the *Three Books of Occult Philosophy,* was ascribed to Henry Cornelius Agrippa. The problem, Waite teases, was that this *Fourth Book* was "…much too informal, and left too much to the discretion of the operator, to be satisfactory for a science so exact as that of Ceremonial Magic."[11] Waite continues his caustic appraisal of it, effectively labeling it as spurious, telling his readers that the *Fourth Book* itself was only "A form of procedure which bequeathed nothing to the imagination and asked no other skill than the patient exactitude of the rule of thumb was necessary to the weakness of the ordinary sorcerer. The *Heptameron, or Magical Elements* ascribed to Peter de Abano is an attempt to supply the want and to offer to the neophyte a complete wizard's cabinet."[12]

A word here about Waite may not be amiss. As is typical of Waite upon the resurgence of his Christian upbringing—which occurred around a decade after the

---

[11] Waite, Arthur Edward. *The Book of Ceremonial Magic. A Complete Grimoire.* University Books, Inc., NY. 1961. page 89.

[12] Ibid. page 89.

dissolution of the Golden Dawn of which he was a member—he attempts through his voluminous writings to lead the reader astray on hard core magical subjects. He does this by combining facts with purposely designed nugatory opinions to produce an argument, the conclusion of which is aimed at swaying the reader away from the ignorance behind such magical activities. As such, the best way to study this individual's potentially valuable but inflammatory writings, *is to reverse what he states.* If he genuinely praises a topic, *be wary of it.* If he denigrates and expresses a tongue-in-cheek attitude toward the subject, *pay close attention to it!* Read it carefully, and understand its content, *not* his interpretation. If you do so, you will quickly uncover much valuable magical and occult knowledge buried not so very deeply in his seemingly negative words.

In the end, Waite was a scholar. He would rant and rave, asserting magical evocation to physical manifestation and other areas of the occult were the inventions of charlatans, and only followed by ignorant believers who would sell their souls for a penny if they could. But his scholarly mind prevented him from tampering with the knowledge he derided. I for one cannot praise the factual content behind his writings enough, despite being labeled a fool for doing so. But then, I am not of the New Age, as the reader well knows.

Waite continues in his introduction to the *Fourth Book*, that it was believed Agrippa wrote the book for the experienced Practitioner of magic. As such, the text does not deal with either specific ceremonial requirements or the specifics of the practice of evocation to physical manifestation. Rather, it only mentions them in a very general way. In order to rectify this and to enable the reader who has not "...tasted of Magical Superstitions, may have them in readiness..." as the opening lines of the *Heptameron* itself tells us, this grimoire was added to the *Fourth Book of Occult Philosophy*. The grimoire goes on to say "In brief, in this book are kept the principles of Magical conveyances," or put more simply, this book shows how to it.

Waite unexpectedly begins to confirm that indeed the _Heptameron's_ promise "...is scrupulously fulfilled; what the operator must do and how he should perform it, so as "draw spirits into discourse," are matters set forth so plainly that the wayfaring man need not err therein." But as is characteristic of Waite, his tongue-in-cheek attitude of derision quickly takes over. After agreeing with the purpose of the text, in an effort to persuade the would-be Operator to work from it, he quickly adds, "Assuming the sacerdotal office of the operator, or a priest for an accomplice, is all so simple that failure could not well be ascribed to a blunder on his part."[13] Nevertheless, the grimoire is completely workable. Its very simplicity demands that it be used. Hence, this is one of the reasons it was chosen here.

The _Fourth Book_ is, for all practical purposes, an extremely concise restatement of some key magical principles found in the famous _Three Books of Occult Philosophy_. Originally, it was believed it was written for the Practitioner who had a substantial background in the theory of magic in general, and as such, would serve as a quick review of those principles. In today's terms, it may be considered like a _Cliff's Notes_ for a college course.

It is a practical book, aimed at helping the Operator prepare for the next magical ritual. Yet the book appears to sit in judgment of itself. It seems to be saying this purpose is insufficient, and that it is not complete as is. The very wording and subject matter of the text cries out an appeal for a practical application of the magical theory, so the reader can experiment and learn through the practical application of the _Heptameron_.

This may very well have been the motivation of Robert Turner, an esoteric scholar, who was the first to append the Heptameron to the original _Fourth Book_ in 1655. The reader should know that the original _Fourth Book of Occult Philosophy_, which appeared around 1560 C.E. and which was ascribed to Agrippa, was not written by him. This is

---

[13] Ibid. page 89.

documented by Johann Wierus, a loyal pupil of Agrippa's, who denounced it as a forgery around 1567 C.E. The *second* 'Fourth Book,' which Turner produced in 1655, actually consists of six separate works, collected by him and placed between the covers of a single volume. This later *'Fourth Book'* contains six chapters: Geomancy; a reprint of the original *Fourth Book* (which Wierus denounced); the *Heptameron; Isagoge;* Astronomical Geomancy; and Of the Magic of the Ancients—Arbatel, who the reader encountered in Chapter Two. To Turner's edition the name *Henry Cornelius Agrippa, His Fourth Book of Occult Philosophy,* was unfortunately appended. In my opinion, not only did this cause considerable confusion for centuries, it confused the purpose for which the original *Fourth Book of Occult Philosophy* was written—as a manual of preparation.

Yet, Turner's *Fourth Book* offers what I feel is a legitimate explanation for his actions. In my copy of the 1655 edition, which I will refer to as the *Turner Fourth Book* hereafter, he explains his position in the Preface. Understanding his view may not seem important now, but as the reader will soon see it is important in understanding the history and purpose not only of the original *Fourth Book*, but the *Turner Fourth Book* and the latter's inclusion, the *Heptameron.* In that preface, dated London, ult. Aug. 1654, Turner seeks to make the Arts Magical more available to the aspiring student by assuring him or her that Magick—the spelling of which the New Age claims to have invented, incidentally—is different from Magicke as he termed it, which he connected with Witchcraft and Sorcery.

Remember, Turner was laboring under the cloud of the Spanish Inquisition, which at that time was still in full force. He and other writers needed a solid justification for their magical views which, after blind-siding the Inquisition's Holy Tribunal, would spread the magical teachings of earlier ages and thus perpetuate them. Turner writes, "Now Witchcraft and Sorcery, are works done merely by the devil, which with respect to some covenant made with

man, he acteth by men his instruments, to accomplish his
evil ends: of these, the histories of all ages, people and
countries, as also the holy Scriptures, afford us sundry
examples."[14]

He then defends 'Magick' by drawing an equation
between it and the Persian term from which it is derived—
Magus. Turner continues, "But Magus is a Persian word
primitively, whereby is exprest such a one as is altogether
conversant in things divine; and as Plato affirmeth, the art
of Magick is the art of worshipping God…. So that the
word Magus of itself imports a Contemplator of divine
and heavenly Sciences; but under the name Magick, are all
unlawful Arts comprehended; as Necromancy and Witchcraft, and such Arts which are effected by combination
with the devil, and whereof he is a party."[15]

In short, it seems at first glance Turner is double-talk-
ing his way around the issue by trying to equate Magus
with Magick, and Magicke with Witchcraft and Sorcery,
and then he drops the ball by saying Magick is also a tool
of Witchcraft and Sorcery after all! A careful reading however, finally reveals the meaning behind his terms. It is the
purpose to which Magick is put, that makes it either the art
of worshipping God or a tool of the devil, which at that
time, was equated with Witchcraft and Sorcery. His
substitution of one spelling of the word for another when
either praising magic or deriding Witchcraft is meaning-
less. We can conclude this when we read, "So that a Magician is no other but…a studious observer and expounder
of divine things; and the Art itself is none other…then the
absolute perfection of Natural Philosophy."[16]

I would like to point out again to be aware that the
contrary writing style as employed by Turner was a typical writing ploy of *all* Middle Ages and Renaissance Era

---

[14] Agrippa, Henry Cornelius. *Fourth Book of Occult Philosophy.*
Kessinger Publishing Company, Montana. Page A2.

[15] Ibid. Page A3.

[16] Ibid. Page A6.

writers on magic. Knowing this may help the individual in their own researches. When studying such texts in order to build a subjective synthesis, learn to read between the lines, and take the *outside* meaning to be the hidden meaning.

Even a casual study of the *Turner Fourth Book* makes it clear that the purpose of his edition was to help the neophyte gain *experience* in magic across the board. In the case of evocation to physical manifestation, he appended the *Heptameron* to the volume as a means of enabling the would-be Practitioner to apply the principles laid down in the original *Fourth Book*. His 1655 classic thus enabled the inexperienced Operator to learn the art of evocation to physical manifestation from the ground up. As with the *Fourth Book of Occult Philosophy* which may have been written by either Agrippa's pupils or written by those of his school of magical thought, the authorship of the *Heptameron* is still in dispute. It was well known during the Middle Ages Era, but it was the Turner 1655 edition of the *Fourth Book* that truly popularized it. As mentioned, the original Fourth Book that appeared around 1560 was simply what I consider to be a very concise exposition of some of the key principles of the *Three Books of Occult Philosophy*. Hence the original *Fourth Book* and the *Heptameron* were separate texts, both of which were either known or unknown to any given Practitioner earlier than 1655. But where did the *Heptameron* itself come from?

All that is really known about its origin is that its author is said to have been one Pietro d'Abano, also cited as Peter de Abano or Peter of Abano in its English form, who lived from 1250 to 1316 C.E. Born in the vicinity of Padua, Italy, he was a skilled, scholarly physician, who was revered by his university students for his wisdom and analytical mind. His attempt to reconcile differences between various medical schools of thought existing at the time was remarkable, although this visionary effort probably added to the severe problems that were to befall him.

After establishing himself at Paris, he was forced to flee and return to his native Italy in order to avoid the

charges of heresy leveled against him by his envious
Parisian medical colleagues. Upon his return to Padua, a
medical chair at the University was created for him. But
the charges of heresy continued to hound him to such an
extent, that when his new rivals heard of the past charges,
they leveled further accusations against him. He was
accused of possessing the famed Stone of the Philosophers, dealing with demons, and acquiring secret knowledge from miniature demon-like creatures he kept
concealed in small vessels. All of this eventually brought
Abano to the attention of the Inquisition. Although the
demonstration of his orthodox Roman Catholic faith
saved him from the tortures of the Holy Inquisitional
Tribunal the first time, he was brought back to face the
Inquisitors a second time, owing to new and expanded
charges of heresy.

This time however, the strain proved too much for
him. He died during the course of the trial. Nevertheless,
he was still convicted of heresy posthumously, and his
image was burned in effigy. It is both ironic and tragic
that it was this man's innocent fascination with rudimentary astrology that brought charges of advanced magical
practice against him. Yet, as Tyson points out in his epic
edition of the *Three Books*, Johannes Trithemius, Agrippa's
teacher, mentions a Clavicle made by de Abano in his own
work, *Antipalus maleficiorum*, circa 1500 C.E. If the Clavicle
that Trithemius mentions at that early date is indeed the
Heptameron, much could indeed be accounted for regarding this strange grimoire.

It is because of Mr. Tyson's comment and my own
extensive research, that I have concluded that while the
Heptameron was not written by d'Abano himself, it was
composed by one or more of his ambitious university
students as a testament to his genius. Such an action was
common for the eras encompassed by the Old System of
Magic, as was demonstrated in the case of the original
Fourth Book of Occult Philosophy. Despite Waite's innocu-
ous arguments to the contrary, it is my opinion that it is
reasonable to assume the *Heptameron* originated sometime

after the death of d'Abano; most likely sometime between the late 14th to the early 15th century C.E.

The *Heptameron* itself does not deal openly with demons. Instead, it treats the nature of the beings it conjures as angelic and beneficent spirits. But, as Waite so aptly puts it, they are described as angels, and threatened as demons. This is a further example of the common ploy used throughout most of the grammars embodied by the Old System of Magic, so the beings conjured by the *Heptameron* are evil beings that are constrained and made to appear through the invocation of the angels, and by calling upon the most holy and ineffable Names of God. Specifically, the process of the Heptameron is divided into two parts. The first entails a method for evoking what are called the "Spirits of the Air" or the "Aerial Spirits" that govern each day of the week. To be clear about it, these beings are in actuality quite demonic. They are constrained however, by a series of angelic conjurations, each of which is particular to a given weekday.

The second part of the book and process is concerned with the specific offices of the demons. Those offices include discovering hidden treasures for the Operator, waging war, uncovering the secrets of friends, enemies, or even the ruling nobility, opening locks and obtaining the love of women, and the acquisition of material wealth and learning about the "decayed sciences." The list of their offices—or powers—goes on and on. In short, this single grimoire professes to be the source from which all material pleasure and luxury can be obtained by the Operator, and as the reader will soon see, in a very real and operable sense, it is.

Having obtained some knowledge of the history and purpose of the *Heptameron* and its later interconnection with the *Fourth Book,* the reader will want to hear a few words concerning the potential power of the former. For over thirty of the forty years I have been involved in occultism and magic, I have experimented extensively with the grimoires. In none of them, including the famous and readily available *Goetia,* have I found an easier, more direct approach to successful evocation to physical manifestation, provided of course, that my ten self-derived Magical Axioms are obeyed.

The implements are simple and few, and relatively easy to produce. The conjurations lead naturally to an ever increasing, automatic exaltation of the mind, which is so necessary for success. The circle, while appearing complex at first glance, is simplicity itself when compared to ones as required, for example, in either the *Clavicula Salomonis* or the *Goetia*. The Perfumes of the Art for each day are readily available and require no 'modern day' magical additions such as Dittany of Crete, in order to enhance manifestation. There are no hours of the day and night to calculate or contend with, such as is offered by Agrippa in the *Three Books*. Nor do you need to worry about their astrological sign and month considerations, as advocated by so many modern authors in their interpretation of the old grimoires. In fact, the few astrological conditions required are so few and easy to accomplish, as to be nearly unbelievable. Yet together, the few requirements laid down in the tract work cleanly, completely, and thoroughly. Provided, of course, the Operator follows the Ten Magical Axioms.

There you have it. With a knowledgeable understanding of the history, purpose and power of the *Heptameron* and its companion, the *Fourth Book*, the reader is now ready to proceed with the magical tract of the *Heptameron* proper, and to begin the **praxis** of magical evocation to physical manifestation.

Chapter Five

The Heptameron Operation — Pulling It All Together

Preparatory Remarks

The edition of the *Heptameron* the reader will be using here is the original 1655 edition appended by Robert Turner to the version of his *Fourth Book,* as it is generally referred to today. It is presented in its entirety so the Operator will not have to worry about it being complete. Nor will you have to worry about butchering, as Agrippa's *Three Books* were by Barrett's production of *The Magus,* and as I have seen in some modern reprints of other texts.

While rigidly preserving the content and syntax of the 1655 edition, I have modernized the spelling of some words where it seemed appropriate. In addition, the Olde English long "s" was replaced with the modern "s" letter. All of this should allow the contemporary eye more ease and understanding. I have also divided the book up into its original two parts. Part One, being the instructions for constructing the Circle of Art, making the Pentacle, the Sword, and the general Conjurations. Part Two consists of the specific conjurations for each day of the week. Additionally, the Circle of Art has been repositioned within the text that describes its construction, in order to avoid any breaks in train of thought. The reader will still have to refer to the names of the angels, their ministers, and so on, in the section for the conjurations of the days of the week, and to refer to the end of the text for the names of the hours and their angels. But the placement I have given it here will make it much more useable than that of the original 1655 Turner edition.

I also added something new, a feature I trust will be of significant help to the soon-to-be Operator of this strange grimoire. Beneath relevant paragraphs, the reader will find a *Commentary* set off in italics. This additional guidance will lend added meaning and insight to the material while providing further instruction necessary to work this particular grimoire efficiently and effectively. These commentaries are also meant to help you understand how to read a grimoire, and apply that new understanding to others you may decide to operate from later on.

Although many of the commentaries will have sole relevance to this specific grammar of magic, the counsel given in others will be found to be applicable not only to other grimoires, but to other magical practices that the Practitioner may become involved in while developing a personal system of magic. It is up to the reader to decide which is which. As I stated early on, it is my intention to give a complete course in the underlying, operational theory of Old System Magic, so that a personal system of magic can evolve over time. As such, this book is not intended to be a one-shot deal. Far from it. Used wisely, it can become the reader's constant companion, a road map on the Path to personal and psychic development. With this small preamble now completed, we move onto the *Heptameron* itself.

Heptameron
or
Magical Elements
of
Peter de Abano

Part One

In the former Book, which Is the fourth Book of Agrippa, it is sufficiently spoken concerning Magical Ceremonies, and Initiations. But because he seemeth to have written to the learned, and well-experienced in this Art; because he doth not specially treat of the Ceremonies, but rather speaketh of them in general, it was therefore thought good to add hereunto the Magical Elements of Peter de Abano: that those who are hitherto ignorant, and have not tasted of Magical Superstitions, may have them in readiness, how they may exercise themselves therein.

Commentary—As pointed out in Chapter Four, the very opening page of the Heptameron could have served as the motivation for Turner being the first to append this grimoire to his own publication of the Fourth Book. *It is clear that the attitude toward Agrippa's* Fourth Book of Occult Philosophy *is one of theory and summary, and not one of practical application, a problem corrected by the* Heptameron *itself.*

As to such terms, "Magical Superstitions" above, and "Magical vanity" in the next paragraph, the reader is reminded that the author of this grammar of magic was writing under the shadow of the Inquisition. During those times it was customary to use such terminology to sidetrack the opposition, however ineffective it may seem to the modern reader. Those were hellish times, produced by an insane Catholicism, the resulting social forces being vastly different from those we live under today. Such double-talk actually caused doubt in the minds of opponents, while serving as loopholes for the individual if they came to the attention of the inquisitional Tribunal.

For we see in this book, as it were a certain introduction of Magical vanity; and as it were in present exercise, they may behold the distinct functions of spirits, how they may be drawn to discourse and communication; what is to be done every day, and every hour; and how they shall be read, as if they were described syllable by syllable.

Commentary—The author of the Heptameron *is justifiably proud of the completeness and pragmatic nature of his grimoire, as it stands in contrast to the* Fourth Book of Occult Philosophy. *He sees it as the inevitable solution to the* Fourth Book's *strictly theoretical content, so that by combining the theory of that book with his grimoire, a complete 'magical tool cabinet' is produced. The modern reader, while finding the* Heptameron *remarkably easy and workable when compared to other grimoires, will still encounter a certain amount of initial ambiguity and difficulty in understanding it. But once again, to the mind of the ancient Operator, it was as readable and understandable as reading a newspaper is for us today. If the reader works with other grimoires later on, he or she will find this same attitude of clarity and simplicity touted in all such texts. It was merely a writing characteristic and mental attitude toward this subject matter that prevailed during those times.*

In brief, in this book are kept the principles of Magical conveyances. But because the greatest power is attributed to the Circles; (For they are certain fortresses to defend the operators safe from the evil Spirits;) In the first place we will treat concerning the composition of a Circle.

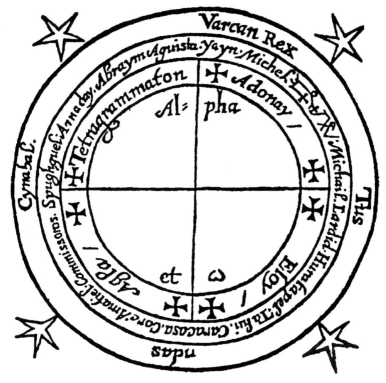

Figure 1
The Circle of Art

Of the Circle, and the composition thereof.

The form of Circles is not always one and the same; but useth to be changed, according to the order of the Spirits that are to be called, their places, times, days and hours. For in making a Circle, it ought to be considered in what time of the year, what day, and what hour, that you make the Circle; what Spirits you would call, to what Star and Region they do belong, and what functions they have.

Commentary 1—Unlike other grimoires wherein the form of the circles and the Names of Power written about it are fixed, the Heptameron *uses a unique scheme whereby names are placed within the circles according to the time of working. By referring to Figure 1 above, the reader will see that the circle is actually a series of four circles—the center one being the 'area of operation'. The circles are a blank, fixed design as described below. The spaces between the circles are then filled in with the appropriate names of angels, seasons of the year, hour, names of the moon and sun, and all the other required aspects in effect at the time the operation is to take place. This is why such a series of circles, permanently drawn on a concrete floor is so desirable for working this grimoire. The circles are normally empty, requiring the Operator to simply 'fill in the blanks' according the Aerial Spirits he or she will be evoking on a specific day of the week. This filling-in process is best done with holy chalk, easily obtained from any catholic church—for a small donation, of course. Such chalk has been blessed by the resident priest, thus bringing the "sacerdotal office" which Waite mentions, into the operation proper.*

It is my suspicion that the Heptameron *was one of the earliest Roman Catholic grimoires that survived the centuries. Such an early magical text, much like the* Sworn Book of Honourius the Magician, *stressed the importance of prayers and circles for protection against the evil spirits evoked to physical manifestation, as opposed to a more complex reliance upon an assortment of objective devices, such as magic rods, knives, and numerous pentacles and seals that are required in such later grammars of magic as, for example, the* Clavicula Salomonis *and the* Goetia. *In the* Heptameron, *while a magic sword and single pentacle are also used, the principal weapon or instrument of protection is the Circle of Art. It represents the physical manifestation of the One who cries out, "I am the Alpha and the Omega. I am the First and the Last. I am He who is, was, and is yet to come," and it places the Operator at the center of this identity with the Creator of the Universe, the Giver and Sustainer of all life, who divided the waters and the earth, and separated them from the heavens, and who dwells in the secret center of the heart of every man and woman. Armed with such conviction, the Operator who has integrated these ideas into his or her own subjective synthesis will indeed be protected against the onrush and enchantments of the most evil of the fallen spirits. For that same God that protects the Operator in his sacred work, is the God that cast the fallen out into the Pit. It is no wonder then, that the circle represents such a powerful weapon and fortress of defense against all hostile spirits, of whatever nature whatsoever.*

Given this purpose and the meaning of the Circle of Art, perhaps the reader can now better understand the ridiculous attitude propagated by the New Age toward this ceremonial tool. The 'astral circles' traced around the Operator in the air, or even visualized on the ground or floor, afford virtually no protection. As with the other purely nonsensical expediencies of so-called modern magic, they not only expose the Practitioner to unnecessary forces, they **guarantee the failure** *of the operation when used with grimoires that belong to the Old System of Magic.*

Therefore let there be made three Circles of the latitude of nine foot, and let them be distant one from another a hands breadth, and in the middle Circle, first, write the name of the hour wherein you do the work. In the second place, write the name of the Angel of the hour. In the third place, the Sigil of the Angel of the hour. Fourthly, the name of the Angel that ruleth that day wherein you do the work, and the names of his ministers. In the fifth place, the name of the present time. Sixthly, The name of the Spirits ruling in that part of time, and their Presidents. Seventhly, The name of the head of the Sign ruling in that part of time wherein you work. Eighthly, The name of the earth, according to that part of time wherein you work. Ninthly, and for the completing of the middle Circle, write the name of the Sun and of the Moon, according to the said rule of time; for as the time is changed, so the names are to be altered.

Commentary 2—The instructions are telling the Operator to construct the outer circle such that its diameter is nine feet, followed by a second, inner circle, and yet a third, so that each is a "…distant one from another a hands breadth…" meaning, about six inches wide. That is, the diameter of each interior circle will be twelve inches less that the preceding circle. By referring to the example the **Heptameron** *gives in Figure 1,* *you can see that the space between the first or outer circle and the second inner circle—in which "Varcan Rex," "Tus," "Andas, and "Cynabal" appears—has an outer diameter of nine feet, and an inner diameter of eight feet. The space between the second and third circles in which "Yayn," "Michael," and so forth are written, will have an outer diameter of eight feet and an inner diameter of seven feet, while the space between the third circle and the area of operation in which "Adonay," "Eloy" and so forth are shown, will have an outer diameter of seven feet and an inner diameter of six feet. This actually makes the diameter of the area of operation to a be a working area of six feet.*

*Notice the Kabbalistic significances of the Circle as they refer to the Holy Tree of Life. The outer circle, nine feet in diameter, corresponds to Yesod and Luna; the realm of the subconscious, wherein all magic occurs, principally because this is the realm in which subjective synthesis and the resulting belief-system of the Operator is built up. The eight foot diameter middle circle corresponds to Hod and Mercury, the aerial correspondence by which the non-dimensional components of the subjective synthesis begin to take form **outside** of the physical, mental, and psychic realms of the Operator. This is followed by the third inner circle, seven feet in diameter, which corresponds to the number 7. Its correspondence is Netzach and the Earth sign, Taurus, whose ruler is Venus. The aerial form taking place in Hod is now 'grounded' by this solidifying, earth influence, not within the circle of course, but **outside** of it, much like a lens focuses parallel rays of light into a single point, and projects it a given distance from the lens. Finally, the area of operation proper, the universe of the Operator. This is the innermost circle wherein the declaration "Alpha et Omega," a truncation of, "I am the Alpha and the Omega, the Beginning and the End, that which was and is, and is yet to be," is boldly stated. It is here wherein the Operator identifies with God, but through his or her identity with their Holy Guardian Angel, whose Sephirah is Tiphareth, which corresponds to the number 6, the diameter of this innermost of the circles.*

And in the outermost Circle, let there be drawn in the four angles, the names of the presidential Angels of the

Air, that day wherein you would do this work; to wit, the name of the King and his three ministers. Without the Circle, in four angles, let Pentagons be made. In the inner Circle let there be written four Divine Names with crosses interposed in the middle of the Circle; to wit, towards the East let there be written Alpha, and towards the West let there be written Omega; and let a cross divide the middle of the Circle. When the Circle is thus finished, according to the rule now before written, you shall proceed.

*Commentary 3—By referring to the "Considerations of the Lord's Day," and the "Tables of the Angels of the Hours" further on in this section, and comparing them to Figure 1, the reader will easily be able to see the placement of the names and sigils for the various angels and spirits within the appropriate circles for operating on a Sunday as in this example. The reader will also note, that the middle circle given in Figure 1 does **not** have all of the names written in it that are called for in the instructions given above. This was simply a convention used by Abano to illustrate only key points in the circle's construction. When making the circle, the Operator will, of course, write in all of the names and sigils, as instructed by the* **Heptameron.** *The "pentagons" are pentagrams as Figure 1 also shows. They are placed at the sub-quarters of the circles as added defense from attack from those points of the compass. That is, they are placed in the Southeast, Southwest, Northwest, and Northeast. For as* The Three Books of Occult Philosophy *state, "A pentangle [pentagram] also, as with the virtue of the number five, hath a very great command over evil spirits, so by its lineature, by which it hath within five obtuse angles, and without five acutes, five double triangles by which it is surrounded."*[17] *Agrippa also draws a correlation to the pentagram being the symbol of Man when his feet are spread apart and his arms outstretched. The resulting human pentagram is thus symbolic of the highest manifestation in existence, Mankind, brought*

---

[17] Agrippa, Henry Cornelius of Nettesheim. *Three Books of Occult Philosophy*. Translated by James Freake, edited and annotated by Donald Tyson. Llewellyn Publications, St. Paul, Minnesota. 1993. page 330.

forth by and from The Highest Itself. As such, the pentagram becomes an expression of Godhead made manifest in a living, breathing form upon the earth plane.

Of the Names of the Hours and the Angels Ruling them.

It also to be known, that the Angels do rule the hours in a successive order, according to the course of the heavens, and Planets unto which they are subject; so that that Spirit which governeth the day, ruleth also the first hour of the day; the second from this governeth the second hour; the third, the third hour, and so consequently: and when seven Planets and hours have made their revolution, it returneth again to the first which ruleth the day.

Commentary 4—In the magic of the Old System as I have defined it in Chapter Two, there are a number of different systems for determining the beginning of any day and the length of each of the hours of that day and night. In the system of hours of the day and night that grew out of the system given in the Three Books of Occult Philosophy, *the day begins with sunrise, and ends at the time of sunset. The hours of the night then begin, ending with the return of the hours of the following day which begins with the next sunrise, and so on. In Agrippa's system, the hours of the day and night are of different length depending upon the time of the year. But there is more to it than that: the hours of the day are not even equal among each other, the same applying to the hours of the night. This subject is covered thoroughly in the* Three Books, *Chapter Thirty-Four.*

As Agrippa explains there, most astrologers divide the space of the day and night into twelve equal parts. But for magical working, it is necessary to use an almanac or other source of information to find the time of sunrise and sunset for a given day. The total time between the two is taken and divided into twelve equal parts, to yield a fixed length of time for each hour of that day. This fixed length of a day hour is then subtracted from one-hundred-and-twenty minutes, to yield the length of time of each hour of the night of that particular day.

While the Three Books *deal with the astronomical basis of Agrippa's complex inequality of the hours of the day and night argument, the system that grew out of these considerations just explained here, works very well for magical work in general and for evocation to physical manifestation in particular. When planning a evocation from the* Heptameron, *the Operator must find the time of sunrise and sunset for the day on which he will be working, figure out the total number of minutes between that particular sunrise and sunset, and divide that total by twelve to arrive at the number of minutes in each of the twelve hours of the day. To the first hour after sunrise the planet ruling that day is assigned, followed by the other six planets of the ancients in turn. For example, if the day being worked on is Sunday, the first hour after sunrise is ruled by the Sun. The second, by Venus, the third, by Mercury, the fourth by Luna, and ending with the twelfth hour, ruled by Saturn. After determining these twelve planetary hours and their rulers for the hours of the day in question, the Operator then subtracts the number of minutes of each (equal) hour of the day from one-hundred-and-twenty, to find the number of minutes in each (equal) hour of the night. In order to assign the planetary rulers to the hours of the night, which begin at sunset, the Operator continues to assign to each hour of the night, in turn, the planet that follows the planet of the last hour of the day. In the case of Sunday the first hour of the night would be Jupiter, since the last hour of the day of Sunday was Saturn. The second and third hours of the night would be followed by Mars, the Sun, and so on. The chart listing this sequence is given in the Three Books, although the explanation given here will make it that much easier to understand the sometimes complex argument and instructions Agrippa gives regarding this matter.*

Therefore we shall speak of the names of the hours.

Hours of the Day	Hours of the Night
1 Yayn	1 Beron
2 Janor	2 Barol
3 Nasnia	3 Thami
4 Salla	4 Athar
5 Sadedali	5 Mathon
6 Thamur	6 Rana
7 Ourer	7 Netos
8 Thamic	8 Tafrac
9 Neron	9 Sassur
10 Jayon	10 Aglo
11 Abai	11 Calerva
12 Natalon	12 Salam

Of the names of the Angels and their Sigils, it shall be spoken in their proper places. Now let us take a view of the names of the times. A year therefore is fourfold, and is divided into the Spring, Summer, Harvest and Winter; the names whereof are these.

‡ The Spring is 'Talvi.' £ The Summer is 'Casmaran.'
♀ Autumne is 'Ardarael.' † The Winter is 'Farlas.'

‡ The Angels of the Spring are: Caratasa, Core, Amatiel, and Commissoros.
‡ The Head of the Sign of Spring is: Spugliguel.
‡ The name of the Earth in the Spring is: Amadai.
‡ The names of the Sun and Moon in the Spring are: for the Sun, Abraym and for the Moon, Agusita.

£ The Angels of the Summer are: Gargatel, Tariel and Gaviel.
£ The Head of the Sign of Summer is: Tubiel
£ The Name of the Earth in the Summer is: Festativi.
£ The Names of the Sun and Moon in Summer are: for the Sun, Athemay, and for the Moon, Armatus.

♀ The Angels of the Autumn are: Tarquam and Guabarel.
♀ The Head of the sign of Autumn is Torquaret.

♀ The name of the Earth in Autumn is: Rabianara.

♀ The Names of the Sun and Moon in Autumn are: Abragini for the Sun, and Matasignais for the Moon.

✝ The Angels of the Winter are: Amabael and Ctarari.

✝ The Head of the Sign of Winter is Altarib.

✝ The name of the Earth in Winter is: Geremiah.

✝ The names of the Sun and Moon in Winter are: Commutaff for the Sun, and Affaterim for the Moon.

The Consecrations and Benedictions: and first of the Benediction of the Circle.

When the Circle is rightly perfected, sprinkle the same with holy or purging water, and say:

"Thou shalt purge me with hyssop, O Lord, and I shall be clean: Thou shalt wash me and I shall be whiter than snow."

Commentary 5—Notice that while the Heptameron *refers to this act of consecration as the 'consecration and benediction of the Circle,' the Operator is actually calling upon God to sanctify him or her while sprinkling the circle on the ground. This is because the altered state of consciousness of the Operator, which commences early on in the rite, now begins to become* **naturally** *exalted. The Operator and the Circle are becoming* **one** *in God, made manifest on the Earth plane of Malkuth. In this exaltation the Operator is touching the divinity within, and is becoming deified. It is in this white heat of exaltation— that will transform into a trance of limitless ecstasy and finally blossom into a state of pure Divine Love as the rite continues— that this new 'One'—the fusion of Godhead and Manhood— now declares through this act of consecration, "By the words which proceedeth from my mouth, are all things made new and holy." Against such a fortress, no evil of whatsoever nature can penetrate. (see Commentary 2.)*

The Benediction of the Perfumes.

"The God of Abraham, God of Isaac, God of Jacob, bless here the creatures of these kinds, that they may fill up the power and virtue of their odours; so that neither the enemy, nor any false imagination, may be able to enter into them: through our Lord Jesus Christ, who liveth and reigneth with Thee, in the unity of the Holy Ghost, God, forever and ever, Amen."

Then let them be sprinkled with holy water.

Commentary 6—The perfumes (incense or herbs) to be used are determined by the day of the working. For instance, if the Operator is evoking the Aerial Spirits of the Lord's Day, he or she will see by looking at the "Considerations of the Lord's Day" in the second part the Heptameron, that the perfume for this day is "red wheat" or "red sanders." A little research will reveal that "red sanders" is red sandlewood, a herb. Other types of sandlewood, for instance, white sandlewood, must not be substituted. As given in the Magical Axiom 1, you use what is called for. Substitutions are not allowed when working with grimoires of the Old System of Magic.

*Of course, the fresher the herb, the better. Why? The Perfume of Art is much more than just an 'offering,' or a means of filling the air with fine particles which can be used by the spirit to assume a physical form. There is an occult principle at work here which is virtually unknown to modern Practitioners, but which was well known to the magicians of the Old System of Magic. That principle involves the occult issue of Alchemy. Although this subject is far too nebulous to discuss in detail here, that part of it that pertains to this present book must be explained to the reader so he or she can operate **knowledgably**.*

*Specifically, there are the three alchemical ingredients composing all matter. They are termed the "Salt, Sulfur, and Mercury" of a substance. Here, they refer to the Salt, Sulfur and Mercury of the Perfume of Art. The Salt is actually the **Body** of the herb. It is not the body you see when you buy or pick the fresh herb. It is what remains of the herb after it has passed through fire, so that only a gray or white ash remains. As such, it is these rarefied particles that will pass into the air and be* *used by the spirit to assume physical form. Ironically, even the Fallen angels require pure substances in order to summon them forth, and such an alchemical body of a herb will do just that. But the issue is even more complex than that. The Sulfur of the herb is its* **Consciousness.** *As the herb burns, this consciousness, whose vehicle in the Herbal Kingdom of Nature of the physical world is an oil, passes into the air along with particles of the body of the herb, enabling the spirit to interact with the Operator* **mentally,** *or* **consciously.** *Finally, the alchemical Mercury of the herb is its* **Life.** *During the burning of the herb, this Life—whose specific vibratory nature is congruent to the nature of the spirit being evoked—enhances the ability of the spirit to interact with the Operator on this Earth plane by providing an agreeable quality for the spirit's nature. Thus, the combination of the alchemical Salt, Sulfur and Mercury of the Perfume of Art, are as critical for the complete success of the rite as is the Circle or any other component of the ceremony. The reader is therefore advised to make certain the Perfume used is as fresh as possible.*

While obtaining the consecrated chalk for drawing the circle on a cement floor, be sure to obtain a quantity of holy water also from the same institution. Since you will be out and about this activity anyway, it will pay you to stop by a church supply store and purchase a large container of 'church incense.' The type you want is called "Dominican Brand Church Incense." It is a common formulation that has the characteristic church odor identified with the Catholic mass and its special services. You will be consecrating it yourself in a simple and special way later on in the Heptameron operation, so be sure to have it on hand.

The Exorcism of the Fire Upon which the Perfumes are to be put.

The fire which is to be used for suffumigations, is to be in a new vessel of earth or iron; and let it be exorcised after this manner.

"I exorcise thee, 0 thou creature of fire, by him by whom all things are made, that forthwith thou cast away every phantasme from thee, that it shall not be able to do any hurt in any thing."

[Then say]: "Bless, 0 Lord, this creature of fire, and sanctify it, that it may be blessed to set forth the praise of thy holy name, that no hurt may come to the Exorcisors or Spectators: through our Lord Jesus Christ, who liveth and reigneth with Thee, in the unity of the Holy Ghost, God, forever and ever, Amen."

Commentary 7—The vessel should be made of iron. It can be any convenient shape, but should be deep enough to restrict hot ashes and sparks from spewing out onto a simple altar-like table, which the Heptameron *implies will be in the circle with the Operator. It will hold the Perfume of Art, holy water, book, and so on. As with the iron vessel for the incense, this altar-like stand should be virgin, that is, new, never having been used previously for any other purpose. This small table should also have a new covering draped over it. Kabbalistic colors can be used here if the Operator desires. For instance, gold or bright yellow for a Sunday operation, lavender or purple for a Monday evocation, and so forth. Otherwise, a simple, new black cloth will do.*

*Note that the vessel is simply sprinkled with holy water in order to purify it before use. But before doing so, be sure to add a quantity of pure, virgin sand to it to serve as a bed for the fire. White quartz sand is best due to its superior insulating qualities. The 'fire' of course is produced by igniting a small cube or disk of self-lighting charcoal, which is also available from any church supply store. The two prayers given above are said over the charcoal **prior** to adding the Perfume of Art to it. That is, the **first** prayer is a Exorcism designed to purify the charcoal **prior** to its being lit. The **second** prayer is said over the charcoal **after** it has been lit. This latter prayer serves as a means of purifying the living fire before it receives the suffumigations or the Perfume of Art.*

Of the Garment & Pentacle.

Let it be a Priest's Garment, if it can be: but if it cannot be had, let it be of linen, and clean.

Commentary 8—Here we see another implication that the Heptameron *is a Roman Catholic grimoire. When the Heptam-*

eron was written, the Operator was either to have been a priest of the Catholic church, or was to enlist the aid of a priest when performing the operation. But notice the latitude given the Operator, since the grimoire can be worked alone, as long as the requirements are followed, which in this case involves the outer ceremonial dress.

The garment actually referred to in this line is called an alb. It is made of pure, white linen, tied at the waist with a white corded sash. It is the first vestment the priest dons prior to putting on the other outer garments appropriate to the operation he is to celebrate. In everyday practice, these other outer garments are determined by the type of mass the priest is going to perform.

If the reader chooses, an actual alb can be purchased, as I have done, from any of the specialty church supply companies found on the world wide web. My alb was imported from Ireland, and is made of pure, hand spun, 100% virgin Irish white linen, girded at the waist with a white corded sash. At first I asked a (former) best friend—a Catholic priest—to wear this during the performance of a Catholic mass prior to my use, which would add a further sacerdotal quality to the vestment. However, in the end, our friendship ended abruptly over this and other matters, and so the alb was not consecrated by him. But as so often happens with these things, another old friend of mine re-surfaced weeks later. He is a Jesuit, who happily obliged me and duly consecrated my alb by wearing it during a Solemn High Mass which I attended, after which he discreetly handed it to me. The reader should know that I am an extremist by nature, and so sought this particular type of added Office to my Vestment of Art. While this is certainly not a necessary requirement of this or any of the other implements, I have added this little story so the reader may at least get an idea of the lengths that can be taken in order to fully operate the grimoires of the Old System of Magic. It is simply offered for what it might be worth.

In any event, the vestment should be made of 100% fine, virgin linen, and girded at the waist by a linen sash of some kind. I do not advise obtaining this garment ready-made from any occult supply store. With the lack of universal quality and cheap substitutions that pervade American society today, the reader cannot be certain what he or she will wind up getting from such a supplier. Instead, I strongly recommend going to a fabric store, picking a suitable pattern for the vestment's design, and purchasing it and the linen from them. The vestment can then either be hand sewn by the Operator, or by employing a seamstress who will do the work perfectly. The garment produced in this way will be pure, last many years, and most importantly, the reader will know what type and quality of material this all-important magical implement is made from. For this is as much a magical weapon or instrument as the Sword or the Pentacle. Remember: there are no shortcuts to evocation, just as there are no shortcuts to success. And in this case, both evocation to physical manifestation and success go hand-in-hand.

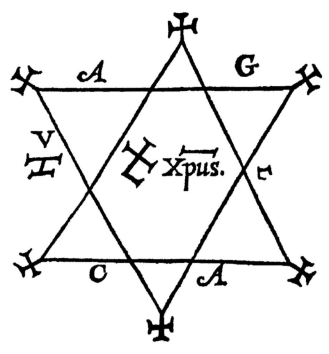

Figure 2
The Pentacle of Protection and Obedience

Then take this Pentacle made in the day and hour of Mercury, the Moon increasing in light, written in parchment made of a kid's skin. But first let there be said over it the Mass of the Holy Ghost, and let it be sprinkled with water of Baptism.

Commentary 9—Please refer to Figure 2. Making this Pentacle is not difficult. The Operator can obtain an eight-and-one-half-inch by eleven-inch sheet of genuine sheepskin parchment from a well stocked art supply store, and trace the Pentacle on it. A six-inch by six-inch figure is quite sufficient, as it can easily be seen by the demon upon its full manifestation. Since the Heptameron *does not call for any special ink to be used in drawing the figure, I have found that a very high quality gold ink is best to trace the image on the sheepskin. My gold ink came from an art supply store that sells the ink in a six-inch barrel tube, the end of which has a broad-tipped point. This type of gold pen allowed me to easily trace out the Pentacle. After the ink dried, I obtained genuine thin leaf gold from the same art store, cut it into strips, outlined the gold Pentacle with Crazy Glue, and pasted the gold foil over the lines of the Pentacle itself. The result is a flashing Pentacle that the spirit cannot fail to see, and which immediately demands its attention and obedience. Between operations, the Pentacle—as with the Sword, Vessel for the suffumigations, Perfume(s) of Art, and indeed all additional equipment used in the working— are to be kept wrapped in white linen cloth that has first been sprinkled with holy water, and then passed through the smoke of the Dominican Brand incense. The holy water 'asperges,' meaning, it removes all unwanted influences from the object, while the suffumigation, or passing the object through the smoke of the incense 'sanctifies' the object and dedicates it to the purpose the Operator has in mind.*

The Pentacle itself is traced on the sheepskin and if the gold leaf overlay is also used, it too is added during the same day and hour ruled by Mercury. The hours in which Mercury rules during its own day, Wednesday, will have to be calculated by the Operator according to the procedure given in Commentary 4. As to the phases of the moon, be careful. Do not perform the Operation or make your Pentacle on the day of the New Moon, or on the day of the Full Moon. On the day of the New Moon, the Moon and Sun are in conjunction or conjoined, meaning they are in the same degree of the same zodiacal sign, that is, they are together. Thus, they act together, but not necessarily in a desirable way. Hence this aspect is to be avoided. The other condition to be avoided for making the Pentacle and for conducting the Operation itself is that astrological condition called Combust. This condition exists when a planet—here, the Moon—is within three degrees of the Sun's longitude. This condition was thought to be extremely adverse by the medieval astrologers, and is discussed thoroughly by Agrippa in The Three Books of Occult Philosophy. *This attitude has carried through into modern astrology today, and for good reason. Agrippa was right. In a Combust state, the force of the Sun is said to overwhelm the force of any planet it is combust with, and so destroy its effects. Again, the Pentacle is not to be made on, nor is the Operation performed on the day of the Full Moon, since the Moon is no longer increasing in light, but begins its descent into its decreasing phases by entering its third quarter. The time to construct the Pentacle is on a Wednesday during the hour of Mercury, anytime between the second day after the New Moon to the day before the Full Moon.*

But the actual construction of the Pentacle is the easy part. Fulfilling the preliminary requirements prior to its construction are perhaps the most strenuous part of the entire Heptameron *operation. In order to clarify the procedure, I'll address each issue separately. Before actually constructing the Pentacle, the sheet of sheepskin upon which it is to be made must be sprinkled with the Water of Baptism. While the* Heptameron *does not make it clear which procedure is to come first, saying the Mass of the Holy Ghost over the parchment or sprinkling with the Water of Baptism, the sprinkling is to be done first. Obtaining this water may be difficult, since it is used for a very specific religious purpose, and hence is not as readily available as is holy water. However, if the Operator attends any Baptism as an observer—which indeed the Catholic church encourages as an added witness to the event—the Water of Baptism will be left in the Baptismal Font **after** the baptism. It is not difficult to fill a small container with that water when everyone else has* *departed, and then leave. In one of my own instances, the priest who performed the baptism came back unexpectedly, and asked me what I was doing. I told him I was a scientist, raised in the Catholic Faith—which is true—and that I wanted the used Water of Baptism to sprinkle on a new project I was beginning, and in this way add the blessings of the church to it. He was so delighted to hear this, that he opened the Baptismal Font and allowed me to take a full pint of the unused Water of Baptism, and then blessed me for my actions! In short, you the operator can easily obtain such used water after the rite of Baptism is performed. It is also my custom to leave a substantial donation at the Font after having obtained what I wanted, in order to be fair to the church, and to ease my own mind. I do not need any lingering feelings of guilt, caused by my own Catholic upbringing, entering into my own subjective synthesis.*

After sprinkling the sheepskin with the Water of Baptism, the Operator must say the Mass of the Holy Ghost over it. This is not difficult in itself, unless the reader is unfamiliar with the procedures of the Catholic Mass. A Catholic Missal is the best source for obtaining instructions on performing your own mass. In order to perform the Mass of the Holy Ghost, you must first perform "The Ordinary of the Mass, Mass of The Catechumens," adding the Votive Mass components of the Mass of the Holy Ghost at the appropriate points, as the Missal will instruct. The reader should be aware that the Catholic mass itself is a kind of template of all masses. Other masses, such as Votive Masses, consist of additional mass components that are added to the standard template for special intentions. In this case, the Votive Mass is the Mass of the Holy Ghost, in which its components are added to the regular mass. While it can be confusing at first, a few hours study of a Missal will make it all clear, in addition to help build individual subjective synthesis. As to the Missals themselves, I strongly recommend the one I use. It is the "Maryknoll Missal", subtitled "Daily Missal of the Mystical Body," edited by the Maryknoll Fathers. I use an original 1956 edition which I had in Catholic school back in those days. It gives each part of the Mass and the component parts of Votive Masses in both English and Latin. This is highly recommended, since the Operator will find a need for

Latin verses in future work. As a final point on this matter, the reader should be aware that the "Mass of the Holy Ghost" will be referred to as the "Mass of the Holy Spirit," even in the 1956 edition of the Maryknoll Missal. This is a Catholic modernization of the term Holy Ghost that occurred in the 1950's.

An oration to be said when Vesture is put on.

"Ancor, Amacor, Amides, Theodonias, Anitor, by the merits of thy Angel, 0 Lord, I will put on the Garments of Salvation, that this which I desire I may bring to effect: through thee the most holy Adonay, whose kingdom endureth for ever and ever. Amen."

Of the manner of working.

Let the Moon be increasing and equal, if it may then be done, and let her not be combust.

Commentary 10—"...increasing and equal" refers to the first day or two of the second quarter of the Moon when the visible face of the Moon is seen as half-full. But "...let her not be combust" refers to that state when the Moon is within three degrees of the Sun, as explained in Commentary 9.

The Operator ought to be clean and purified by the space of nine days before the beginning of the work, and to be confessed, and receive the holy Communion.

Commentary 11—By "...clean and purified..." the Heptameron is referring to both outward as well as inward cleanliness. The following conditions of preparation for evocation as given below, are actually found in all Old System Magic grimoires, and are reproduced here to aid the reader in his or her understanding. While it is best to follow them as closely as possible, it is up to the individual to determine just how far he or she will go to keep to the fasting and cleanliness regimen.

During the nine days preceding the Operation, the Operator should quit all social activities of every sort, tending only to necessary business matters, and completing those as quickly as possible each day, but without any undue stress.

Then the Operator should seek solitude as much as possible, praying in a way that is comfortable, while in keeping with the Catholic nature of this grimoire. As an example, the Operator could spend time either reading and contemplating the Psalms, *or studying the* Heptameron *text carefully, committing to memory the required conjurations and prayers, or a combination of both of these activities. Long walks in secluded, quiet woods and mountains while contemplating the enormity of the upcoming evocation, is also another type of prayer the Operator can engage in. Of course, drinking alcohol, consuming excessive quantities of food, and taking any illegal drugs is to be scrupulously avoided. In fact, the diet should be simple, raw vegetables constituting the main course, with only modest amounts of meat added as a side dish. No more than two such meals should be eaten in any twenty-four hour period, although fresh fruit or additional raw vegetables can be added if the Operator must have them. Rest should be moderate, neither being too long or too short, and interaction with one's friends and even family members should be kept to an absolute minimum. Sexual activity of any kind is also to be strictly avoided. As called for, the Operator is to receive the Sacraments of Confession and Holy Communion, these, a day or two before the actual operation. If the receiving of Confession and Communion is hard for the reader, let me assure you, that it is harder for me. Having broken with the church nearly four decades ago for intensely personal and severe reasons, it takes all my dedication to follow through with these requirements. But I look at it rationally. If there is a box, locked with a combination lock that contains something I want, I will dial the numbers of that combination no matter how much I object to the box being locked, or to the long sequence of numbers that must be dialed in order to open the lock, after which I will then take from the box what I want. It is as simple as that. So decide what you want, let no inner stirrings or outer circumstances deter you, and in due time, you will have your heart's desire. The reader would do well to remember this when inner stirrings of objections begin to cause anxiety and emotional discomfort.*

Let him have ready the perfume appropriated to the day wherein he would perform the work. He ought also to have holy water from a priest, and a new earthen vessel with the fire, a vesture and Pentacle; and let all these things be rightly and duly consecrated and prepared. Let one of the servants carry the earthen vessel full of fire, and the perfumes; and let another bear the book; another the Garment and Pentacle;

*Commentary 12—The above instructions of using servants in the operation are to be read and understood in reverse. That is, during the dangerous times of the Inquisition—and indeed throughout the Medieval Ages and Renaissance—it was customary for a magician to work alone. The risk of involving one, two, three or more other individuals in his magical work, was simply too great. People talk. They brag. They try to exaggerate their knowledge of magic in order to intimidate others and get their way by posing a threat of what they can do through magic. This falls upon the ears of the Inquisitors, and before the Operator knows it, the Inquisitional Tribunal has arrested him and begun the interrogation process. Thus, in the case of this grimoire, the lone Operator is being given permission to use servants if he dares. It is much like stating the obvious today. Everyone knows the obvious. No one wants to hear it, but it is stated anyway. In fact, while I have worked with others in different areas of magic, aside from two evocations to physical manifestation, I have always conjured alone. My assistant in those two evocations (the Catholic priest mentioned earlier) was the exception to the rule. I must give him credit here. He not only held fast and firm during the manifestation while supporting my evoking, but during one rite he prevented me from making a very, very major mistake that could have ended, who knows how? But ordinarily, when the Operator involves another individual or several, he cannot predict what they will do when the manifestation occurs. And I assure you, that when the operation reaches its height, the last thing you want to face on this earth is an assistant running through the circle, breaking it, and destroying the circle, which is the major instrument of protection. Learn from my four decades of experience. **Evoke by yourself!***

and let the master carry the Sword; over which there must be said one Mass of the Holy Ghost; and on the middle of the Sword, let there be written this name † AGLA †, and on the other side thereof, this name † ON †.

Commentary 13—The Sword of Art can be of any convenient length, but it should be long enough to intimidate when pointed, as if it could be extended safely through the circle to injure the spirit if required, while yet keeping the Operator at a safe distance. Because of this consideration, I recommend a sword between forty and fifty inches in length, a length of forty-five inches being ideal. It must also be double-edged and razor sharp principally because sharp edges threaten to further 'divide and dissect' the spirit's nature, which is already unstable; already divided as it were. These beings fear further division of their qualities as much as we fear losing our awareness of ourselves or our memories. This sharpness, added to the martial qualities of destruction, bloodshed, and slaughter embodied in the weapon through its millenniums of use in warfare, has a powerful effect on the demon. Its cooperation is further enforced by holding the Sword of Art in the right hand which is the side of the Holy Tree of Life that contains Geburah, and therefore, Mars, the God of War. Be sure the sword is not so heavy that you cannot wield it and point it at the spirit with your outstretched arm. Such an action must never be done without strength, and this includes the physical strength with which you wield the weapon.

*The sword is to be made during the day and hour ruled by Mars, the Moon being waxing to full phase—that is, during its first or second phase—and like the Pentacle, anytime between the second day after the New Moon to the day before the Full Moon. Luna should also be in a Fire sign of the Zodiac. It is first sprinkled with holy water, the names inscribed, and then suffumigated with the Dominican Brand incense, **not** some herb or incense that corresponds to Mars. Why? Because the magical name AGLA, written on one side of the blade, and on the other side, the name ON—which is an abbreviation of the most holy, ineffable Name of God, TETRAGRAMMATON—are names that were appropriated by those priests of the Catholic church for use in their private magical practice, which was still within* *the church's liturgical framework. Since the operation is Catholic, the normal Kabbalistic thought pattern does not apply here. This is a vital Key in being able to interpret and work with any Old System grimoire successfully. The context of the ritual or ceremony must be **understood** in terms of the **subjective synthesis** of its creators. Carte blanche attitudes, so prevalent in the New Age today, will produce their corresponding effects—nothing, across the board.*

*While the names can be painted on, I recommend inscribing them deeply into the blade, and then painting them over with a deep, dark red or magenta enamel paint, the same color blood possesses when it pours out of a fresh, fatal, deep wound. The materialized demon will recognize this Kabbalistic significance, along with the meaning of the weapon and the sharp edges, through the Will of the Operator. So done, it cannot fail to produce a genuine threat to, and ensure the obedience of, the spirit. The Operator **must** maintain these conditions to succeed.*

And as he goeth to the consecrated place, let him continually read the Litanies, the servants answering:

v. Lord, have mercy,   r. Lord, have mercy,
v. Christ have mercy,   r. Christ, have mercy,
v. Lord, have mercy,   r. Lord, have mercy,
v. Christ, hear us,   r. Christ, hear us,
v. God the Father of heaven, have mercy on us,
r. have mercy on us,
v. God the Son, Redeemer of the world, have mercy on us,
                              r. have mercy on us.
v. God the Holy Spirit have mercy on us,
                              r. have mercy on us
v. Holy Trinity, one God, have mercy on us,
                              r. have mercy on us
v. Holy Mary pray for us sinners, now and at the hour of our death, Amen.

Commentary 14—"v" refers to the "verse" the Operator will say aloud as he and his assistants proceed to the circle, which has been prepared beforehand, and which contains the appropriate names and sigils for the time of the operation. "r" refers to the "refrain" or "response" the assistants say aloud in answer to the Operator—or Master, as he is called—if he chooses to use assistants. In the case of the wise Operator who works alone, he or she simply repeats both verse and refrain on the way to the circle or the "Place of Working," as the site of evocation is also called in the grimoires.

And when he cometh to the place where he will erect the Circle, let him draw the lines of the Circle, as we have before taught: and after he hath made it, let him sprinkle the Circle with holy water, saying, "Wash me 0 Lord, and etc."

Commentary 15—The above instructions in The Heptameron*—and indeed, in many other Old System Magic grimoires—cause beginners no end of confusion. In the previous section, "Of the Manner of Working," the verses and refrains were said "And as he (the Operator) goeth to the consecrated place..." Yet the "consecrated place" is only consecrated by having made the circle in advance, and thereby dedicated it to the purpose to be fulfilled! So how can the circle be constructed in advance of the operation, and then be constructed again? There is a compound answer to this seeming dilemma, which is really very simple. As to the first explanation. As I mentioned earlier, it was customary to perform evocations in deep, secluded woods, usually at night, far away from prying eyes and out of earshot. Due to the complexity of the circle, the lack of light in nighttime operations, and the shortness of the hour of operation in which the rite was to be performed, the Operator would go to his chosen secluded spot, trace out the circle in advance, and when returning to the place to perform the rite, would* **retrace** *the* **outer circle** *with the sword, thereby 'refreshing' it with the force of the hour of the evocation that was now at hand. In the second case, if the Operator was to conjure in a cellar in a remote house, he or she would "erect the circle" in advance as it is properly termed, and when returning to it in order to perform the rite, would retrace the* **entire** *structure quickly with the Sword of Art, thereby 'refreshing' it with the force of the hour of evocation which was now at hand. In short, erect the circle in advance, and retrace it in its entirety with the sword, quickly,* *immediately before beginning the evocation. The line, "Wash me O Lord, and etc." refers to the prayer of consecration of the circle, "Thou shalt purge me with hyssop, O Lord, and I shall be clean: Thou shalt wash me and I shall be whiter than snow."*

The Master therefore ought to be purified with fasting, chastity, and abstinence from all luxury the space of three whole days before the day of the operation.

Commentary 16—That is, during the last three days of the nine day fasting and abstinence period, the Operator is to intensify this self-purification process. All luxury of any kind is to be completely avoided. As an example, in my own case, I receive or speak to no one except my wife, take no telephone calls, do not review any mail—either the post office delivered or email type— and enter prolonged periods of contemplation in which I go over and over the dynamics of the rite that will soon be performed. I live an extremely quiet life, reading the Psalms *and the* Old Testament. *I also perform a stricter fasting regimen. This fast consists of drinking only one six ounce glass of orange juice in the morning, and one six ounce glass of apple juice at night. No solid food of any kind is eaten. This fasting is maintained until the operation is completed, after which only modest amounts of solid food are slowly reintroduced into my body over the next three days. As the reader studies other grimoires from the Old System of Magic, he or she will discover that the idea behind this strict fast is rooted in the belief that as the physical body grows weaker, the spiritual (or, psychic, in my view) grows stronger. I have found this reasoning to be quite correct in my own magical work in general, and certainly, in evocation to physical manifestation.*

And on the day that he would do the work, being clothed with pure garments, and furnished with Pentacles, Perfumes, and other things necessary hereunto, let him enter the Circle, and call the Angels from the four parts of the world, which do govern the seven planets, the seven days of the week, colours and metals; whose names you shall see in their places.

Commentary 17—The above instructions cause some confusion at first. As it reads, it seems to be saying that the Operator is to call upon the angels from the four parts of the world of **each** *day, along with their colors, metals, and so on, even though the operation will be for done for a* **specific** *day, for example, on a Thursday. The answer comes in the final line, "...whose names you shall see in their places." This means that the Operator is* **only** *to call upon the angels* **of the day of the operation,** *along with the metals, colors, and so on, and* **also** *announce the* **name of the "heaven"** *as given in the conjuration for the day being worked.*

And with bended knees invoking the said Angels particularly, let him say, "O Angels supradicti, estote adjutores meae petitioni, and in adjutorium mihi, in meis rebus and petitionibus."

Commentary 18—This prayer is to be said aloud with a fervor that would seem to tear the world asunder. The intensity will come automatically, as at this point, the Operator's highly altered state of consciousness will begin to enter a profound state of exaltation, that will soon turn into ecstasy. This ecstatic state will remain until the state of Bliss is reached at some point in the rite, after which the final transformation into Divine Love will occur, as spoken of in the Magical Axioms.

Be certain to use the Latin language where it is given throughout the Heptameron text. You must also, of course, understand the meanings of these words, and so will have to translate them for yourself. While I could give the translation for this and the other Latin verses to follow, I will not do this here. There are two reason for this. First, working out such translations are a necessary exercise in building one's state of subjective synthesis. Second, in the Latin language, as in the English language, there are a number of possible interpretations based upon the various meanings of the words and their positions in the sentence. The resulting translation each individual will work out, therefore, will be different; a property of the individual's mental structure and psychic matrix, so to speak. As such, it will have a special meaning for the individual, and in the end, will serve to exalt the mind during recitation. Such is the reward of individual effort when working the grimoires of the Old System of Magic.

Then let him call the Angels from the four parts of the world, that rule the Air the same day wherein he doth the work or experiment.

Commentary 19—All of these names will be found clearly given in the conjurations of each day of the week that are to follow in Part Two of the Heptameron.

And having implored especially all the Names and Spirits written in the Circle, let him say:

"0 vos omnes, adjuro atque contestor per sedem Adonay, per Hagios, 0 Theos, Ischyros, Athanatos, Paracletos, Alpha et Omega, et per haec tria nomina secreta, Agla, On, Tetragrammaton, quod hodie debeatis adimplere quod cupio"

These things being performed, let him read the Conjuration assigned for the day wherein he maketh the experiment, as we have before spoken;

Commentary 20—The conjuration for the day being worked is now recited according to the day of the week being worked, as given in Part Two. Of course, the Operator will have memorized it thoroughly, as he or she has done with all of the general prayers and consecrations. Usually, at this point, the Operator will be struggling to recall those words, as the state of ecstasy or Bliss will have begun to overtake him or her.

Be aware that there will be no manifestation at this point, since the Conjuration of the Day—as given in Part Two—is actually an invocation of the holy angels, and not of the aerial spirits of the day. The Conjuration of the Day is recited first, since it is a plea to the holy angels. The Operator is invoking them to come to his or her aid, and to help them in this work of Art. By calling upon these Beings of Light through the formal and peculiar structure of the Heptameron rite, the Operator is entreating these divine beings to open the channel between the world of the spirits and the world of Malkuth, and to force these aerial beings of the day to come unto the Operator.

But if they shall be pertinacious and refractory, and will not yield themselves obedient, neither to the Conjuration assigned to the day, nor to the prayers before made, then use the Conjurations and Exorcism following:

An Exorcism of the Spirits of the Air.

"We being made after the image of God, endued with power from God and made after his will, do exorcise you, by the most mighty and powerful name of God, EL, strong and wonderful, N., and we command you by Him who spake the word and it was done, and by all the names of God, and by the name + ADONAI + EL + ELOHIM + ELOHE + ZEBAOTH + ELION + ESERCHIE + JAH + TETRAGRAMMATON + SADAI + Lord God Most High: we exorcise you, and powerfully command you that you forthwith appear unto us here before this Circle in a fair human shape, without any deformity or tortuousity; come ye all such, because we command you by the name YAW and VAU, which Adam heard and spoke; and by the name of God, AGLA, which Lot heard, and was saved with his family; and by the name JOTH, which Jacob heard from the angel wrestling with him, and was delivered from the hand of his brother Esau; and by the name ANAPHEXETON, which Aaron heard and spoke, and was made wise; and by the name ZEBAOTH, which Moses named, and all the rivers were turned into blood; and by the name ESERCHIE ORISTON, which Moses named, and all the rivers brought forth frogs, and they ascended into the houses of the Egyptians, destroying all things; and by the name ELION which Moses named, and there was great hail, such as had not been since the beginning of the world; and by the name ADONAl, which Moses named, and there came up locusts, which appeared upon the whole land of Egypt, and devoured all which the hail had left; and by the name SCHEMA AMATHIA, which Joshua called upon, and the sun stayed his course; and by the name ALPHA and OMEGA, which Daniel named, and destroyed Bel and slew the dragon; and in the name EMMANUEL, which the three children, Sidrach,, Misah, and Abednego, sung in the midst of the fiery furnace, and were delivered; and by the name HAGIOS; and by the seal of ADONAI; and by ISCHYROS, ATHANATOS, PARACLETOS; and by these three secret names, + AGLA + ON + TETRAGRAMMA-TON + I do adjure and contest you; and by these names, and by all the other names of the living and true God, our Lord Almighty, I exorcise and command you by Him who spoke the word and it was done, to whom all creatures are obedient: and by the dreadful judgment of God; and by the uncertain sea of glass, which is before the divine majesty, mighty and powerful; by the four beasts before the throne, having eyes before and behind; and by the fire round about his throne; and by the holy angels of heaven; by the mighty wisdom of God, we do powerfully exorcise you, that you appear here before this Circle, to fulfill our will in all things which shall seem good unto us; by the seal of BALDACHIA, and by this name PRIMEUMATON, which Moses named, and the earth opened and swallowed up Corah, Dathan, and Abiram: and in the power of that name PRIMEUMATON, commanding the whole host of heaven, we curse you, and deprive you of your office, joy, and place, and do bind you in the depth of the bottomless pit, there to remain until the dreadful day of the last judgement; and we bind you into eternal fire, and into the lake of fire and brimstone, unless you forthwith appear before this Circle to do our will: therefore, come ye, by these names + ADONAI + ZEBAOTH + ADONAI + AMIORAM +; come ye, come ye, come ye, ADONAI commandeth; SADAY, the most mighty King of Kings, whose power no creature is able to resist, be unto you most dreadful, unless ye obey, and forthwith affably appear before this Circle, let miserable ruin and fire unquenchable remain with you; therefore come, in the name of ADONAI + ZEBAOTHM + ADONAI + AMIORAM +; come, come, why stay you? hasten! ADONAI, SADAI, the King of Kings commands you: + EL + ATY + TITCIP + AZIA + HIN + JEN + MINOSEL + ACHADAN + VAY + VAAH

+ EY + EXE + A + EL + EL + EL + EL + A +HY +HAU
+HAU +HAU + VAU + VAU + VAU + VAU +"

Commentary 21—This is the first actual conjuration proper of the aerial spirits of the day. The reader should notice that "N," given at the beginning of the 'Calling' as a conjuration is also termed, refers to the "Name" of the aerial spirits of the day. In this case, the "Angels of the Air" given in each of the daily conjurations in Part Two, are considered angels. It is they who are to be named here. For example, in a Sunday working, the Operator would call out, where "N," is given in the conjuration—

"Varcan, Tus, Andas, and Cynabal, and all ye, his Ministers, and indeed and verily, all ye spirits of the Air of this day!"

I have never know this 'Call template,' which I composed decades ago, to fail. Also note that the term 'we' is used in the conjuration, in case the Operator has the nerve to work with assistants, as I have already remarked upon in Commentary 12.

The reader will also notice that the conjuration is actually called an Exorcism in the text. The reason for this is that in the Heptameron, matters proceed quickly. In this very first Calling, the process of cursing and invoking the "Curse of Chains"—which appears as a separate, later action in such later grimoires as the Goetia—is used immediately. The Operator is thereby showing his or her sincerity, resolve, and determination from the start. Unlike latter grimoires, in which the aerial spirits are differentiated into separate beings—again as in the case of the Goetia, for example—there is no such distinction of these beings made in the Heptameron. It was customary in the earliest grimoires to get down to business immediately, and begin cursing or exorcising, as part of the conjuration or summoning process. You should also be aware that the insertion of a cross-symbol, "+," between each divine name, was used in early grimoires both to separate the names, as well as an instruction for the Operator to draw a cross in the air with a magical weapon, which in this case would be the Sword of Art. While this action may not be necessary, I do this, as it enables me to focus my mind and thereby gain greater control over the Bliss, which by this time is reaching a incredible fever pitch.

A few words regarding the pronunciation of the divine and angelic names is now in order. The New Age spends an exasperating amount of time on different methods of "vibrating Words of Power," as they term the Names of God, angelic beings, and other words of power such as the "Barbarous Words of Evocation." This vibration scheme is completely unnecessary. It is simply another of their constructs designed to explain why—after one of their evocations—there is either no physical phenomena or manifestation save for some imagined feeling of something having been present, or what have you. The fact of the matter is, the energy contained in the divine names and words of power is there by virtue of the words themselves, and contained in the living breath of the Operator who is calling upon them in his or her state of sublime Bliss—a state in which their individual part of Godhead is the One doing the Calling. Nothing else is needed, save for that genuine ecstasy now turned into the white hot fire of Bliss, and the virtue contained in the words themselves.

At this point in the rite, the manifestation usually begins. It is not crystal clear yet, but it will be unmistakable that a form is beginning to take shape in the swirling incense smoke that has drifted from the incense vessel within the circle, and has begun to course through the room. Unlike the New Age insistence that the spirit will appear in a certain quarter of the compass depending upon the Kabbalistic attributions of the planet ruling the day of working, the apparition can come from any quarter. Hence the Operator must keep vigilant, lest he or she is taken by surprise. But this is not all that occurs. The appearance of colored lights floating in the air around the circumference of the outermost circle, flashes of green, gold, and yellow rays of light coming out of thin air and firing throughout the room, along with various sounds, will begin to occur as well. The sounds are not creaks or anything that could be mistaken for the normal noises a house might make. Rather, the sounds are animal in nature, although not from any animal the Operator has ever heard of before. Poltergeist phenomena is also likely at this point, although the objects will not be thrown toward, and therefore will not pass, the boundary of the Circle of Art. A common type of phenomenon in this regard is the repeated slamming of any doors in the cellar room—if the operation occurs indoors—or screeching sounds; as if sharp claws are being drawn over a glass surface. Grunts, and low guttural growls are also common. All of these occurrences are to be welcomed by the Operator as a sure sign the evocation is proceeding as it should. But the Operator must hold to their ground, all the while allowing the mind to drift into further intensified states of Bliss, which will eventually fade into the purest ecstasy of Divine Love. All the while, the Operator must retain conscious awareness of the events and control over the mind. At this point, begin the second conjuration below, amidst the unfolding drama which is in the process of shattering one's former concept of reality.

A Prayer to God, to be said in the four parts of the world, in the Circle.

AMORULE + TANEHA + LATISTEN + RABUR + TENEHA + LATISTEN + ESCHA + ALADIA + ALPHA and OMEGA + LEYSTE + ORISION + ADONAI +; 0 most merciful heavenly Father! Have mercy upon me, although a sinner; make appear the arm of thy power in me this day against these obstinate spirits, that I, by thy will, may be made a contemplator of thy divine works, and may be illustrated with all wisdom, to the honor and glory of thy Holy Name. I humbly beseech thee, that these spirits which I call by thy judgment may be bound and constrained to come and give true and perfect answers to those things which I shall ask of them; and that they may do and declare those things unto us, which by me may be commanded of them, not hurting any creature, neither injuring or terrifying me or my fellows, nor hurting any other creature, and affrighting no man; and let them be obedient to those things which are required of them. [Then standing in the middle of the Circle, stretch out thy hand towards the Pentacle, saying]: ¶By the Pentacle of Solomon I have called you; give me a true answer.

Then let him say: ¶BERALANENSIS + BALDACHIENSIS + PAUMACHIA + APOLOGIA SEDES+, by the most mighty kings and powers, and the most powerful princes, genii, Liachidae, ministers of the Tartarean seat, Chief prince of the seat of Apologia, in the ninth legion, I invoke you, and by invoking, conjure you; and being armed with power from the supreme Majesty, I strongly command you, by Him who spoke and it was done, and to whom all creatures are obedient; and by this ineffable name TETRAGRAMMATON + JEHOVAH, which being heard the elements are overthrown, the air is shaken, the sea runneth back, the fire is quenched, the earth trembles, and all the host of the celestials, and terrestrials, and infernals do tremble together, and are troubled and confounded; wherefore, forthwith and without delay, do you come from all parts of the world, and make rational answers unto all things I shall ask of you; and come ye peaceably, visibly and affably now, without delay, manifesting what we desire, being conjured by the name of the living and true God, + HELIOREN +, and fulfill our commands, and persist unto the end, and according to our intentions, visibly and affably speaking unto us with a clear voice, intelligible, and without any ambiguity.

Commentary 22—The manifestation will solidify further at this point, the sounds, sights, and physical phenomena in the room reaching a fever pitch. Hold fast. The state of Bliss will either have faded into the ecstasy of pure Divine Love, or will be on the verge of doing so. There is no secret formula for predicting exactly when the states from ecstasy to Bliss will resolve into the state of pure Divine Love, due to the individual's nature, level of psychic development, and the level of perfection their state of subjective synthesis and its resulting subconscious belief system has reached. But know that having reached this point in the rite, all is proceeding well. At some time, between this point in the ceremony and the full manifestation, the state of pure Divine Love will be reached, after which the Operator must then be ready to contend with the Control and Command aspects of the evocation.

Visions & Apparitions.

These things being duly performed, there will appear infinite visions, apparitions, phantasms, and so on, beating of drums, and the sound of all kinds of musical instruments; which is done by the spirits, that with the terror they might force some of the companions out of the Circle, because they can effect nothing against the exorcist himself; after this you shall see a infinite company of archers, with a great multitude of horrible beasts, which will arrange themselves as if they would devour the companions; Nevertheless, fear nothing.

Commentary 23—However unbelievable it may sound, the sounds, sights, and physical phenomena occurring at this point in the rite will redouble. Between the rapidly oncoming state of pure Divine Love, the struggle to retain consciousness, and the events unfolding around the Operator, there will be even more of the visions and apparitions Abano speaks of. Neither my colleagues who work from the Heptameron nor I, however, have ever had quite the effects spoken of above. There are no musical instruments. Instead, the screeches become much louder and more frequent. There are no beating of drums, but instead, heavy, numerous, strong poundings against the walls of the room occur. There are no archers nor horrible beasts, although there are a myriad of faces—if that is what they can be called— unbelievable grotesque faces flicking in and out of the air around the circle. Once again, hold fast.

Perhaps you can see now why I recommend working alone. Notice the line, "...that with the terror they might force some of the companions out of the Circle, because they can effect nothing against the exorcist himself." Unless you are absolutely certain you can count on an assistant, the reader must realize they risk much, as Abano warns here. The Operator, although powerfully affected by the visions and events unfolding around him, is protected from assault by his state of deification, as well as by the circle. But the assistant is not. He or she has not risen to identification with the Godhead within them, and because of this, are in mortal danger. If they run and break through the barrier of the circle—well, that is a matter I leave for the reader to speculate upon.

Then the exorcist, holding the Pentacle in his hand, let him say:

"Avoid hence these iniquities, by virtue of the banner of God."

Then will the spirits be compelled to obey the exorcist, and the company shall see them no more.

Commentary 24—Not exactly. The visions, sounds and apparitions do not simply depart in the twinkling of an eye. They become subdued, but do continue for awhile until, at last, the aerial spirits of the day of operation achieve full manifestation.

Then let the exorcist, stretching out his hand with the Pentacle, say:

"Behold the Pentacle of Solomon, which I have brought into your presence, behold the person of the exorcist in the middle of the exorcism, who is armed by God, without fear, and well provided, who potently invoketh and calleth you by exorcising; come, therefore, with speed, by the virtue of these names: + AYE + SARAYE + AYE + SARAYE +; defer not to come, by the eternal names of the living and true God, + ELOY + ARCHIMA + RABUR + and by the Pentacle of Solomon here present, which powerfully reigns over you; and by the virtue of Celestial spirits, your lords; and by the person of the exorcist, in the middle of the exorcism; being conjured, make haste and come, and yield obedience to your master, who is called 'Octinomous.'"

This being performed, immediately there will be hissings in the four parts of the world, and then immediately you shall see great motions; which when you see say:

Commentary 25—This occurs each and every time. In addition to the visions, apparitions and other sounds that are fading away but still present, the Operator will hear an enormous hissing, in the quarter of the compass in which the aerial spirits will fully manifest. When I heard it for the first time, I thought a gas line suddenly sprung a leak, until I realized the house I was in had hot-air heating, provided by coal.

Just as the Heptameron describes, the Operator will then see a swirling motion, as if a bright cloud, either white, gray, yellow, or gold, is coming out of a hidden nowhere, and is beginning to grow larger and larger. Regardless of the day worked, and the aerial spirits summoned thereby, these 'clouds' are always and only of these colors. Usually, it is at this point—but remember, it can be sooner—that the state of sublime Bliss ruptures into that of pure Divine Love. The state of emotional intoxication is beyond description, as certainly as it is almost beyond human endurance. It is this all consuming white hot-fire of passion within the Operator then, that allows the channel between the world of the spirits and ours, to finally and fully open, as I previously discussed. The Operator must now proceed with the finale of the manifestation by screaming forth the following, which will be utterly natural due to the state he or she is presently in—

"Why stay you? Wherefore do you delay? What do you? Prepare yourselves to be obedient to your master in the name of the Lord, BATHAT or VACHAT rushing upon ABRAC, ABEOR coming upon ABERE."

Then they will immediately come in their proper forms; and when you see them before the Circle, show them the pentacle covered with fine linen; uncover it and say—

"Behold your confusion if you refuse to become obedient."

And suddenly they will appear in a peaceable form, and will say:

"Ask what you will, for we are prepared to fulfill all your commands, for the Lord hath subjected us hereunto."

Commentary 26—The aerial spirits will then take their proper form before you outside the circle. It is customary to hold the Pentacle, covered with a piece of fine linen in your left hand, while placing your right hand on the linen prior to unveiling it. After the unveiling, the Operator will see their forms so con-

cretely, he or she may think they are objective, solid, beings as real as any other, in the room. Be not deceived. There is a danger here which I call the "Trance of Manifestation." Remember, you are in a divine-induced state of euphoria. This is a state of pure Divine Love, and being semi-divine, there will be an impulse coming from that part of God within you to take mercy on the Fallen spirits, and to leave the circle and give them benediction. For God—which the Operator certainly is not, but whose consciousness is now divinely dissolved in rapture—can do such an action. Hold fast to what thread of self-consciousness you still possess while in this state, and prepare for the next battles—that of Control and Command.

Then let the exorcist say: —

"Welcome spirits, or most noble princes, because I have called you through him to whom every knee doth bow, both of things in heaven, and things in earth, and things under the earth; in whose hands are all the kingdoms of kings, neither is there any able to contradict his Majesty. Wherefore, I bind you, that you remain affable and visible before this Circle, so long and so constant; neither shall you depart without my license, until you have truly and without any fallacy performed my will, by virtue of his power who hath set the sea her bounds, beyond which it cannot pass, nor go beyond the law of his providence, of the most High God, Lord, and King, who hath created all things. Amen.

Commentary 27—It is at this point that a strange mystical experience will envelop the Operator. Something occurs within the Operator which is projected to the spirits just as the 'Welcome' and further threat in the above statements are made. It is the tug of war between the Operator and spirit, as spoken of in Axiom 6. It will feel as if the Operator and spirit are pulling at the ends of a cord that is connected to the Operator's solar plexus. Remember, do not attempt to force control by any act of will, as stated in Axiom 6. You establish control not by forcing, not by trying to establish the control, but by simply maintaining a conscious hold over your rapture or state of pure Divine Love, and by simply watching the tug-of-war feeling continue between you and the entity. In short, it will be your **passive resistance** *that will force the entity to surrender its attempts to control the situation, and to surrender its will to you. It will all happen in the twinkling of an eye. You are now a divine being, and the spirit is subject to your will. It will relent. (The reader would also do well to reread Axiom 4 at this point as well.)*

One final point here. Although not dealt with in the Heptameron proper, the spirit or spirits—according to their aerial nature one or more may appear at first, but at least one will remain—will ask the Operator what he or she wishes, and will remind the magician that he and his ministers and legions can only fulfill that which is in their office—or powers—to fulfill. Keep the dialogue short, as will be discussed next.

Then command what you will, and it shall be done. Afterwards license them thus: —

"+ In the name of the Father, + and of the Son, + and of the Holy Ghost, go in peace unto your places; peace be between us & you; be ye ready to come when you are called."

Commentary 28—Your first command, while yet enduring the state of pure Divine Love, must be to have the spirits assume a more pleasing appearance. All other sounds, apparitions, and the like will have ceased, and literally, a mindshattering silence will fall over the scene in which the Operator and the spirits are the only players. Do not ask them to take on human form, unless it is within their office to do so, as in the case of the spirits of Mercury and Venus. But a command to take on a "more pleasing form" will at least tone down some of the more grotesque characteristics exhibited by the aerial spirits of other days of the week.

As given in Axiom 6, it is now time to deliver your Charge to the spirits. Be certain your Charge is as all encompassing and as brief as possible, as described in Axiom 6. And above all things, keep to your point—the fulfillment of your desire, and the conditions upon which it is to be fulfilled—and end the evocation to physical manifestation as quickly as is reasonably possible, by giving the License to Depart. Be sure to repeat this

License at least three times, and certainly, until the spirits have completely vanished. Although the Operator will still be intoxicated with the state of pure Divine Love—and which will continue for three days or so after the rite has ended—he or she must remain within the circle, burning Dominican Brand (church) incense, and offering prayers of thanksgiving to God for having allowed the rite to have taken place, and to have taken place successfully. As the Operator does so, he or she will feel a rapid clearing of the air and the room, as if a great emptiness now fills the void between the walls and ceiling. This feeling will be unmistakable, as the air itself will grow clearer, despite the heavy incense smoke in it. When this point has been reached, the Operator may then safely leave the circle. The evocation to physical manifestation is now over.

HERE ENDS PART ONE OF—
Heptameron
or
Magical Elements of Peter de Abano

PART TWO
Heptameron
or
Magical Elements of Peter de Abano

Preparatory Remarks

The pages to follow give the conjurations of the aerial spirits for each day of the week as set down by the *Heptameron*, as ascribed to Abano. It contains all the names of the angels, planetary symbols, as well as the sigils of the beings that are to be placed in the various Circles composing the Circle of Art. In the original text of the *Heptameron*, regarding the appearance of the spirits of each of the seven days of the week, the author states, "But in what manner they appear, is spoken already in the former book of Magical Ceremonies."

In both the original *Fourth Book of Occult Philosophy*—said to have been penned by Agrippa or one of his students—as well as in the Turner Fourth Book, this statement appears. It is thereby referring the reader to the *Fourth Book* itself—of either edition—since that book presents the descriptions of these beings when they manifest. Since the *Fourth Book* is not being reprinted here, I have taken the descriptions of these beings from that book, and inserted them at the end of the conjuration of each day of the week. I have done this so the reader will have a complete working text between the covers of this book, as well as for the sake of completeness.

Lastly, I have added an "Author's Note" where applicable, in order to make a point given in the text clear, or to add such miscellaneous information that may be of help to the reader. As with the Commentaries, these remarks are set off in italics.

Considerations of the Lord's day.

The Angel of the Lord's day, his Sigil, Planet, Sign of the Planet, and the name of the fourth heaven.

Figure 3
The Magical Sigils and Images of The Lord's Day

— The Angels of the Lord's day are: Michael, Dardiel, and Huratapal.

— The Angels of the Air ruling on the Lord's day are: Varcan, King: and Tus, Andas, and Cynabal, as his Ministers.

— The wind which the Angels of the Air above-said are under is the North-wind.

— The Angels of the fourth heaven, ruling on the Lord's day, which ought to be called from the four parts of the world are: —at the East: Samael, Baciel, Atel, Gabriel, and Vionairaba; —at the West: Anael, Pabel, Ustael, Burchat, Suceratos, and Capabili; at the North: Aiel, Aniel, [vel Aquiel], Masgabriel, Sapiel and Matuyel and at the South: Haludiel, Machasiel, Charsiel, Uriel and Naromiel.

— The perfume of the Lord's day is Red Wheat [or Red Sanders]. *(Author's Note: That is, Red Sandalwood. Remember, not white or any other kind.)*

Ω The Conjuration for the Lord's day.

I CONJURE and confirm upon you, ye strong and holy angels of God, in the name + ADONAI + EYE + EYE + EYA + which is he who was, and is, and is to come, + EYE + ABRAY +; and in the Name + SADAY + CADOS + CADOS + sitting on high upon the Cherubim; and by the great name Of God himself, strong and powerful, who is exalted above all the heavens; + EYE + SARAYE + who created the world, the heavens, the earth, the sea, and all that in them is, in the first day, and sealed them with his holy name + PHAA + ; and by the name of the angels who rule in the fourth heaven, and serve before the most mighty Salamia, an angel great and honorable; and by the name of his star, which is Sol, and by his sign, and by the immense name of the living God, and by all the names aforesaid, I conjure thee, Michael, 0 great angel! who art chief ruler of this day; and by the name + ADONAI + the God of Israel, I conjure thee, 0 Michael ! v. That thou labor for me, and fulfill all my petitions according to my will and desire in my cause and business.

The Spirits of the Air of the Lord's day, are under the North wind; their nature is to procure Gold, Gems, Carbuncles, Riches; to cause one to obtain favor and benevolence; to dissolve the enmities of men; to raise men to honors; and to carry or to take away infirmities. [But in what manner they appear, it is spoken already in the former book of Magical Ceremonies.]

(Author's Note: As explained in the Preparatory Remarks, in each of these conjurations I am giving the verbatim account of the appearances of the spirits of each day, according to the Fourth Book. The appearances of the spirits of the Lord's Day are as follows. Owing to the day being Sunday, the ruling planet is the Sun, according to Kabbalistic convention—)

Shapes familiar to the Spirits of the Sun. —

The Spirits of the Sun for the most part appear in a large, full and great body sanguine and gross, in gold color, with the tincture of blood. Their motion is as the Lightning of Heaven; their sign is to move the person to sweat that calls them. But their particular forms are: A King having a Scepter riding on a Lion; A King crowned; A Queen with a Scepter; A Bird; A Lion; A Cock; A yellow or golden Garment; A Scepter. Caudaius.

Considerations of Monday.

The Angel of Monday, his Sigil, Planet, the Sign of the Planet, and the name of the first heaven.

Figure 4
The Magical Sigils and Images of Monday

— The Angels of Monday are: Gabriel, Michael, and Samael.

— The Angels ruling the Air on Monday are: Arcan, King; and Bilet, Missabus, and Abuzaha as his Ministers.

— The wind which the said Angels of the Air are subject to is the West-wind.

— The Angels of the first heaven, ruling on Monday, which ought to be called from the four parts of the world: —from the East: Gabriel, Gabrael, Madiel, Deamiel, and Janael; from the West: Sachiel, Zaniel, Habaiel, Bachanael, and Corabael; from the North: Mael, Vuael, Valnum, Baliel, Balay, and Humastrau, and from the South: Curaniel, Dabriel, Darquiel, Hanun, Anayl, and Vetuel.

— The perfume for Monday is Aloes. (*Author's Note: This is Lingnum Aloes wood. The reader may have heard how expensive and rare this wood is, in their New Age travels. Be not deceived. The source given here provides the fresh, strong herb, and inexpensively. It is available on the world wide web from http://www.alchemy-works.com*)

Ω The Conjuration of Monday.

I CONJURE and confirm upon you, ye strong and good angels, in the name + ADONAI + ADONAI + ADONAI + ADONAI + EYE + EYE + EYE + CADOS + CADOS + CADOS + ACHIM + ACHIM + JA + JA +

strong + JA + who appeared in Mount Siani with the glorification of King + ADONAI + SADAI + ZEBAOTH + ANATHAY + YA + YA + YA + MARANATA + ABIM + JEIA +, who created the sea, and all lakes and waters, in the second day, which are above the heavens and in the earth, and sealed the sea in his high name, and gave it its bounds beyond which it cannot pass; and by the names of the angels who rule in the first legion, and who serve Orphaniel, a great, precious, and honorable angel, and by the name of his star which is Luna, and by all the names aforesaid, I conjure thee, Gabriel, who art chief ruler of Monday, the second day, v. That thou labor for me, and fulfill all my petitions according to my will and desire in my cause and business.

The Spirits of the Air of Monday, are subject to the West-wind, which is the wind of the Moon: their nature is to give silver; to convey things from place to place; to make horses swift; and to disclose the secrets of persons both present and future:

The forms familiar to the Spirits of the Moon. —

They will for the most part appear in a great and full body, soft and phlegmatique, of color like a black obscure cloud, having a swelling countenance, with eyes red and full of water, a bald head, and teeth like a wild boar. Their motion is as it were an exceeding great tempest of the Sea. For their sign, there will appear an exceeding great rain about the Circle. And in particular their shapes are: A King like an Archer riding upon a Doe; a little Boy; A Woman-hunter with a bow and arrows; A Cow; A little Doe; A Goose; A Garment green or silver-colored; An Arrow; A Creature having many feet.

Considerations of Tuesday.

The Angel of Tuesday, his Sigil, his Planet, the Sign governing that Planet, and the names of the fifth heaven: —

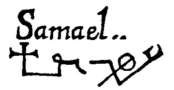

Figure 5
The Magical Sigils and Images of Tuesday

— The Angels of Tuesday are : Samael, Satael, and Amabiel.

— The Angels of the Air ruling in Tuesday are: Samax, King; and Carmax, Ismoli and Paffran as his Ministers.

— The wind to which the said Angels are subject to is the East-wind.

— The Angels of the fifth heaven ruling on Tuesday, which ought to be called from the four parts of the world are: —at the East: Friagne, Guael, Damael, Calzas, and Arragon; at the West: Lama, Astagna, Lobquin, Soncas, Jazel, and Irel; at the North: Rahumel, Hyniel, Rayel, Seraphiel, Mathiel, and Fraciel; and at the South: Sacriel, Janiel, Galdel, Osael, Vianuel, Zaliel.

— The perfume for Tuesday is Pepper. *(Author's Note: This is simple black pepper, but course ground is best. Since this type of pepper burns more slowly, it is less irritating to the eyes. Properly speaking, the spirits of Tuesday must be summoned out-of-doors, as the caustic nature of even course ground black pepper is simply too irritating for conducting the rite in an enclosure.)*

Ω The Conjuration of Tuesday.

I CONJURE and call upon you, ye strong and good angels, in the names + YA + YA + YA + HE + HE + HE + VA + HY + HA + HA + HA + VA + VA + VA + AN + AN + AN + AIA + AIA + AIA + EL + AY + ELIBRA + ELOHIM + ELOHIM +; and by the names of the high God, who hath made the sea and dry land, and by his word hath made the earth, and produced trees, and hath set his seal upon the planets, with his precious, honored, revered and holy name; and by the name of the angels governing in the fifth house, who are subservient to the great angel Acimoy, who is strong, powerful, and honored, and by the name of his star which is called Mars, I call upon thee, Samael, by the names above mentioned, thou great angel ! who presides over the day of Mars, and by the name + ADONAI + the living and true God, v. that thou labor for me, and fulfill all my petitions according to my will and desire in my cause and business.

The Spirits of the Air of Tuesday are under the East-wind: their nature is to cause wars, mortality, death and combustions; and to give two thousand Soldiers at a time; and to bring death, infirmities or health.

The familiar shapes of the Spirits of Mars. —

They appear in a tall body, cholerick, a filthy countenance of color brown, swarthy or red, having horns like Harts horns, and Griphins claws, bellowing like wild Bulls. Their motion is like fire burning; their sign Thunder and Lightning about the Circle. Their particular shapes are: A King armed riding upon a Wolf; a Man armed; A Woman holding a buckler on her thigh; A Hee-goat; A Horse; A Stag; A Red Garment; Wool; A Cheeslip.

Considerations of Wednesday.

The Angel of Wednesday, his Sigil, his Planet, the Sign governing that Planet, and the name of the second heaven.

Figure 6
The Magical Sigils and Images of Wednesday

— The Angels of Wednesday are: Raphael, Miel, & Seraphiel.

— The Angels of the Air on Wednesdaty are: Mediat [or Modiat], King; and Suquinos, and Sallales as Ministers.

— The wind to which the said Angels of the Air are subject is the South-West wind.

— The Angels of the second heaven governing Wednesday, which ought to be called from the four parts of the world are: —at the East: —Mathlai, Tarmiel, and Baraborat; at the West: Jeresous, and Mitraton; at the North: Thiel, Rael, Jariahel, Venahel, Velel, Abuiori, and Ucirnuel; and at the South: Milliel, Nelapa, Babel, Caluel, Vel, and Laquel.

— The fumigation of Wednesday is Mastick.

Ω The Conjuration of Wednesday.

I CONJURE and call upon you, ye strong and holy angels, good and powerful, in a strong name of fear and praise, + JA + ADONAI + ELOHIM + SADAY + SADAY + SADAY + EIE + EIE + EIE + ASAMIE + ASAMIE +; and in the name of ADONAY, the God of Israel, who hath made the two great lights, and distinguished day from night for the benefit of his creatures; and by the names of all the discerning angels, governing openly in the second house before the great angel Tetra, strong and powerful; and by the name of his star which is Mercury; and by the name of his seal, which is that of a powerful and honored God; and I call upon thee, Raphael, and by the names above mentioned, thou great angel who presides over the fourth day: and by the holy name which is written in the front of Aaron, created the most high priest, and by the names of all the angels who are constant in the grace of Christ, and by the name and place of Ammaluim, v. that thou labor for me, and fulfill all my petitions according to my will and desire in my cause and business.

The Spirits of the Air of Wednesday are subject to the South-West-wind: Their nature is to give all Metals; to reveal all earthly things past, present, and to come; to pacify judges; to give victories in war; to re-edify; and to teach experiment and all decayed Sciences; and to change bodies mixt of Elements conditionally out of one into another; to give infirmitied or health; to raise the poor, and cast down the high ones; to bind or loose Spirits; to open locks or bolts: such-kind of Spirits have the operation of others, but not in their perfect power, but in virtue or knowledge. *(Author's Note: "decayed Sciences" refers to the physical sciences as we know them today. That is, physics, astronomy, chemistry, and mathematics. These sciences were considered decayed because they were not of heavenly or so-called spiritual quality; another indication of the religious tone and attitude of the early days the Heptameron was in use. "...but not in their perfect power, but in virtue or knowledge," refers to the belief that mercurial influences could not, in and of themselves, operate to open lock directly. That is, a mercurial spirit would not appear and perform such a feat for the Operator. Instead, the spirits would so influence the mind of the Operator that he or she would suddenly receive the knowledge of how to perform that action by themselves.)*

The familiar forms of the Spirits of Mercury. —

The Spirits of Mercury will appear for the most part in a body of a middle stature, cold, liquid, and moist, fair, and with an affable speech; in a human shape and form; like unto a Knight armed; of color clear and bright. The motion of them is as it were silver-colored clouds. For their sign, they cause and bring horror and fear unto him that calls them. But their particular shapes are: A King riding upon a Bear; A fair youth; A Woman holding a distaffe; A Dog; A Shee-Bear; A Magpie; A Garment of sundry changeable colors; A Rod; A little staffe. *(Author's Note: In my opinion, the appearance of the spirits of Mercury are by far the most terrifying at first, as are the physical phenomena that accompany their full manifestation. After being constrained however, they are most pleasing. Their assumption then is as that of a 'fair youth' given above. They are indeed powerful, and dispense the Virtues of their Office liberally and graciously.)*

Considerations of Thursday.

The Angel of Thursday, his Sigil, Planet, the Sign of the Planet, and the name of the sixth heaven.

Figure 7
The Magical Sigils and Images of Thursday

— The Angels of Thursday are: Sachiel, Castiel, and Asasiel.

— The Angels of the Air governing Thursday are: Suth, King; and Maguth, and Gutrix as his Ministers.

— The wind which the said Angels of the Air are under is the South-wind.

— But because there are no Angels of the Air to be found above the fifth heaven, therefore on Thursday say the prayers following in the four parts of the world —

— At the East: O great and most high God, honored be thy name, world without end.

— At the West: O wise, pure, and just God, of divine clemency, I beseech thee, most holy Father, that this day I may perfectly understand and accomplish my petitions, work and labor; for the honor and glory of thy holy name, who livest and reignest, world without end. Amen.

— At the North: O God, strong, mighty, and wonderful, from everlasting to everlasting, grant that this day I bring to effect that which I desire, through our blessed Lord. Amen.

— At the South: O mighty and most merciful God, hear my prayers and grant my petitions.

— The perfume for Thursday is Saffron.

Ω The Conjuration of Thursday.

I CONJURE and confirm upon you, ye strong and holy angels, by the names + CADOS + CADOS + CADOS + ESCHEREIE + ESCHEREIE + ESCHEREIE + HATIM + YA +, strong founder of the worlds; + CANTINE + JAYM + JANIC + ANIC + CALBOT + SABBAC + BERISAY + ALNAYM +; and by the name + ADONAI +, who created fishes and creeping things in the waters, and birds upon the face of the earth, flying towards heaven, in the fifth day; and by the names of the angels serving in the sixth host before Pastor, a holy angel, and a great and powerful prince and by the name of his star which is Jupiter, and by the name of his seal, and by the name of + ADONAY +, the great God, Creator of all things, and by the name of all the stars, and by their power and virtue, and by all the names aforesaid, I conjure thee, Sachiel, a great Angel, who art chief ruler of Thursday, v. that thou labor for me, and fulfill all my petitions according to my will and desire in my cause and business.

The Spirits of the Air of Thursday, are subject to the South-wind; their nature is to procure the love of women; to cause men to be merry and joyful; to pacify strife and contentions; to appease enemies; to heal the diseased, and to disease the whole; and procureth losses, or take them away. (*Author's Note: The reader will no doubt have noticed the considerable differences in the Offices of these spirits as opposed to New Age 'Qabalistic' planetary attributions. The ancient Kabbalah of Reuchlin, Waite, Levi, and other Old System Magic magicians and Kabbalists is much richer than the crib sheet approach postured and promulgated by modern magic. The reader would do well to study these older texts, if you desire to build a solid Kabbalistic foundation, and construct a powerful, effective, and efficient subjective synthesis.*)

The familiar forms to the Spirits of Jupiter. —

The spirits of Jupiter do appear with a body sanguine and cholerick, of a middle stature, with a horrible fearful motion; but with a mild countenance, a gentle speech, and of the color of Iron. The motion of them is flashings of

Lightning and Thunder; their sign is, there will appear men about the circle, who shall seem to be devoured of Lions. Their particular forms are: A King with a Sword drawn, riding on a Stag; A Man wearing a Mitre in long raiment; A Maid with a Laurel- Crown adorned with Flowers; A Bull; A Stag; A Peacock; An azure Garment; A Sword; A Box-tree.

Considerations of Friday.

The Angel of Friday, his Sigil, his Planet, the Sign governing that Planet, and the name of the third heaven.

Figure 8
The Magical Sigils and Images of Friday

— The Angels of Friday are: Anael, Rachiel, Sachiel.

— The Angels of the Air reigning on Friday are: Sarabotes, King; and Amabiel, Aba, Abalidoth, and Flaef as his Ministers.

— The wind which the said Angels of the Air are under is the West-wind.

— The Angels of the third heaven, ruling on Friday, which are to be called from the four parts of the world are: at the East: Setchiel, Chedusitaniel, Corat, Tamael, and Tenaciel; at the West: Turiel, Coniel, Babiel, Kadie, Maltiel, and Huphaltiel; at the North: Peniel, Penael, Penat, Raphael, Raniel, and Doremiel; and at the South: Porna, Sachiel, Chermiel, Samael, Santanael, and Famiel.

— The perfume of Friday is Pepperwort.

Ω The Conjuration of Friday.

I CONJURE & confirm upon you, ye strong & holy angels, by the names ON + HEY + HEYA + JA + JE + SADAY + ADONAY +, and in the name SADAY who created four-footed beasts, and creeping things, and man, in the sixth day, and gave to Adam power over all creatures; wherefore blessed be the name of the Creator in his place; and by the name of the angels serving in the third host, before Dagiel, a great angel, and a strong and powerful prince, and by the name of his star, which is Venus, and by his seal which is holy; and by all the names aforesaid, I conjure upon thee, Anael, who art the chief ruler this day, that thou labor for me, and fulfill all my petitions according to my will and desire in my cause and business.

The Spirits of the Air of Friday are subject to the West-wind; their nature is to give silver; to excite men, and incline them to luxury; to reconcile enemies through luxury; to make marriages; to allure men to love women; to cause, or take away infirmities; and to do all things which have motion.

Familiar shapes of the Spirits of Venus. —

They do appear with a fair body, of middle stature, with an amiable and pleasant countenance, of color white or green, the upper part golden. The motion of them is as it were a most clear Star. For their sign, there will seem to be maids playing without the Circle, which will provoke and allure him that calleth them to play. But their particular forms are: A King with a Scepter riding upon a Camel; A Maid clothed and dressed beautifully; A Maid naked; A Shee-goat; A Camel; A Dove; A white or green Garment; Flowers; the herb Savine. (*Author's Note: The spirits of Venus are the most alluring of all. Great care must be used when they manifest, so the Operator does not fall for their attempts to draw him or her from the Circle. Their voices are so melodic, it might remind the Operator of the legends of the Sirens of old who lured sailors to their death through a shipwreck on rocky coastlines. This is another reason to operate alone. The Operator will have enough difficulty controlling their own human nature during this manifestation, without having to worry about what a "servant" or assistant might do once these spirits take form.*

I should make another point here. By now the reader has become aware of the multitudinous shapes and activities that occur during the 'process of manifestation,' as indeed it is a process. But it is not linear, meaning, one part of the manifestation does not (necessarily) occur first, another second, and so on. Despite this, I have found that there is a general trend which, by knowing in advance, may help the Operator during this critical phase of the evocation. The "motion" in the room generally occurs first, followed by the appearance of ghost-like apparitions—here, the maids playing about the outer circle's circumference—and then the solid appearance of the spirit. In this case, as an example, the manifestation of a King with a Scepter riding upon a Camel. If the Operator receives this normal type of manifestation, all is well and good. All too often however, one of the more strange manifestations of the spirit will occur, such as—in this case—a white or green garment, or even a talking herb. It may sound humorous, trying to have a dialogue with a talking garment or herb, but I assure you, it is not. The Operator's reality has been altered so greatly already, that additional stress caused to his or her perceptions could very well prove too much to endure. Thus, in these instances, the Operator must immediately charge the spirit to assume a more pleasing, understandable form. In this case, a human form. After such a charge, the spirit will immediately change its appearance to—in this case—either the King with a scepter riding upon a camel, a lovely woman dressed beautifully, or a beautiful, naked woman. Once again, the Operator must maintain control over themselves while in the state of Divine Love, as the Control aspect of the evocation is about to commence.)

Considerations of Saturday, or the Sabbaoth.

The Angel of Saturday, his Sigil, his Planet, and the Sign governing that Planet.

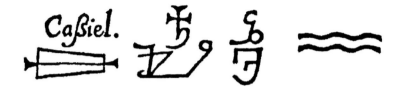

Figure 9
The Magical Sigils and Images of Saturday

— The Angels of Saturday are: Cassiel, Uriel, and Machatan.

— The Angels of the Air ruling on Saturday are: Maymon, King; and Abumalith, Assaibi and Balidet as his Ministers.

— The wind which the said Angels of the Air are under is the South-West-wind.

— The fumigation of Saturday is Sulphur.

It has already been declared in the considerations of Thursday, that there are no Angels ruling the Air, above the fifth heaven: therefore in the four Angles of the world, use those Orations which you see applied to that purpose on Thursday.

At the East: O great and most high God, honored be thy name, world without end. And so on.

℧ The Conjuration of Saturday.

I CONJURE & confirm upon you, Caphriel or Cassiel, Machator, and Seraquiel, strong and powerful Angels; and by the name + ADONAY + ADONAY + ADONAY + EIE + EIE + EIE + ACIM + ACIM + ACIM + CADOS + CADOS + IMA + IMA + IMA + SALAY + JA + SAR +, Lord and Maker of the World, who rested on the seventh day; and by him who of his good pleasure gave the same to be observed by the children of Israel through-out their generations, that they should keep and sanctify the same, to have thereby a good reward in the world to come; and by the names of the angels serving in the seventh host, before Booel, a great angel, and powerful prince; and by the name of his star, which is Saturn; and by his holy seal, and by the name before spoken, I conjure upon thee, Caphriel, who art chief ruler of the seventh day, which is the Sabbaoth, that thou labor for me, and fulfill all my petitions according to my will and desire in my cause and business.

The Spirits of the Air of Saturday are subject to the South-West: their nature is to sow discords,, hatred, evil thoughts and cogitations; to give leave freely, to slay and kill every one, and to lame or maim every member. *(Author's Note: The word, "cogitations" refers to one's ability to judge; to think and to reason. As such, the reference is that the spirits of this day increase the Operator's faculty in this regard.*

Notice also that even though the Heptameron is a Roman Catholic grimoire, the Jewish Sabbath is referred to specifically, and the conjuration gives a very dignified description of the day and its origin. It was customary for the Catholic originators of the grimoires, even during those dangerous times of the Inquisition Tribunal, to nevertheless pay honor to the Hebrews and their Jewish religion. This was a carryover of the Kabbalistic influence the works of such early writers as Ruechlin made upon the early Christian magicians.)

The shapes familiar to the Spirits of Saturn. —

They appear for the most part with a tall, lean, and slender body, with an angry countenance, having four faces; one in the hinder part of the head, one on the former part of the head, and on each side nosed and beaked: there likewise appeareth a face on each knee, of a black shining color: their motion is the moving of the wind, with a kind of earthquake: their sign is white earth, whiter than any snow. The particular forms are: A King having a beard, riding on a Dragon; An old man with a beard; An old woman leaning on a staff; A Hog; A Dragon; An Owl; A black Garment; A Hook or Sickle; a Juniper-tree. *(Author's Note: By far, these are the most serious spirits to deal with. Unless the Operator can genuinely, honestly, and realistically justify the need to deal with these beings, he or she is advised in the strongest terms to leave them alone. Unless you are thoroughly experienced in evocation to physical manifestation and can control your mind during the state of Divine Love, I warn you to leave these powerful beings severely alone.)*

TABLES OF THE ANGELS OF THE HOURS,
according to the course of the day.

SUNDAY

Hours, day	Angels	Hours, night	Angels
1. Yayn	Michael	1. Beron	Sachiel
2. Janor	Anael	2. Barol	Samael
3. Nasnia	Raphael	3. Thaun	Michael
4. Salla	Gabriel	4. Athir	Anael
5. Sadedali	Cassiel	5. Mathun	Raphael
6. Thamur	Sachiel	6. Rona	Gabriel
7. Ourer	Samael	7. Netos	Cassiel
8. Tanic	Michael	8. Tafrac	Sachiel
9. Neron	Anael	9. Sassur	Samael
10. Jayon	Raphael	10. Aglo	Michael
11. Abay	Gabriel	11. Calerna	Anael
12. Natalon	Cassiel	12. Salam	Raphael

MONDAY

Hours, day	Angels	Hours, night	Angels
1. Yayn	Gabriel	1. Beron	Anael
2. Janor	Cassiel	2. Barol	Raphael
3. Nasnia	Sachiel	3. Thaun	Gabriel
4. Salla	Samael	4. Athir	Cassiel
5. Sadedali	Michael	5. Mathon	Sachiel
6. Thamur	Anael	6. Rana	Samael
7. Ourer	Raphael	7. Netos	Michael
8. Tanic	Gabriel	8. Tafrac	Anael
9. Neron	Cassiel	9. Sassur	Raphael
10. Jayon	Sachiel	10. Aglo	Gabriel
11. Abay	Samael	11. Calerna	Cassiel
12. Natalon	Michael	12. Salam	Sachiel

TUESDAY

Hours, day	Angels	Hours, night	Angels
1. Yayn	Samael	1. Beron	Cassiel
2. Janor	Michael	2. Barol	Sachiel
3. Nasnia	Anael	3. Thanu	Samael
4. Salla	Raphael	4. Athir	Michael
5. Sadedal	Gabriel	5. Mathon	Anael
6. Thamur	Cassiel	6. Rana	Raphael
7. Ourer	Sachiel	7. Netos	Gabriel
8. Tanic	Samael	8. Tafrac	Cassiel
9. Neron	Michael	9. Sussur	Sachiel
10. Jayon	Anael	10. Aglo	Samael
11. Abay	Raphael	11. Calerna	Michael
12. Natalon	Gabriel	12. Salam	Anael

WEDNESDAY

Hours, day	Angels	Hours, night	Angels
1. Yayn	Raphael	1. Beron	Michael
2. Janor	Gabriel	2. Barol	Anael
3. Nasnia	Cassiel	3. Thanu	Raphiel
4. Salla	Sachiel	4. Athir	Gabriel
5. Sadedali	Samael	5. Mathon	Cassiel
6. Thamur	Michael	6. Rana	Sachiel
7. Ourer	Anael	7. Netos	Samael
8. Tanic	Raphael	8. Tafrac	Michael
9. Neron	Gabriel	9. Sassur	Anael
10. Jayon	Cassiel	10. Aglo	Raphael
11. Abay	Sachiel	11. Calerna	Gabriel
12. Neron	Samael	12. Salam	Cassiel

THURSDAY

Hours, day	Angels	Hours, night	Angels
1. Yayn	Sachiel	1. Beron	Gabriel
2. Janor	Samael	2. Barol	Cassiel
3. Nasnia	Michael	3. Thanu	Sachiel
4. Salla	Anael	4. Athir	Samael
5. Sadedali	Raphael	5. Maton	Michael
6. Thamur	Gabriel	6. Rana	Anael
7. Ourer	Cassiel	7. Netos	Raphael
8. Tanic	Sachiel	8. Tafrac	Gabriel
9. Neron	Samael	9. Sassur	Cassiel
10. Jayon	Michael	10. Aglo	Sachiel
11. Abay	Anael	11. Calerna	Samael
12. Natalon	Raphael	12. Salam	Michael

FRIDAY

Hours, day	Angels	Hours, night	Angels
1. Yayn	Anael	1. Beron	Samael
2. Janor	Raphael	2. Barol	Michael
3. Nasnia	Gabriel	3. Thanu	Anael
4. Salla	Cassiel	4. Athir	Raphael
5. Sadedali	Sachiel	5. Maton	Gabriel
6. Thamur	Samael	6. Rana	Cassiel
7. Ourer	Michael	7. Netos	Sachiel
8. Tanic	Anael	8. Tafrac	Samael
9. Neron	Raphael	9. Sassur	Michael
10. Jayon	Gabriel	10. Aglo	Anael
11. Abay	Cassiel	11. Calerna	Raphael
12. Natalon	Sachiel	12. Salam	Gabriel

SATURDAY

Hours, day	Angels	Hours, night	Angels
1. Yayn	Cassiel	1. Beron	Raphael
2. Janor	Sachiel	2. Barol	Gabriel
3. Nasnia	Samael	3. Thanu	Cassiel
4. Salla	Michael	4. Athir	Sachiel
5. Sadedali	Anael	5. Maton	Samael
6. Thamur	Raphael	6. Rana	Michael
7. Ourer	Gabriel	7. Netos	Anael
8. Tanic	Cassiel	8. Tafrac	Raphael
9. Neron	Sachiel	9. Sussur	Gabriel
10. Jayon	Samael	10. Aglo	Cassiel
11. Abay	Michael	11. Calerna	Sachiel
12. Natalon	Anael	12. Salam	Samael

(Author's Note: The reader will find the list of these names of the hours of the day and night and their angels also in the section, "Of the Names of the Hours and the Angels Ruling Them," earlier in this chapter. You may also notice a difference in the spelling of some of the names in that earlier section compared to the spellings given here, as well as words capitalized out of sequence, periods where they do not belong, and other grammatical features that do not constitute "good English" as we know it today. The problem of the spelling is to be expected when dealing with the problem of transcription through the centuries, and poses no problem. In all cases, the Operator should use the spelling of the names of the hours of the day and night, and their angels, as they appear in this latter listing. As to the capitalization and other grammatical errors, I have inserted them here exactly as they appear in the original Heptameron. This was done in order to give the reader the flavor of the times in which this grammar of magic was written, as well as to preserve the text as it originally appears.)

But this is to be observed by the way, that the first hour of the day, of every Country, and in every season whatsoever, is to be assigned to the Sun-rising, when he first appeareth arising in the horizon: and the first hour of the night is to be the thirteenth hour, from the first hour of the day. But of these things it is sufficiently spoken. *(Author's Note: Admittedly, this is an awkward way to refer to the 'thirteenth hour,' which is actually the first hour of the night. That is, it is the next hour after the twelfth hour of the day. By referring to Commentary 4 on calculating the hours of the day and night, any problem the reader should experience with this issue should be readily resolved.)*

HERE ENDS THE HEPTAMERON
OR
MAGICAL ELEMENTS of Peter De Abano

Chapter Six

Handling the Success and Dealing with the Slingshot Effect

The reader may well be saying at this point, "Well, maybe I could use a little coaching in handling the Slingshot Effect, but why would I ever need any help on handling success? There can't be anything dumber than that!" The question seems logical on the surface. But like an iceberg, ninety percent of the issue lies below the surface. This is why I decided to add this final chapter to a book that is designed to help the reader fulfill his or her material, intellectual, and emotional desires. Things are not always as they seem. While what follows here may appear to be philosophical, I assure you that in the end—after you have conducted your first evocation to physical manifestation from the *Heptameron*—you will agree with me that the advice offered herein is nothing short of intensely practical.

Right now, as you are scanning these lines, I am willing to bet that you are no different from the rest of humanity. You have needs. You have wants. You have desires that are combinations of both needs and wants. You may even possess such a high level of self-honesty that you can clearly distinguish between your needs and wants, and understand that the two are—as in so many instances—light years apart. Yet, you still covet them, and for reasons of your own, have justified them.

Ultimately, you are correct in doing so. For unlike the society in which you live, which seeks to placate the crippled mentalities of their dull populace with instant gratification fads and quick-fix, passing fancies, you have set your own course and intend to follow it through to its inevitable conclusion. Nor do you accept the empty dictates and reasons for suffering in the here-and-now in exchange for the promise of a better afterlife, spouted from the church steeples, synagogue roof-tops, and temple ramparts of dead religions still masquerading as living, vibrant, paths to spiritual wholeness and salvation.

You have seen the cons and lies in the grinning deathmasks of their pseudo self-righteous priests, ministers, and rabbis. And you have rightly and justly rejected them and their dogmas that only lead to increased coffers for themselves and their churches, while maintaining power over you, your thoughts, and therefore, over your entire life. Instead, not only have you determined to set your own course, you are grimly committed to following it; a course of action that will produce a satisfying, exciting and full life that in the end, will make your stay upon this earth something to be remembered.

These secret determinations and judgments were the factors that led you to this book. I salute you for your attitude and courage in taking the responsibility for your own life—material, intellectual, emotional, and psychic— forget the 'spiritual' nonsense—and placing it into your own hands. But as you have seen throughout this book, additional instructions must be offered even to the most courageous among my readers, so that they know how to handle the finer points of what is now looming large on their magical horizon.

In your first evocations, be extremely careful when satisfying only your wants. Of course, there is nothing wrong with this. I will certainly not caution you in that watered-down Christian ethic that presents itself in the New Age literature as, '...as long as it does not interfere with the Will of another...' That is nonsense. Everyday, in every way, in all walks of life, one person, one town, one state, and one country is interfering with the Will of another. It is a function and reflection of the workings in Malkuth, and as much a part and substance of this plane of existence, as is the hardest and most brilliant diamond that was ever found. As well it should be.

No, I am not trying to blind you with the 'Thou Shalts' or 'Thou Shalt Nots' of the religious scoundrel or the New Age fraud. Rather, I am cautioning you to hold off on your fulfillment of *pure* wants in the beginning. The reason for this is quite practical and tactical.

After your first success in evocation to physical manifestation from the *Heptameron*, you will—for weeks afterward—remain in that twilight state of magical consciousness wherein all things are not simply possible or even probable, but inevitable. It is this altered awareness, the product of the altered state of consciousness achieved during the Operation, that will be creating permanent brain changes within both your mind and your very being. You will be seeing clearly, but not necessarily *realistically*. You be 'psychically intoxicated' as I like to put it, by the knowledge that you can, indeed, have or be whatever you want. The only limitations you will have are those you put upon yourself. But remember. Everything has a price.

In terms of your everyday reality, I am cautioning you not to fall into the something for nothing trap so aptly demonstrated in American society. That lie exists only in this country. It is not an enduring part of hard core reality—the reality in which you live. Since society surrounds you every day, it will effect your overall attitude, including the new attitude produced by your success with evocation to physical manifestation. You will think, "I can have this, and I can have that." In the long run you can and will, but not *now*. Not immediately. Be on guard.

Let the changes going on within you enter into your mental and life streams fully, and gel properly and completely before deciding upon "What do I get next!" To allow these internal changes and their gelling to occur easily and safely, withdraw as much as possible from the daily insanities of those around you. Seek quiet and Peace in which to grow, because during this time of inner change, many of the wants you viewed as needs, and needs that you viewed as wants, will exchange places.

This alone will leave you with an entirely new concept of who you are, where you are, where you are going, and how you will get there. In addition, your entire psychic makeup will undergo a radical transformation—a very positive one—that will lead you down new paths of self-discovery and awareness, and into deeper and deeper levels of understanding 'who' and indeed 'what' you really are. In fact, you will find that 'you' are not 'who' you thought 'you' were. Nor 'what' you were. You will come to the realization that truly, you are a work in progress, and quickly come to understand that progress will take time and nurturing, just as changing from one occupation to another requires time and practice to acquire and properly use a new set of skills.

But the societal aspect of the something for nothing lie, extended into your future evocation plans, is only part of the temptation into which you could fall. Compared to the more sinister aspect to be dealt with here, it could even be called the superficial part of your potential problem. For the sinister part involves the evoked spirits—or demons, or Fallen angels—because in fact, that is what they really are. While you will send them back to their own world by the License to Depart, and in this way be free of them, you will not—and I strongly repeat—will *not* be free of their influence, until the object of your want, desire, or need, has been fulfilled completely and in all of its parts.

Their fulfillment of your needs is one thing. In terms of the Slingshot Effect, the events that *may* yet occur even with a near-perfect evocation will be—as I said in Axiom 7—mild, in the case of having a need fulfilled. But if you play around with having some flippant 'want' gratified—even though full manifestation, Control and Command were established—the possibility of having a mild Slingshot Effect will skyrocket. It will be as if you rationalized away the fact that the evocation did not begin well, and yet persisted through to its conclusion.

This is because these beings are—as I have explained—by their very natures, highly resistant to following any Will other than their own. Once again. It is not that they see you as an enemy to be destroyed outright. But their changeable, unstable natures and willfulness, will still enter into their actions in fulfilling your ends. In the case of a 'need,' I suspect the deeper levels of your subconscious subjective synthesis actually aid them in doing what they must, as you innately view the need as justified. In the case of a 'want,' that same subjective synthesis operates *both* for and against you, much like a contestant on a game show who cannot make up their mind what gifts to select when they win the contest. Some gifts are practical and are needed, but are no fun. Others are just plain fun, but stir up feelings of guilt. Between these two extremes, the tug-of-war goes on, always producing dissatisfaction with whatever gifts are selected.

Make no mistake about it. The more negative emotions—both conscious and subconscious—you will experience regarding the legitimacy and fulfillment of your wants, the more means and ways your subjective synthesis will automatically offer up to the spirits in order to trip you up. So whatever you do, build your set of experience and working acumen in evocation to physical manifestation gradually, over a reasonable period of time, by having what you currently perceive as needs fulfilled first.

Remember. Your wants and needs will change. They will shift identities, the needs becoming wants and vice versa, in addition to genuine needs, perceived wants, and earnest desires actually changing into other needs, wants, and desires. You may or may not believe me at this point. Nevertheless, I tell you here and now that the path of power and progress you are to embark upon—should you choose to work the *Heptameron*—will give you enough with which to contend, without mudding up your own waters of self interest.

As to the Slingshot Effect itself. As I have explained, as long as you follow the Magical Axioms, produce full manifestation, and establish Control and Command, you have nothing to fear from the more overt displays of the Slingshot Effect. Of course, there is always the possibility that you *could* experience mild effects even from a thoroughly well conducted evocation. But as I stated, those effects will most probably be so mild you may hardly be aware of them. Nevertheless, be vigilant during the days following the evocation, and certainly, until the object you sought from the evocation is fully and completely manifested in your life.

Yet, even when some of these effects do occur from a well conducted rite, in time, you will merely muse at them, realizing how much they too can be part of the overall process of evocation and personal growth. Because in fact, that is what evocation and all Old System Magic—as well as true Hermetic Magic—is about. Personal growth. This is the path you could very well choose to set your foot upon. If you do, I wish you well. For I can guarantee you a life like no other, filled with more wonders and amazing experiences than you could possibly imagine at this moment. Your life will be full of the treasures uncovered on your journey of Self discovery, from the material wealth and benefits received through your magical work, and from the new visions and vistas that will fill your mind, heart, and eyes—both the inner and outer.

I leave you, my loyal reader, who has passed through so much in this book, with a final recommendation. It has always been my contention that as long as you must breathe your last breath yourself, let no person, no institution, no group or organization, tell you how to live your life. Obey the laws of the country in which you are in, only for the sake of expediency in not being interfered with by those who would rather see you under the heel of their boot.

Live according to your own inner sense of ethics and morals, not as 'a beast of the fields,' indulging in every excess your newly derived power from evocation to physical manifestation most certainly can confer upon you. Those ideals—the self-designed, inwardly created codes of morality and ethics—are not dirty words after all. They are guideposts along the path you have chosen to travel.

And after having lived your life, having seen things and journeyed to those furthermost limits of human experience where few mortals have ever dared to go, let your epitaph read, "I lived my life as I wanted to, where I wanted to, and how I wanted to. I created my own Way, lived it by a code I set for myself, and traveled this Path alone. Let criticism and its servants be damned!"

Suggested Reading List

Agrippa, Henry Cornelius of Nettesheim. *Three Books of Occult Philosophy*. Translated by James Freake, edited and annotated by Donald Tyson. Llewellyn Publications, St. Paul, Minnesota. 1993

Agrippa, Henry Cornelius. *Fourth Book of Occult Philosophy*. Kessinger Publishing Company, Montana.

Assagioli, Roberto, M.D. *The Act of Will*. Penguin Books, NY. 1973

Assagioli, Roberto, M.D. *Psychosynthesis*. Penguin Books, NY. 1976

Barrett, Francis. *The Magus, or Celestial Intelligencer; being a complete system of Occult Philosophy*. Introduction by Timothy d'Arch Smith (1967). Citadel Press Book. Reprint Samuel Weiser, Inc., York Beach, Maine. 1989

Barry, Kieren. *The Greek Qabalah. Alphabetic Mysticism and Numerology in the Ancient World*. Samuel Weiser, Inc. York Beach, Maine. 1999

Betz, Hans Dieter, editor. *The Greek Magical Papyri in Translation including the Demonic Spells*. Vol. One: Texts. 2nd ed. The University of Chicago Press, Chicago. 1996

The Book of the Goetia or The Lesser Key of Solomon the King. From numerous manuscripts in Hebrew, Latin, French and English by the Order of the Secret Chief of the Rosicrucian Order. 1903 translation. The Occult Publishing House, Chicago.

Brenner, Charles, M.D. *An Elementary Textbook of Psychoanalysis.* Bantam Doubleday Dell Publishing Group, Inc., NY. 1995

Brill, Dr. A.A., editor and translator. *The Basic Writings of Sigmund Freud.* Random House, Inc., NY. 1995

Casaubon, Meric. Dr. *John Dee's Actions with Spirits (1659).* Stephen Skinner, ed. Askin Publishers, London. Distributed by Samuel Weiser Inc., NY. 1974

Davidson, Gustav. *A Dictionary of Angels including the fallen angels.* The Free Press, MacMillan, Inc. NY. 1971

Faraone, Christopher A. and Dirk Obbink, eds. *Magika Hiera. Ancient Greek Magic and Religion.* Oxford University Press, NY. 1991

Flowers, Stephen Edred, PhD., ed. *Hermetic Magic. The Postmodern Magical Papyrus of Abaris.* Samuel Weiser, Inc. York Beach, Maine. 1995

Fowden, Garth. *The Egyptian Hermes. A Historical Approach to the Late Pagan Mind.* Princeton University Press, Princeton, NJ. 1986

Freke, Timothy and Peter Gandy. *The Hermetica. The Lost Wisdom of the Pharaohs.* Penguin Putnam, Inc., NY. 1997

Freud, Sigmund. *General Psychological Thought. Papers on Metapsychology.* Simon & Schuster, NY. 1997

Freud, Sigmund. *An Outline of Psycho-Analysis.* W.W. Norton & Co., NY. 1989

Gaster, Dr. Moses. *The Sword of Moses. An Ancient Book of Magic.* Holmes Publishing Group. 2000

Griffith, F. Li. and Herbert Thompson, eds. *The Leyden Papyrus. An Egyptian Magical Book.* Dover Publications, Inc., NY. 1974

Grimoirium Verum. Translated from Hebrew by Plangierè, Jesuite Dominicaine. Originally published by Alibeck the Egyptian at Memphis, 1517. Trident Books, Seattle, Washington. 1997.

The Grand Grimoire. Translated by Gretchen Rudy. Co-published by Trident Books and Ars Obscura, Seattle, Washington. 1996

Hermetica, volumes 1 through 4 (Corpus Hermeticum). The Ancient Greek and Latin Writings which contain religious or philosophic teachings ascribed to Hermes Trismegistus. Introduction, Texts, and translation by Walter Scott. Kessinger Publishing Group, Montana.

Honourius. *The Sworn Book of Honourius the Magician (as composed by Honourius through counsel with the Angel Hocroell).* Prepared from two British Museum manuscripts. Edited and translated by Daniel J. Driscoll. Heptangle Books, Gilette, NJ. 1977

Horney, Karen, M.D. *Self-Analysis.* W.W. Norton & Co., NY. 1994

Hyatt, Christopher S., Ph.D. *Undoing Yourself with Energized Meditation and Other Devices.* The Original Falcon Press, Tempe, Arizona. 1982.

Hyatt, Christopher S., Ph.D. *The Psychopath's Bible: For the Extreme Individual.* The Original Falcon Press, Tempe, Arizona. 2004.

James, Geoffrey, editor and translator. *The Enochian Evocation of Dr. John Dee.* Heptangle Books, Gillette, NJ. 1988

James, William. *Psychology. The Briefer Course.* Dover Publishing, Inc., NY. 2001

Jung, Carl G. and M.-L. von Franz, Joseph L. Henderson, Jolande Jacobi, and Aniela Jaffé. *Man and His Symbols.* Bantam Doubleday Dell Publishing Group, Inc., NY. 1968

Jung, C.G. (1875–1961) *Memories, Dreams, Reflections.* Random House, Inc., NY. 1989

Jung, C.G. *Psychology of the Unconscious.* Dover Publications, Inc., NY. 2002

Kaplan, Aryeh, translator and commentary. *Sefer Yetzirah. The Book Creation in Theory and Practice*, revised ed. Samuel Weiser, Inc., York Beach, Maine. 1997

King, Francis. *The Rites of Modern Occult Magic*. The MacMillan Co., NY. 1970

Laycock, Donald C. *The Complete Enochian Dictionary. A Dictionary of the Angelic Language as revealed to Dr. John Dee and Edward Kelly*. Weiser Books, Boston, MA / York Beach, Maine. 2001

The Lesser Key of Solomon or Lemegeton Clavicula Salomonis. Detailing the Ceremonial Art of Commanding Spirits Both Good and Evil. Joseph H. Peterson, ed. Weiser Books, York Beach, Maine. 2001

Levi, Eliphas (1810–1875). *The Book of Splendours. The Inner Mysteries of Qabalism. Its relationship to Freemasonry, Numerology, and Tarot*. Samuel Weiser, Inc., York Beach, Maine. 1984

Levi, Eliphas. *The Great Secret or Occultism Unveiled*. Samuel Weiser, Inc. York Beach, Maine. 2000

Levi, Eliphas. *The Mysteries of the Qabalah or Occult Agreement of the Two Testaments*. Samuel Weiser, Inc., York Beach, Maine. 2000

Levi, Eliphas. *The Science of Hermes*. Translated by A.E. Waite. The Alchemical Press. Holmes Publishing Group, Edmonds, WA. 1996

Levi, Eliphas. *Transcendental Magic. Its Doctrine and Rituals. (1910)* Kessinger Publishing, LLC, Kila, MT.

Luck, Georg, translation, annotation, and introduction. *Arcana Mundi. Magic and the Occult in the Greek and Roman Worlds*. The Johns Hopkins University Press, Baltimore. 1985

Mathers, S.L. MacGregor, translator. *The Book of the Sacred Magic of Abramelin the Mage as delivered by Abraham the Jew unto his son Lamech A.D. 1458*. Dover Publications, Inc., NY. 1975.

Mathers, S. Liddell MacGregor. *The Key of Solomon the King (Clavicula Salomonis)(1888).* Translated and edited from manuscripts in the British Museum by S.L. MacGregor Mathers. Samuel Weiser, Inc. NY. 1974

Mathers, S.L. MacGregor, translator and editor. *The Grimoire of Armadel.* Introduction by William Keith. Samuel Weiser, Inc. York Beach, Maine. 1998.

Mathers, S.L. MacGregor, translator. *The Kabbalah Unveiled.* Penguin Books, London. 1991

Morley, Henry. *The Life of Henry Cornelius Agrippa. Doctor and Knight, Commonly Known as a Magician vols 1 & 2 (1856).* Kessinger Publishing Group, Montana

Newcomb, Jason Augustus. *21st Century Mage. Bring the Divine Down to Earth.* Weiser Books, Boston, MA/York Beach, Maine. 2002

Pennick, Nigel. *Magical Alphabets. The Secrets and Significance of Ancient Scripts—Including Runes, Greek, Ogham, Hebrew and Alchemical Alphabets.* Samuel Weiser, Inc. York Beach, Maine. 1992

Regardie, Israel. *The Complete Golden Dawn System of Magic.* The Original Falcon Press, Tempe, Arizona. 2003

Regardie, Israel. *The Tree of Life. A Study in Magic.* Samuel Weiser, Inc., NY. 1971

Regardie, Israel. *What You Should Know about the Golden Dawn.* Foreword by Christopher S. Hyatt. Falcon Press, Phoenix, Arizona. 1987

Reuchlin, Johann. *On the Art of the Kabbalah.* University of Nebraska Press, Lincoln, Nebraska. 1993

Robinson, James M., general editor. *The Nag Hammadi Library. Revised edition. The definitive new translation of the Gnostic scriptures.* Harper Collins Publishers, San Francisco. 1988

Scholem, Gershom. *Kabbalah. A definitive history of the evolution, ideas, leading figures and extraordinary influence of Jewish mysticism.* Penguin Books, NY. 1978

Scholem, Gershom, editor. *Zohar. The Book of Splendor. Basic Readings from the Kabbalah.* Schocken Books, NY. 1977

The Sixth and Seventh Book of Moses (or Moses' Magical Spirit Art Known as the Wonderful Arts of the Old Wise Hebrews, Taken from the Mosaic Books of the Cabala and the Talmud for the Good of Mankind). Egyptian Publishing Co. Kessinger Publishing Co., Montana.

Turner, Robert. *Elizabethan Magic. The Art and the Magus.* Element Books Limited, Great Britain. 1989

Waite, Arthur Edward. *The Book of Ceremonial Magic. A Complete Grimoire.* University Books, Inc., NY. 1961

Waite, A.E. *The Holy Kabbalah. A Mystical Interpretation of the Scriptures.* Carol Publishing Group. 1995

Westcott, William Wynn (1848–1925). *Collectanea Hermetica Parts 1–10.* Introduction by R.A. Gilbert. Samuel Weiser, Inc., York Beach, Maine. 1998